HOT PROPERTY

HOT PROPERTY

CARLY PHILLIPS

THORNDIKE
CHIVERS

LIBRARY OF CONGRESS CATALOGING-IN-PUBLICATION DATA

Phillips, Carly.
  Hot property / by Carly Phillips.
    p. cm. — (Thorndike Press large print romance)
  ISBN-13: 978-1-4104-0953-9 (alk. paper)
  ISBN-10: 1-4104-0953-8 (alk. paper)
    1. Baseball players—Fiction. 2. Women public relations personnel—Fiction. 3. Large type books. I. Title.
PS3616.H454H675 2008
813'.6—dc22   2008028415

BRITISH LIBRARY CATALOGUING-IN-PUBLICATION DATA AVAILABLE

Published in 2008 in the U.S. by arrangement with Harlequin Books S.A.
Published in 2009 in the U.K. by arrangement with Harlequin Enterprises II B.V.

U.K. Hardcover: 978 1 408 42131 4 (Chivers Large Print)
U.K. Softcover: 978 1 408 42132 1 (Camden Large Print)

Dear Reader,

I love writing, but no series has given me more joy than the Hot Zone, maybe because of the many personal connections for me in these books. Uncle Yank is based on my grandpa Jack, may he rest in peace, and macular degeneration runs in my family. Giving Uncle Yank a love of life despite his limitations has truly been a labor of love. From your many wonderful letters, I sense you have the same warm, fuzzy feeling for the Jordan sisters and the Hot Zone characters as I do. Thank you so much for letting me know!

Thank you, too, for being diligent, intelligent, smart readers. You picked up on inconsistencies in this series that are — frankly — embarrassing for me. As I explained to those of you who wrote me about the errors, I wasn't trying to see if you were paying attention (although you definitely were!). All I can say is that I'm human. I have tried to address the inconsistencies in this story and have clarified that both Annabelle and Micki have daughters.

Hot Property is the last in the Hot Zone series of books. John Roper (Micki's best friend and high-maintenance client) and Amy Stone (Riley's cousin from Florida) are about to meet — and when they do, sparks fly!

So enjoy the heat and the fun, and the next time you write to me, I hope it's because you miss these characters as much as I will!

Best wishes always and happy reading!

Carly

www.carlyphillips.com

e-mail: carly@carlyphillips.com

I write best when I'm on vacation. Maybe it's the sand, the surf or maybe it's the company.

This book is dedicated to The Smith Family — Gary, Tracey, Matthew and Robbie, the greatest (and funniest) family friends ever. Thanks for giving a Table for Four new meaning.

As always, to Phil, Jackie, Jen, Buddy and Bailey — for making me crazy and keeping me sane . . . all at the same time.

To the editor who knows me best and always makes me better, Brenda Chin; and to Janelle Denison, for all you do, they're all for you!

And to the Plotmonkeys: Janelle, Julie Leto and Leslie Kelly — www.plotmonkeys.com — for having a brain when mine is fried. Love you guys!

PROLOGUE

Amy Stone was surrounded by testosterone. Not everyday, average testosterone but the heavy-duty testosterone that could only belong to athletes. She couldn't stop staring at the quarterbacks, the baseball stars and other large, muscular guests attending her cousin Riley's wedding reception. The bride, Sophie Jordan, her sisters and their friends appeared unfazed by so many hot men in one place. As publicists for the Hot Zone, a PR firm specializing in athletes, they were probably used to the sight. As a single woman more accustomed to living and working as a social director at a Fort Lauderdale retirement community owned by her relatives, Amy was out of her element.

But that was about to change. Starting in January, Amy would be working at the Hot Zone, too, and she'd have to learn how to handle herself around these big-shot athletes without melting at their feet. She'd already made a few trips to the city and had begun settling into the apartment Micki Jordan Fuller had leased to her. After spending the holidays with her family, Amy would be leaving her easy life behind.

She'd turned twenty-five on Halloween — there was some irony there, she was sure — and she'd woken up, looked at her life and realized a change was long overdue. She belonged in a crowd of young people, not refereeing irreverent retirees who preferred skinny-dipping to swimming with bathing suits and Long Island iced teas to the nonalcoholic variety. But she was worried about the trouble her mother and her friends could get into left on their own.

Which reminded her . . . She scanned the area looking for her family. The acreage was huge, the view beautiful. Amy couldn't find her mother or her aunt Darla, but she consoled herself with the notion that if she couldn't see or hear them, they couldn't be causing a ruckus. That had to be a good sign. Especially since the reception was being held at the Brandon, Mississippi, estate of *Senator* Harlan Nash, the man who'd raised Riley as his own son.

She prayed her mother and aunt would behave for a change. As she'd instructed

10

them this morning, no nude bathing in the fountain, no playing tag in the yard. Her relatives lived to enjoy life. And they did — a little too much sometimes, which often got them into trouble, making them all the object of public ridicule. It had often been a point of contention between her parents when her father was alive. When Amy had made the decision to move back home and had taken the job as director, aka babysitter, she'd known her father, who'd died when she was twelve, would approve.

The sun beat down on her head and she envied the senator's guests who had parasols to shade themselves from the heated rays. The humidity was really getting to her. Her skin was sticky beneath her dress as she strode to the bar.

"Can I get you a drink?" a deep male voice asked.

Amy turned, shading her eyes against the glare of the sun, and stared into the most gorgeous face she'd ever seen on a man. His eyes were a deep shade of green, his features more chiseled than rugged, and when he smiled, dimples embraced his white teeth and oh-so-sexy smile.

"I was just about to order a cola," she said.

"I think I can manage that for you." His easygoing smile grew wider. "Do not go anywhere."

Amy wouldn't dream of it. It was one thing to be surrounded by testosterone, another to have one of these men turn his attention her way. Heat suffused her and her pulse rate kicked up so she found it hard to breathe. Amy wasn't a nun and she'd been with her share of men, but she'd never dated a guy as rugged and . . . well, hot as this man.

He eased his way between the people at the bar and quickly returned with her drink in one hand, one for himself in the other. "Here you go."

She accepted the glass. "Thank you."

"My pleasure." He nodded and tipped his glass, clinking it against hers. "So, pretty lady, are you a guest of the bride or the groom?"

She tried not to preen under the compliment, but he'd gotten under her skin already. "I'm a guest of the groom. Riley is my cousin," she explained, before taking a cool, welcome sip of her soda.

"Are you related to the senator?" he asked.

"No, actually, Spencer Atkins is my uncle." Riley had a complicated family situation, but Amy figured this man, probably an athlete, knew of renowned sports agent, Spencer Atkins, who was Riley's biological father. "What about you? Which side of the family do you know?"

"I'm a guest of both, actually."

"Which would make you a client of the Hot Zone PR and Athletes Only?" she said, referring to her uncle's sports agency.

"Not only beautiful but perceptive, as well."

She was certain she blushed. "What sport do you play?"

"You don't know who I am?" His eyes widened. "I'm wounded," he said in an affected tone with a little boy's hurt in his expression. But immediate laughter let her know he was just teasing.

Amy smiled, enjoying his sense of humor and easygoing personality. The attraction went without saying. The man was definitely irresistible.

"John Roper, New York Renegades center fielder at your service." He tipped his head toward her, then extended his hand.

"Amy Stone." She placed her palm inside his. Searing heat branded her, sizzling up her arm and into her chest, knocking the wind out of her completely.

Wow.

She'd *never* had such an intense reaction to a man before. She caught a whiff of his sensual cologne, which caused an erotic spike in her body temperature. "It's nice to meet you, John."

A cute smile pulled at his lips. "It's nice to meet you, too, Amy Stone." His voice dropped a husky octave.

She ran her tongue over her dry lips. "So what table are you seated at?" she asked him.

He'd been holding her gaze with a look hot enough to melt the ice sculptures she'd seen earlier, but suddenly he twisted his body, looking around before turning back to her again. "Listen, the seating is . . . um . . . complicated."

"Tell me about it. It's a wedding. Seating is always complicated. I'm just hoping I'm not at the same table as my mom and her sister." Amy had picked up her place card earlier, but she hadn't seen her relatives since they'd left the ceremony to ask where they were seated. Amy rolled her eyes at her predicament and laughed.

John didn't join her. "It's not that kind of complicated." He mulled something over in his mind for a while before finally speaking. "I just didn't expect to meet someone like you here," he said, warmth and something inherently more in his tone.

"Tell me about it." She hadn't come here with a date or intending to meet a man,

14

either, but she was definitely glad she had met one. Now she didn't have to survive those awkward moments during slow songs. If John didn't ask her to dance, maybe she'd just ask him instead. Though that sounded more like something her mother would do than Amy, this man was worth stepping out of her comfort zone for. A tingle of anticipation rippled through her at the thought of a slow dance, his arms wrapped around her waist. . . .

He bent his head close to hers. She inhaled and his aftershave filled her with deep yearning. He leaned closer. For a whisper? Not a kiss, it was way too soon.

But her heart pounded in anticipation.

"Roper! Roper!" A shrill female voice called out his name.

The chance for her to discover his intentions disappeared as Amy and John jerked back and turned toward the sound. A beautiful woman walked, teetering on high heels, across the lawn, making a beeline his way. Her long dress kept catching beneath her shoes, and although she held up the hem with both hands, the trip was obviously a difficult one.

"There you are," she said. "Didn't I ask you to stay on the patio? I told you I didn't want to ruin my dress on the lawn." She whined through heavily glossed lips that turned downward in what was obviously meant to be a pretty pout.

It *was* pretty, though Amy hated to concede the point. The other woman was model-thin and attractive in a waiflike sort of way, elegant despite her awkward trek across the lawn. And judging from the possessive way she aligned herself against John, she was his date.

His date. Disappointment rushed through her. All the while he'd been initiating conversation and coming on to her — at least that's how she'd read his words and his body language — he'd had another woman waiting for him.

How naive could she be, thinking a hot baseball player would be interested in a country bumpkin? And that's what she felt like compared to the chic woman standing next to him. She resented the emotion, hating that she allowed herself to feel inferior.

"I leave you alone for five minutes and I find you racking up another conquest in my absence," the other woman said.

"I —" He paused. Obviously he couldn't find an acceptable excuse because there was none.

Amy's heart beat hard and fast while nausea overwhelmed her. She turned and started for the house, trying to get as far away as she could get from John Roper.

"Amy, wait!" He called after her. "I know this looks bad, but —"

She refused to turn around. It looked like what it was. He'd brought a date to the party, but he'd definitely come on to *her.*

He caught her arm, forcing her to face him.

His date followed, coming up beside them. "You're worried about her and not me? You *jerk!* I flew out to this godforsaken place to be with you and this is how you repay me? By trying to hook up with a local bimbo?"

Before anyone could blink, the woman grabbed his drink from his hand and deliberately poured it down his shirt.

"Come on, Carrie. This is a Hugo Boss shirt!" He pulled at the stained material and glared at his date. "Was that really necessary?"

She forced a smile. "I think it was."

Amy couldn't believe this. The crowd around them grew silent and began to edge closer for a better look. Amy cringed. She hated being the center of attention and she resented that this man had done it to her now.

"You two obviously need privacy." This time she ran from the circus act that was

17

John and his date.

She slowed as she approached the patio, disappointment in John Roper and the way this day had turned out as strong as the sun overhead. She'd really been attracted to him, but she didn't need a man like that in her life. She would begin her new job as a publicist for the Hot Zone, operating behind the scenes. But she definitely had to grow a thicker skin if she was going to deal with this kind of high-maintenance client on a daily basis.

A commotion broke out on the other side of the patio and Amy glanced over. Apparently the bride had decided to toss the bouquet early. She squinted for a better view and groaned aloud.

Amy's mother, Rose, and Aunt Darla both jumped for the prize and were now rolling on the lawn, both determined to claim the flowers. Neither wanted the tradition that went along with the bouquet, since they'd sworn off remarriage. And they weren't interested in the flowers, either. They just wanted the attention due them from catching it.

On one side of the house was John and his date. On the other side wrestled the crazy redheaded sisters who needed someone to separate them and give each a time-out.

This day couldn't possibly get any worse.

But when the New Year arrived and with it, her new life, Amy swore to make it her mission not only to succeed, but to thrive.

CHAPTER ONE

One month later

Sports agent Yank Morgan sat in the back-seat of his Lincoln and rubbed a hand over his scruffy beard. Scruffier now since his wife, Lola, had thrown out his razor to prevent him from accidentally slitting his throat. Dang woman had also somehow discovered where he'd hidden his spares. Apparently an almost-blind man had no privacy in his own bathroom.

Normally he'd be angry, but considering his eyesight had gotten worse, he was forced to admit Lola had a point. Macular degeneration was messing with the balance of power in his marriage. Telling a woman she was right about anything, though, especially his woman, would be the equivalent of relinquishing his throne. And that wasn't happening at home or at work.

"We're here, Mr. Morgan," J.D., the ex-football player he'd hired as his driver, said.

"Want me to walk you inside?"

Yank shook his head. "No, thanks. It's bad enough you had to drive me here. I don't need you as my guide. I got Noodle for that." His Labradoodle sat beside him and Yank patted her furry head. He'd got the dog when she was a pup, but now she was the size of her standard poodle mother.

"Be careful. I don't want to end up at the emergency room again because you tripped over something you and the mutt didn't see."

"She's not a mutt, she's a mix of two pure breeds," Yank said proudly as he opened his car door.

"I still say you should have bought a real guide dog and not a pet." J.D. came around and met him.

Yank frowned. "Keep sounding like my wife and you'll have to find yourself a new job."

J.D. merely laughed. "You say that every day," he said as he helped Yank out of the car.

Yank did his best to ignore the indignity of needing aid at basic tasks. A man accepted what a man had to accept. "You remind your father we're playing poker tonight," Yank said.

Nobody asked how Yank played without

being able to see the cards, and Yank refused
to discuss it. He'd rather lose money every
month than give up the things he loved. And
J.D.'s father, Curly, had been in Yank's
poker game for years, even before Yank had
become his nieces' guardian when they were
little girls.

J.D. scratched Noodle's fluffy fur and
helped Yank pull the dog out of the car.
"You think I need to remind Dad of something he's been doing every month for most
of his life? At least now with Lola around I
know he won't be smoking. You and my
father. Neither one of you listen to your
doctors," J.D. muttered.

"Wait till you get older before passing
judgment. I'll only be about fifteen minutes." Yank pulled his heavy jacket tighter
around him and let the dog lead him toward
the door of the gym.

Part Labrador retriever, part poodle,
completely dense when it came to being in
charge, Noodle wasn't the guide dog Yank
should have gotten, but he enjoyed the
pretense. It was fun making people think he
was a little bit crazy. There were worse ways
to spend his life, he thought, laughing.

He made his way to the weight room in
the back of the gym. The trainers and em-
ployees were used to him visiting clients and

23

bringing Noodle along. He headed for where he knew he'd find John Roper, letting years of experience lead the way. The main part of the gym was noisy and crowded, but as he approached the private rooms in the back, Yank could hear that there weren't as many people there.

Which Yank figured was the reason his not-so-star baseball player client John Roper chose to work out here and now. Unfortunately, the televisions were on and the sound coming from the speakers told Yank that morning sports talk-show host, Frank Buckley, was spouting off at the mouth as usual.

"Spring training is around the corner and this New York Renegade fan still hasn't gotten over John Roper's disastrous last season or his role in the Renegades Game 5 World Series loss. Call in and let me know if your lack of expectations match mine for the highly overpaid hero. The Buck Stops Here, folks."

The television station went to commercial at the same time Roper yelled aloud, "Somebody shut that damn thing off before I rip the speakers off the wall."

When nobody moved, Yank added his two cents. "Can't you hear the man? Shut off the noise or we'll sue you for intentional infliction of emotional distress."

The weights clanged hard as Roper dropped them to the floor. "Morgan, what are you doing here?" he asked.

"Visiting the dumbbells." Yank laughed at his own joke.

Roper didn't.

"You still upset over Buckley the Bastard's tirade? Grow up and get over it," Yank said. He'd already tried coddling Roper through his rough patch and it hadn't worked. He was moving on to tough love.

"Someone dropped off a Roper bobble-head doll with my doorman. Damn thing had a knife stuck in the shoulder."

Yank groaned. The fans wouldn't let Roper forget his nightmarish last season. He hadn't been able to hit or throw, and to make things worse, he'd sprained his shoulder in a failed attempt to stop a game-winning home run by slamming it into the center field wall. This in addition to striking out earlier when the bases were loaded and the Renegades had a chance at the go-ahead run. Their team had lost, the fans needed a scapegoat, and they'd chosen the highest-priced center fielder in the game to sacrifice. Not that the man wasn't in a slump, but losing had been a team effort.

Now Buckley insisted on continuing the

torture in the off-season. Roper had every right to be pissed. He didn't need Buckley riling up the fans against him in his daily tirades.

"Are you sure Buckley doesn't have a personal grudge?" Yank asked.

Roper rose to his feet, looming large over Yank. "I screwed his ex-girlfriend. She just didn't see fit to mention she was no longer his ex on the night in question."

Yank chuckled. "He oughta let it go."

"She's his wife now," Roper said.

"Shit."

"Yeah," Roper agreed. "You do realize that if this was a lesser market, nobody would pay attention to anything Buckley said?"

Yank shook his head. "But it isn't a lesser market. It's New York." And that said it all.

Athletes were like movie stars here, back- and front-page news and fodder for gossip. "You used to love the attention," Yank reminded him.

Prior to his funk, Roper had been known for being a high-maintenance outfielder. E-Sports TV, Magazine and Radio named Roper among the top metrosexual athletes of the year. Yank didn't get why grown men like Roper spent good money on the best clubs, gyms and hairdressers. What normal man had his back waxed? Yank had no idea.

But Roper's good-looking mug had made them both a boatload of money, so Yank wasn't about to complain.

"I did love the attention," Roper said. "Until my talent went south." Roper leaned forward on the bench, elbows on his knees, and stared ahead at nothing in particular. "So what are you really doing here?" Roper asked.

"I came to cheer you up. I don't want the media to see you down and I sure as hell don't need you taking a swing at one of them, no matter how much they provoke you."

"That sounds like a message from Micki."

Yank's niece, Michelle, was Roper's close friend, as well as his publicist. She was the resident expert at the Hot Zone for keeping her high-maintenance client out of trouble and out of the press.

Then again, maybe some good press was exactly what Roper needed. "I have a present for you. Here's a gift certificate." Yank pulled a piece of paper from his back pocket. "Go get yourself a massage and a manicure."

"Not in the mood."

Yank didn't know what else to do in order to help his dejected client. "Don't you want to look your best for the annual Hot Zone

New Year's party?"

"I'm not going."

Yank smacked him upside the head. "You sure as hell are. You're going to hold yourself up and make like life's grand. Attitude is everything and right now yours sucks."

Yank couldn't see well but he figured Roper was scowling at him about now. "I'm sure you're having a rough time after the series, but obviously something more has you bent out of shape. The happy-go-lucky guy I know wouldn't be sulking like a pansy."

Roper rose and Yank felt the other man's height close beside him.

"You want to know what's bothering me? Where should I start? I could live with last year's disaster if I thought I was definitely coming back, but we both know the shoulder's not healing the way it should. That means my career may be shorter than we'd anticipated. Not a financial problem given my huge contract, right?"

"Unless you pissed it away . . ." Yank said, not at all serious.

"You know me better than that. But my family's working hard at doing it for me."

Yank blinked. "Ever hear *just say no?*"

"You try telling them that."

Yank wasn't worried about Roper's future.

The younger man had come to him for investment advice and Yank knew he'd diversified wisely. But if his career was shortened due to injury and his family was going through his money like water, Yank could understand the man's distress. "Slow 'em down, then," Yank suggested.

"Yeah, I'm trying," Roper muttered. "Do me a favor? Tell Micki I need time to myself. If she doesn't quit worrying and sending you around to check on me, I'm going to let the Hot Zone go. Who knows? If I can't play this season, I may not need a PR firm at all."

Yank frowned. "Micki's not worried about you as a client, you ass. She's worried about you as a friend."

"I know that," Roper said, sounding more subdued and apologetic. "I appreciate her concern, but there's nothing she can do unless she's got a magic cure for the shoulder."

Even Yank knew when to give a man space, and John Roper needed it more than Yank had realized. "I'll make you a deal," he said to the man he both liked and admired.

"What's that?"

"Come to the party and I promise nobody will be talking business. You could use some time to relax. No media invited. What do you say?"

Roper remained silent for too long.

Obviously the man was tense and strung tight if he couldn't bring himself to say he'd come to a party. "When was the last time you got laid?" Yank asked, voicing the first question that came to mind.

"None of your damn business."

Yank chuckled at the quick answer. "Then it's been too damn long."

Yank had seen the symptoms in other good men, as well. Men who spent too much time alone and needed a woman in their lives. Not that he'd know . . . No sir, but he knew Roper needed a distraction from focusing on his World Series screwup or the start of spring training in February.

Too bad Yank had already hooked up his three nieces with solid men. But just because his girls were taken didn't mean Yank couldn't work his magic with Roper and another woman.

But who could he find to put up with a man who liked things orderly and neat, designer and upscale? He went through the women in his office, then smacked himself for being so dense. He should have thought of the female solution to Roper's problems sooner.

Amy Stone, the niece of his partner, Spencer Atkins. She was feisty, pretty and single, and only an idiot could have missed the sparks between Amy and Roper at Sophie's wedding. Roper's date had been a bimbo but not an idiot, Yank thought, recalling the drink she'd spilled down Roper's shirt and their immediate exit right afterward. And since Amy had just moved to the city and taken a position at the Hot Zone, she didn't know many people in town. Yes, sir, Amy was his answer.

He didn't intend to tell Roper, though. Yank loved surprises. "Come to the party," Yank insisted.

"You'll leave me alone if I do?"

Yank nodded. "Scout's honor," he said, raising his hand.

Roper shrugged. "Okay, then. Why the hell not?"

Yank tugged on Noodle's leash, and as they walked out the door, Yank whistled, pleased with his handiwork.

J.D. met him by the car. "Why are you in such a good mood?"

"Because I'm not a Boy Scout and I never have been," Yank said, laughing. John Roper was about to benefit from Yank being a lying, meddling son of a bitch.

Amy loved Florida. She enjoyed the warm

weather all year, the ease of never having to wear a winter jacket. It was one of the reasons she'd stayed down South instead of going away to college. She also was a person who appreciated comfortable surroundings, and her home and family in Florida represented the familiar.

Her father had died of a heart attack when she was young. But thanks to her mother and aunt, and her uncle's frequent visits, she'd never felt alone or neglected. Still, she'd been old enough to remember her father and she'd always felt his absence in her life. While her mother was wild, spirited and free, her father had been more reserved, the epitome of good manners.

When she was a kid, she'd had some wild antics of her own, like when her father had insisted they give the puppy she'd found to the pound. Granted it was a no-kill shelter, but she'd wanted that dog, and to prove her point, she'd picketed — with signs — from the garage roof below her bedroom window. He had insisted she come down before she fell off, making his disapproval with her technique clear along with his fear for her safety. He preferred she use traditional, safe methods to make her point instead of alerting the neighbors and causing them to panic and call both him and 9-1-1.

She laughed at the memory, because it had been one of the few times she'd made use of her mother's genes — the ones she usually kept hidden inside her. From that point on, she'd tried to please her father and rein in any wildness. Even after he was gone, Amy had never stopped trying to please him.

Being a social worker, helping out others in need, was something she knew her father would have been proud of. When she'd lost that job, thanks to one of her mother's more outrageous stunts, she'd been devastated and she'd retreated home to lick her wounds. While there, she fell into the habit of looking out for her mother and her friends, again something her father would have approved of. She'd ended up as the social director of the seniors' community and she had to admit the job had been a good fit for her.

But she'd spent enough time watching over her mother and she missed being with people her own age. Amy had woken up on her birthday and realized not only hadn't she accomplished her old dreams, she'd forgotten to make new ones. Uprooting herself from the familiar was the first step in forging a new life. One that included a new career — with the Hot Zone thanks to her uncle Spencer and the generosity of the Jordan sisters in giving her a chance.

Now, on New Year's Eve, she stepped off the elevator at the Park Avenue offices of the Hot Zone and glanced at the guests, the male ones in particular, and an immediate feeling of déjà vu swept over her. Just like at Sophie and Riley's wedding, she felt out of her element. Would she ever get used to being surrounded by buff, hot men? She hoped not, she thought, as she glanced around at her new normal.

The coat-check woman greeted her and took her jacket. A server offered her a glass of champagne, which Amy declined. She wanted a clear head for all the new faces and names she'd encounter, as well as access to her memories of those she'd already met at the wedding. Those memories were vivid. Especially the ones of John Roper and how disappointed she'd been by his deception. Of course, maybe he'd have told her about his date given more time.

And maybe he hadn't leaned close enough to kiss her cheek, she thought, still disappointed by the outcome. No matter how much she wanted to believe he'd been as blindsided by their attraction as she'd been, that he couldn't help but act on it, date or no date, she knew she was deceiving herself.

In all likelihood, the man was exactly what he seemed to be — a guy trying to juggle more than one woman at a time.

The man was a superstar athlete, a celebrity who was probably used to women falling at his feet. Amy had grown up listening to her uncle's stories of his famous clients. And Amy had inadvertently played the role of doting admirer. But that wasn't who she was. Amy wasn't into the glitz, glamour and fame celebrity brought.

She exhaled a stream of air, annoyed at herself for giving Roper any thought at all. She forced herself to focus to the holiday decorations that lingered from Christmas and the pretty silver balls hanging from the ceiling. A professionally decorated tree sat in the corner twinkling with lights that were sure to be taken down soon after the first of the year. The decor outdid anything she, her mother and aunt back in Florida had managed to set up in the clubhouse each year.

"Amy?"

She turned at the sound of her name above the noise of the happy crowd. Sophie Jordan approached quickly, a warm smile on her face. No matter how many times Amy saw Sophie, she was always shocked by her beauty and perfection. Tonight her honey-blond hair was pulled back in a neat knot, her face beautifully made up.

Amy hugged Sophie, the sister who was the organizer behind the Hot Zone. She had met Sophie for the first time in Florida last year. Though Sophie wasn't as touchy-feely as Amy, she hugged right back.

"You look happy. Marriage to my cousin must agree with you," Amy said, taking in Sophie's glowing face.

Sophie grinned. "Well, marriage to Riley *is* pretty darn good."

"I just bet it is. Where is my cousin, anyway?"

"He'll be here soon."

"And your sisters?" Amy glanced over Sophie's shoulder. "Are they around here somewhere?"

"Unfortunately Micki's still on the island — her husband, Damian, owns a slice of paradise. Her daughter had a respiratory infection and Damian insisted on taking the family to a warmer climate for a little while. From what they say, it seems to be helping. But Annabelle is here working the crowd. I'm sure you'll see her soon."

Amy nodded. "Well, please send Micki my love."

"I will. And you can do it yourself at the first staff meeting in a few days."

Amy already knew she was stepping into a high-profile, high-pressure place with loyalty and dedication in spades, and she wanted to play a successful part. Nepotism might have gotten her the job, but only proving herself would keep her here. She was definitely ready for the challenge.

"Well, look who's here!" a booming male voice said. Her uncle's partner, Yank, pulled her into a big hug at the same time Amy caught sight of his wife, Lola, standing behind him.

Amy waved to the other woman, who smiled right back.

"Just tell me your crazy mother and aunt are still at home in Florida," Yank said as he stepped back.

Lola groaned. "Ignore him. He's had a drink or two and doesn't know what he's saying." She smacked her husband on the shoulder.

"I'm stone-cold sober. You've been watering down my drinks all night." He leaned closer to Amy. "She thinks just because I can't see, my taste buds have gone, too."

And he thought Amy's relatives were crazy? She shook her head and laughed. "No problem, Lola. I've heard from Uncle Spencer that Yank says whatever's on his mind." She shot the older man a grateful look. "Thank you for giving me a chance here," she told him.

Yank grinned, obviously pleased. "You see? The only one who's got a problem with me is you," Yank said to his wife.

Sophie rolled her eyes. "Okay, you said your hellos, Uncle Yank. How about giving me a chance to introduce Amy to some other people at the party?"

"I'd like that." Amy rubbed her hands together.

"Why not start with someone she knows and ease her in. John Roper's over there in the corner," Yank said without much tact.

Amy's stomach flipped. "Oh, I think we can skip over him," Amy said, only partially meaning it. A traitorous part of her wanted to get a glimpse of him again.

"Nonsense. Amy wouldn't want him to think he was avoiding her, considering he's been eyeing *her* since she walked into the room," Yank said.

"He has?" Amy asked, then wished she could bite her tongue and take it back. Still, she had to admit it stroked her ego to know Roper's eyes had been on her since she'd arrived. She had to force herself not to glance at the corner and look over at *him*.

Lola scowled at her husband. "Leave Amy alone," she instructed.

"Lola's right," Sophie said. "But tell me something. Just how would you know where Roper is, considering you can't see well enough to identify anyone?" Sophie perched her hands on her hips and eyed her uncle warily.

"She's got your number, old man," Lola said, laughing.

"Who are you calling old?" he grumbled.

Lola ignored him, meeting Sophie's gaze instead. "Actually, Yank's been checking up on Roper ever since he arrived. I feel like the man's personal GPS system."

"Speaking of guides, where is Noodle?" Sophie asked.

"One of the staff took the dog out for a walk." Lola gestured toward the windows overlooking the city. "They'll be back soon."

Sophie nodded. "Gotcha. Well, I can understand your concern for Roper. We've all been worried about him lately. The papers have been brutal."

Despite her better judgment, Amy's curiosity got the better of her. "Why? What's going on?"

The other three stared at one another, wide-eyed and surprised.

"I guess New Yorkers forget that not everyone else's world revolves around sports," Sophie said, realization dawning.

"You know that the Renegades made it to the World Series?"

Amy nodded. She just hadn't kept up with the details since the opposing team hadn't been from Florida.

"Roper went into the post season in a serious slump," Sophie said in a low whisper. "He didn't play well at all in the series, struck out in the clutch and injured his shoulder in an attempt to stop a home run. The team lost the series and Roper became the media scapegoat."

"Ouch." Poor man, she thought, then caught herself. The *poor man* didn't need her pity, that much she knew for sure.

Despite herself, Amy's gaze came to rest on the sexy guy who had made her pulse kick up a notch and her mouth go dry.

And he still had a female cozying up to him just like the last time.

"He doesn't look happy," Sophie murmured.

She was right. Despite the attention of a woman who appeared to be hanging on his every word, Roper appeared dazed and bored.

"How odd," Lola said. "Normally Roper loves every bit of attention he can get, female or otherwise."

Amy pursed her lips and kept silent. She'd

once been all too happy to shower him with that attention. Thanks to the scene made by his date at the wedding, everyone here knew it.

"Must be today's paper that's getting to him," Yank said. "Lola read it to me earlier. The *News* ran a list of New Year's resolutions. Said if Roper didn't get a renewed dose of talent from Santa, he should resolve to take a one-way ticket to Siberia as his contribution to the team."

"That's awful," Amy said, shocked by the brutal treatment despite her feelings about Roper at the moment.

"That's New York," Sophie replied. "Something you'll be getting used to, I promise."

Amy nodded. "Still, I can't imagine being the center of such negative press day in and day out."

Yank shrugged. "In this city, it comes with the territory. The bigger the contracts, the worse the scrutiny and the higher the expectations. Let's go save him," Yank said. He practically gave Amy a shove forward, calling Roper's name at the same time.

So much for steering clear of him, Amy thought. And one glance his way had her wondering why she wanted to.

"I'm sorry," Sophie whispered, catching

up with her.

"Not a problem," Amy said with a forced smile as they walked forward.

Yank Morgan trailed right along with them until Lola deliberately pulled him away for a scolding.

Amy chuckled at the family dynamic, one to which she could relate. But she had something more important to focus on now than Yank and Lola.

Roper's gaze locked on Amy's and her insides twisted with the familiar sense of awareness he'd invoked in her once before.

"Ladies, please come rescue me from wedding talk," Roper said, reaching out and putting an arm around Sophie's shoulder.

But he never broke eye contact with Amy.

"Wedding?" Sophie asked, her voice rising. "I didn't know you were even seeing someone special."

Wedding? A voice inside Amy's head echoed and her stomach cramped.

"As in, you and a member of the opposite sex making a permanent commitment? Someone give me a fan. I think I'm going to faint." Sophie waved a hand in front of her face, mocking him and chuckling at the same time.

"Did you hear that, John? They think *you're* getting married." The woman by his side, a different woman from the last one Amy had seen him with, laughed in real amusement.

When she turned around, Amy realized the other woman was much younger than she'd originally thought. Certainly younger than Amy and definitely younger than John Roper.

"John's not my fiancé, he's my brother," the other woman explained.

Amy let out a breath she hadn't realized she'd been holding. She wanted to dismiss the wave of relief washing over her, but she couldn't. Roper wasn't getting married and she could breathe again. Obviously, despite her frustration with him over their first meeting, the attraction was still there, strong as ever.

"Ah, now that makes more sense." Sophie nodded in understanding. "I couldn't see you taking yourself off the market, and I definitely couldn't see the papers missing out on the courtship."

"Ha, ha," Roper muttered.

While they were sparring, Amy took a moment to look at the younger woman with fresh eyes. With the family connection made, Amy saw the resemblance now — the sandy-blond hair, the shape and color of their green eyes and the matching dimples.

"Sabrina, meet everyone here." Roper inclined his head towards his sibling. "Everyone, meet my sister, Sabrina." He finished the introductions with a quick wave of his hand.

"Nice to meet you all." Sabrina smiled, once again reinforcing the family resemblance. "I wish I could stay and hang out, but I've got to go find my fiancé."

"Nice to meet you," Amy murmured, but Roper's sister had taken off before she could hear the reply.

Sophie glanced at her watch. "I should follow her lead. Riley should have been here by now."

"Go on. I'll take good care of Amy while you're gone."

Sophie shot Amy a look of concern, but Amy didn't want the other woman worrying about her or thinking she couldn't handle herself with one of Hot Zone's clients.

Amy put on her brightest smile. "Say hi to Riley and tell him I'll catch up with him in a few minutes," Amy said.

"Are you sure?" Sophie's gaze bounced between Amy and Roper.

Roper pushed off from where he was leaning against the wall and rose to his full, overwhelming height.

"Don't worry about me," Roper said, treating Amy to a wink and a grin that caused a tingling straight down to her toes.

"I wasn't. Amy?" Sophie asked.

"Go find my cousin and give him a kiss for me." She dismissed the other woman's worry with an encouraging smile.

Sophie turned to Roper. "You know that Riley will kick your ass if you misbehave, so be good to Amy. She's new in town."

He cocked an eyebrow, throwing a sexy look her way. "When am I ever not good?"

Which was exactly what had Amy on edge. But she was a big girl. She could handle herself, as well as John Roper.

Sophie frowned, but after a lingering glance at Amy, took off to find her husband, leaving them alone.

Roper stepped closer. And Amy knew she was in deep trouble.

CHAPTER TWO

When Yank insisted Roper show up at this gig, he'd agreed under duress. Now Roper realized fate wanted him here so it could present him with the one thing he needed — a distraction from his career problems, his sister's wedding and his brother's constant whining about a loan. Amy Stone provided that distraction. Apparently life had given him a second chance, and he decided to take this as the first positive sign in ages. Maybe things were looking up after all.

He vividly recalled the instant attraction he'd felt for Amy the first time he'd laid eyes on her. And the stirring in his body told him *that* much hadn't changed. He'd gone to the wedding out of obligation, still in a funk over the blown World Series. But one look at the pretty brunette and all thoughts of his problems had fled. She'd been a breath of fresh air in his down-and-out life. He'd actually forgotten all about his date, mostly because she was simply arm candy and hadn't meant anything to him at all. Not that that was an excuse. Although Roper liked women, all women — blond, brunette or redhead, natural or from a bottle — when he looked at Amy, the punch in the gut had been harder and more defined.

He hadn't lost sight of the fact that he'd made an ass of himself the last time they were together and he owed her an apology for what had transpired. Now, with everyone gone, he and Amy were alone in their own corner of the party and she met his gaze head-on, not blinking or backing down.

He admired the fact that he couldn't rattle her and refused to rush his perusal. She had tanned skin only someone from a southern state could manage, a fresh, unjaded look in her eyes, and curly hair that didn't appear overly set with sprays or products. He could definitely get into tangling his hands in the soft brown curls.

But most of all he wanted to be with a woman who in all likelihood didn't keep up with New York sports news and Roper's humiliations. One who wouldn't pity him, judge him or want something from him in any way. Of course, he was getting ahead of himself. Chances were good she hadn't forgiven him for the scene at the wedding, and he couldn't blame her.

"So how have you been?" he asked once they were alone, or as alone as they could be in a room full of people.

"Just fine, and you?" She folded her arms across her chest, causing her cleavage to swell above the glittery gold tank she wore beneath a white silk blouse.

He knew Amy's movement was unintentional, and he had to admit her lack of pretense was one of the things he found most appealing about her. "I've been better," he admitted, opting for honesty.

But he didn't want to get into his recent problems. He cleared his throat and asked, "Been in town long?" Not his best line, but he wanted to change the subject.

She shook her head. "Not very."

She wasn't making this easy. For the first time, he was uptight around a woman and unsure of how to reach her. "So, um, when do you leave?" he asked.

She raised an eyebrow. "Anxious to get rid of me already?"

He shook his head, exhaling hard. "I'm blowing this big-time. Let's backtrack, okay? It's good to see you again."

"Same here." She immediately pursed her lips.

He'd bet she wished she could take that comment back, but he liked her refreshing honesty.

She turned, obviously scanning the crowd.

He followed her gaze but couldn't pinpoint anyone or anything that would have distracted her. "Looking for someone?"

"As a matter of fact, I am," she said as she pivoted back to face him. "I was trying to locate your date."

A grin tugged at his mouth. "What makes you think I brought one?" he asked.

"Experience."

"Touché."

She shrugged. "I can't imagine you spending New Year's Eve alone." She reached her hand out, tapping a finger against his pink Ralph Lauren dress shirt.

She was bolder than he thought she'd be, but the slight trembling of her fingers told him the movement was forced. He'd bet she didn't want him to think he could get to her again.

Well, hell. *She* got to him. "You wound me," Roper said.

"You'll live."

He laughed hard, something he hadn't

done in way too long. "I suppose I deserved that."

She grinned. "You supposed right." Her hand lingered. Her pink fingernails were short and blended with the color of his shirt.

His flesh burned hot underneath the material. He couldn't tear his gaze from her delicate fingertips lingering so close to the buttons that would let his skin touch hers.

She followed his stare, glanced down, realized she hadn't removed her hand and snatched it away, leaving him to wonder if she'd felt the same searing heat.

She cleared her throat. "Well, your shirt's clean so I assume you've been a good boy. You haven't ticked off your date, at least not yet. So where is she? Ladies' room? Buffet table?"

They were bantering easily and he was glad. But he'd like for her to get to know him better so he could erase the bad first impression he'd made. "If I admit that was tacky and I apologize, can we start over?" he asked.

"That depends." She narrowed her gaze, assessing him in silence, but assessing him nonetheless.

Roper decided the fact that she couldn't take her eyes off him was a good thing. At least it was mutual. He couldn't stop staring at her, either. The more he thought about it, the more he realized she'd be good for him. A welcome break from physical therapy for his sprained shoulder and from wondering whether or not he'd return in time for spring training.

"I didn't come with a date," he admitted, refocusing on Amy. "Lesson learned the hard way." Thank God.

She inclined her head. "That's a start," she murmured.

"What if I told you I was so taken by you at the wedding that I couldn't help myself, date or no date?"

She swiped her tongue over her lightly glossed lips. "I'd say you were pushing it and would be better off with just the apology."

"Even if I was telling the truth?"

"Especially then," she said, her voice huskier than before.

He stepped closer, so close he could examine each freckle on her nose and cheeks. "Come on, give me another chance. Let's start fresh." On impulse, he reached out and ran his finger down the tip of her nose. Skin touched skin and his hand sizzled on contact.

Her eyes widened with awareness, but she didn't back away.

Pleased, he tipped his head even closer. "So what do you say?"

She bit down on her lower lip, pausing in thought.

The seconds that he waited were the longest of his life.

"For the sake of peace, why not?" she finally said.

He had the second chance he'd sought, he thought with relief. "Can I get you some punch?"

She wrinkled her nose. "I think I'm going to stay away from alcohol. Besides, I should really get —"

A loud bell-like sound clanged, drowning out her voice.

"What's that?" Amy yelled over the noise.

"Sounds like a fire alarm."

And he must have been right because the guests, talking loudly among themselves, headed for the front of the offices leading to the hallway.

"Let's get moving," he said.

"Are you serious? We're twenty floors up!" Panicked, she grabbed for her heels.

"What are you doing?"

"I was going to take off my shoes so I could run downstairs easier!"

He swallowed a laugh, knowing her fear was real. "In my experience, more often than not it's a false alarm."

She narrowed her gaze. "Haven't you ever seen *The Towering Inferno?*"

He chuckled aloud this time. "It's a bad seventies movie, not reality. But you have a point. Let's get going. If the shoes don't hurt, you can keep them on. We're not going to be running. Just moving quickly."

She nodded.

"Shoes on or off?" he asked, talking loudly to compensate for the clanging bell.

"On. The heels aren't that high. I'll be fine."

Before she could make a run for the stairs or push through the crowds, Roper slipped his hand into hers and took control. He led her to the fire exit along with the rest of the guests and they maneuvered the long walk down in silence, punctuated by the alarm but with no hint of smoke or fire. Finally they stepped into the front lobby and were greeted by firemen in uniform directing people to the sidewalk across the street.

From what Roper could gather, the fire chief thought it was a false alarm, but until they checked out the building, they couldn't be sure. Everyone needed to evacuate.

Outside, he caught up with one of his teammates.

Jorge Calderone lifted a hand in greeting.

"Someone say Yank Morgan trip on his Noodle and accidentally pull on the fire alarm," he said in his heavy accent.

Roper shook his head and laughed. "You're kidding. Was the old man hurt?"

"He's fine. But Sophia *mucho* angry that he ruined the party."

Roper thought of perfectionist Sophie and said, "I just bet she is."

"I'm not staying to freeze my ass off out here. See ya, *mi amigo.*" Jorge strode away without looking back.

Roper turned to Amy. "I'd have introduced you to my friend but he took off too fast."

"Not a problem." Her voice shook as she spoke and she had wrapped her arms around her upper body as she shivered in the below-freezing temperatures.

He slipped his sport jacket off and wrapped it around her shoulders.

She smiled appreciatively. "Thanks. I left my jacket at the coat check when I arrived, and my body is used to much warmer temperatures."

"I should have figured as much. Can I take you somewhere for dinner? I know a nice place with good food." The party might be over, but he wasn't ready to part ways with Amy just yet.

"No thanks. I really should just go home, change and get warm. Oh, no." She swung around and glanced back at the building.

"What's wrong?"

She shut her eyes, frustration clear in her expression. "I left my key in my coat pocket."

He shoved his hands into his front trouser pockets for warmth. "I'm sure the hotel would issue you another one, unless your ID is in your pocket, too?"

"No. But I'm not talking about a hotel key card. I'm talking about the actual key to my apartment."

"Wait, you live here? In New York?" Suddenly he was wary. Earlier when he'd pursued her, somewhere in the back of his mind was the knowledge that Amy was in town for a short time. No hopes, no expectations to add to his burdens. Except, apparently, he was wrong.

"I just moved here. I'm subletting Micki's apartment since it's too small for her whole family and they stay at Damian's when they're in the city, anyway." Amy hopped from foot to foot in order to keep warm. "I take it Micki didn't mention it?"

Roper shook his head. He was going to strangle his best friend for the omission. If he'd known Amy was a permanent resident, he wouldn't have restarted his flirtation. He was looking for a quick fix and a good time. Not a relationship with a woman nearby who, though she kept her distance now, would undoubtedly begin to expect something more eventually. He'd had enough of that already.

"I could talk to Sophie or Yank and see if they have an extra key, but they look tied up with the firemen," she said, glancing over his shoulder. "I guess I'll just wait."

Her eyes were wide, her cheeks flushed red from the cold and her curls were tousled around her pretty face. Oh, hell, who was he kidding? Even if he had known she'd moved to town, he'd have had a hard time staying away. Besides, he wasn't going to overthink this, just make the most of it.

She shivered and he stepped toward the curb, hailing the first yellow cab that appeared and opening the door so she could get in first.

"Where are we going?" she asked.

"My place." Where she could warm up before he took her back to her building to see if the doorman or super had a spare key.

It was New Year's Eve and he wanted to keep her with him for a while longer.

Amy hadn't agreed to go to his apartment.

She just wanted to get warm. She settled into the taxicab seat, then Roper sat down beside her. His body heat rippled through her, warming her when just seconds before she was chilled inside and out.

He rattled off an address to the driver.

"Wait."

"You need warm clothes and maybe some hot food before dealing with Micki's grouchy doorman," he said, before leaning forward and telling the driver to go.

She knew better than to sound like an ungrateful brat, considering she was freezing, hungry and she had nowhere else to go. "Good point. Thanks." Teeth chattering, she leaned back in her seat for the duration of the ride to his high-rise farther uptown.

When she finally walked into his apartment twenty minutes later, she was immediately reminded that she still wasn't used to city living. In her old world, one-floor ranch homes were the norm. Her house in Florida hadn't been huge, but because everything was spread out on one level, the square footage seemed larger. Her father had left her mother with enough insurance money to let them live comfortably, and once her uncle had bought the real estate he'd turned into a retirement community along with his fellow investors, he'd insisted his sisters move there, as well. Amy had lived in one of the smaller units, paying token rent. Here in New York, her new apartment was small and quaint.

Roper's place was enormous. She sensed how large it was just by looking across, past the sliding doors to the terrace off the living room. Then there was the decor. In a masculine cocoa-and-cream color scheme, the living room held a plush suede sofa and ottoman, two club chairs and a rectangular marble cocktail table in the center. A massive large-screen TV hung on the wall across from the sitting area, while behind the couch, framed artwork made the room come alive.

"Like it?" Roper asked as he tossed his keys into a bowl in a practiced movement.

"It's gorgeous."

He grinned. "Thanks. I decorated it myself." The pride in his voice was unmistakable.

"I'm impressed." What other hidden talents did he have? Amy wondered.

He shrugged. "Why pay a professional if I can just as easily do it myself? That's my motto. Anyway, let me get you something to change into. My sister leaves comfortable clothes here in case she's too lazy to go home, which used to happen pretty often

before she met her fiancé. She won't mind
if you borrow them."

Amy rubbed her hands up and down her
arms, covered only by her thin blouse.
"Thanks."

"After you warm up, we'll talk about what
to eat. I'll be right back."

She turned to study her surroundings
once more, her gaze coming to rest on the
trophies in a dark wood cabinet with glass
doors. MVP, Golden Glove and other no-
table mentions were inscribed on plaques
with John Roper's name.

He walked back into the room with a stack
of clothes in his hand. "Take your pick."

"Nice set of awards. Once again, you've
impressed me," she said as she accepted a
sweat outfit.

"I hope the awards aren't the only things
you like about me, because you know what
they say, all good things come to an end."
He studied her through narrowed eyes.

"I don't know you well enough to know
what I like about you." She knew better
than to mention the career problems she'd
just learned about tonight.

"Good answer." He smiled and his eyes
softened, warming her a bit more.

She supposed it couldn't be easy to meet
women and not know whether they were

interested in him or in his status and money. Amy had no use for either. She'd grown up comfortable and didn't need excessive luxury, although what her mother couldn't afford, her uncle had always provided. But Amy never took having material things for granted. Love and family were much more important than money. But he didn't know enough about her to understand she was a genuine person and she knew better than to try to convince him with mere words.

She had already seen there was more to Roper than the player she'd assumed him to be. Like his ability to apologize for mistakes and his chivalry in bringing her back here to warm up with seemingly no ulterior motive.

"Let's get to know each other better over a good meal. While you change, I'll fix us up something to eat," he said.

"There's no need for you to go to any trouble. We can order in. It's easier. And I ought to know — I've been living on take-out."

Although she had essentially been the caretaker in the family, keeping everyone busy and out of trouble, she'd also been spoiled by living near her mother and aunt. They'd served her home-cooked meals and delivered them to her doorstep if she wanted to be alone. She hadn't had to worry about fixing things for herself, which was a good thing, because she was a hazard in the kitchen. Here in New York, she'd been too busy making Micki's apartment her own and learning her way around the city to attempt making meals, too.

"That settles it, then. I'm definitely cooking. It relaxes me, and besides, it's healthier than eating the fried food and heavy sauces you'll find in takeout."

She couldn't help but laugh. "A man who cooks? Now, *there's* something to like about you. I knew that list wouldn't be all that hard. I'll change and then maybe you can give me some pointers in the kitchen."

"I'd be happy to." His eyes sparkled with pleasure. "Bathroom's down the hall on your right." He pointed toward the back of the apartment.

She headed to change in his spare bathroom, something her apartment didn't have, and a few minutes later she returned to the kitchen dressed in sweats that were a little snug but much warmer and more comfortable than the outfit she'd worn to the party.

She stood in the doorway and took in the gorgeous state-of-the-art kitchen. "Wow. My mother would be impressed."

"I'm impressed, too." His gaze traveled

leisurely over her, his eyes darkening with distinct approval. "You dress down as well as you dress up. The rumpled, fresh-out-of-bed look suits you," he said with a sexy grin.

Her face warmed at the compliment and her body followed suit.

"I didn't realize you were that much taller than my sister," he said, taking in the sweats that she'd rolled around her calves.

She glanced down at her bare ankles. "Well, at least capris are in style."

"They are and they look great on you."

"Thanks." A flush rose to her cheeks. She could say the same about how good he looked, too.

He'd opened the first few buttons on his shirt and rolled up his sleeves, giving him an edgy, sexy look. "So let's get started. You said you wanted lessons. I take it cooking's not your thing?"

She sighed and lifted her hands uselessly in the air. "Nope. They say children learn by watching, but I'm afraid I never picked up Mom's talent. Not even the basics."

"Well, then, sit and I'll teach you."

She realized he'd already taken out presliced chicken strips and now he was slicing fresh vegetables on a cutting board. A wok sat ready and waiting for him to use.

"Starting with precut and sliced food

helps," she said, laughing.

He raised an eyebrow. "So you're that much of a novice, hmm?"

"And you're that much of an expert?"

He nodded.

Everything about the man took her by surprise. A really pleasant surprise.

She settled herself onto a barstool near the island, where he was working.

"I buy presliced chicken because my schedule's so hectic I never know how much time I'll have. On a night like tonight, it comes in handy. You can buy precut vegetables, as well, but it takes me no time and I'd rather eat fresh. Now I'm nearly ready to toss the vegetables into the wok."

She blinked at how fast he'd prepared a meal that would have taken her an hour minimum. "Maybe I should be taking notes," she mused as she reached over and plucked a carrot from the cutting board.

"Hey, quit nibbling or you won't be hungry enough to enjoy my masterpiece." He playfully smacked at her hand, but she was faster.

She nabbed another carrot before he could stop her.

In two steps he stood by her side, his presence big and overwhelming, the heat in his eyes matching the desire pulsing through her veins. From the moment she'd laid eyes on this man, she'd been seduced by his looks. What sane woman wouldn't be?

But in the short time she was with him tonight, she'd seen glimpses of the everyday guy he really was. She really liked what she saw.

He reached for the carrot and she tucked it tighter into her hand.

"Give it up," he ordered, clearly amused by her game.

She bit the inside of her cheek. "Make me."

He tickled her but she held on fast, eagerly anticipating his next method of extraction.

Their eyes met and held. Her pulse pounded hard in her throat and the anticipation of his lips hot and hard on hers sent tremors quaking through her body.

She slid her tongue over her mouth, moistening her lips, waiting, hoping . . .

The jarring ring of the telephone broke the thick silence surrounding them. His head jerked toward the sound.

Needing space, Amy jumped up from her chair. "You should answer it," she said, her voice unusually shaky.

He shot her a glance filled with equal parts heat and regret before grabbing the portable phone behind him. "Yeah," he barked into the phone, then listened to whoever was on the other end.

"Sorry. Happy New Year to you, too, Mom. Why aren't you out at one of those Hollywood parties you love so much?"

Hollywood? That was an interesting tidbit of information, Amy thought. And far better to focus on that than how close they'd come to kissing.

"Oh, right. Time difference. I forgot. I'm distracted, that's all." His gaze settled on Amy, his stare deep and consuming, letting her know he hadn't forgotten what had almost happened between them. What could still happen if she let it.

He cleared his throat. "That's okay. What's going on?" he asked. His expression darkened the longer his mother spoke. "No, Mom, I'm not giving Ben money to invest in a gym."

He listened, then said, "Because giving money to my brother is like throwing it away, that's why." Roper pinched the bridge of his nose. "Have you forgotten about all the failed businesses that I did subsidize for him? Never mind. I can't talk about this now. I have company."

He winked at Amy, but she didn't miss the fact that his previously playful side had disappeared.

"Yes, Mom, *female company.* Just how long am I supposed to compensate Ben because I made it in the majors and he didn't?"

Obviously his mother wasn't listening to what Roper said, and Amy winced. As an only child, she wasn't used to dealing with siblings. But she *was* used to coping with stubborn adults who acted like kids and who wouldn't take no for an answer. She was being given an inkling into Roper's family dynamics, and they seemed to be in as much turmoil as his career.

"I didn't say family wasn't important, Mom. Go to your party and we'll talk about this tomorrow," he said, his voice softening.

He obviously loved his mother. He also had a complex family situation, but really, who didn't? She'd had to leave home to get a life, but that didn't mean she wasn't worried about every move Rose and Darla made. She loved them, but there were times they grated on her nerves, pushing every emotional button she possessed.

Roper obviously felt the same way about his family. His life wasn't easy, she thought. She quietly slipped the carrot they'd fought over into her mouth and waited for him to finish his call.

"Yes," he said, raising a finger toward Amy

to indicate he'd be off soon. "Yes, I know. Go enjoy and forget about it for now. Oh, and Mom? Happy New Year," Roper said.

He hung up the phone and turned her way. A flush highlighted his cheekbones and a muscle ticked on one side of his face. "Nothing like a call from Mom to kill the mood," he said too lightly.

Amy figured he needed a minute or two to calm down, so she let him turn away and place the food into the heated wok.

She tried to use the minutes wisely, reminding herself she wasn't going to be taken in by his charm, something he possessed and no doubt knew how to use in spades. After all, he was not just an athlete but a showman. Yet already she was coming to know him better and to like him despite all common sense. She tried to calm her still-racing heart, but Roper's effect on her was very strong. And the whole night lay ahead. . . .

CHAPTER THREE

Roper could not believe his mother was bugging him about helping Ben yet again. On New Year's Eve. Just as he was finally going to kiss Amy.

Still wound tight, he tossed the last handful of vegetables into the wok with too much force and oil splattered up at him. He stepped back to avoid being hit.

"Families can be a bitch," Amy said at last, breaking the tension.

He turned toward her. "Especially mine."

"Um . . ." She bit down on the bottom lip he'd been on the verge of devouring minutes before. "If you missed my mother and aunt in action, then I'm sure you heard the wedding stories. I hardly think I'm in a position to judge other people's relatives." She laughed, lightening his mood in an instant.

He didn't know another woman capable of getting into his head that way. He ought to be wary, but right now, he was just grateful. "You've got a point. My mother likes to lay on the guilt when I don't give Ben what he wants."

"Your brother played baseball, too?" Amy leaned forward and perched her chin in her hands.

He stared into her curious gaze. Discussing his personal life with anyone, especially women, had always been a big no-no. Inevitably something private made it into the papers after the relationship ended. He'd learned it early in the minors and had never violated the rule since.

Yet here he was, ready to talk to Amy. He drew a deep breath and forged ahead before he could stop himself. "Ben never made it past the minors. He blames me for inheriting talent from my father. His father, his and Sabrina's, wasn't good for much of anything. He walked out on my mother and us kids, which frankly wasn't much of a loss. But after baseball, Ben just ventured from job to job. You know the expression *jack of all trades, master of none?*"

She nodded in understanding, listening without judging, which only made him want to tell her more. "Over the years Ben's come to me for money for one investment after another, promising me a huge return. At first I thought he'd find something that gave him financial security. Eventually I realized that would never happen, but I helped him out, anyway, just because I could."

While he spoke, he took plates from the cabinet and she helped him set the table.

"You're a good brother," she said. "Uncle Spencer's taken care of his sisters the same way. He bought the retirement complex that my mother and her sister live in. It keeps them out of trouble. Or should I say, it confines their trouble. Anyway, it seems to work."

"Real estate is a smart investment. Ben's last idea was a franchise that would put condom machines in restrooms around the country. My brother was calling himself the future Condom King of America."

Amy pursed her lips to keep from laughing.

Roper grinned. "You can let it out. It's ridiculous, I know. But at my mother's insistence, I gave him the franchise money and he promptly passed it on to a guy who ran away with the cash. Last my detective heard, he was sunning himself in Mexico, avoiding extradition for embezzlement. Meanwhile there were a lot of disappointed, broke future Condom Kings he'd bilked out of large amounts of cash."

"So you'd like to help him but can't

because he's stubborn and invests in pipe dreams. Meanwhile you feel guilty that you won't help him anymore because he's still your family."

He gave her a quick nod. She'd nailed his dilemma perfectly, he thought, not all that surprised at her insight. But he was uncomfortable with how well she understood him. He stirred the vegetables and poured them into a bowl, covering it with foil to keep warm while he cooked the chicken.

Eventually the silence got to him. "So there you have the story of my life. How about you? Any brothers or sisters to tell tales about?"

She shook her head. "I'm an only child."

"Lucky you." A few more preparatory steps and he served the food, dividing up the meal and putting it on their plates.

She sat down at the table to eat. "I wouldn't say I was lucky. It was pretty lonely growing up by myself."

He tipped his head to one side. "I never looked at it that way." He'd had Ben to fight with and toss a ball to. And he'd had Sabrina trailing after him with doting eyes.

"That's because right now you have issues with your brother."

"Here's the thing." He set two full glasses of water on the table. "I love my family, but everyone needs something from me. They pull at me from every direction and like you said, I feel guilty not responding on the minute."

"Because you always have before."

"Exactly." He placed his hand on the top of his chair. "Now, how about some champagne? It *is* New Year's Eve."

She crinkled her nose in that cute way she had whenever she wasn't sure she wanted to do something. "Maybe just one glass."

He obliged, pulling a bottle from the fridge, popping the cork, pouring and finally sitting down beside her at the table. "A toast," he said, raising his glass.

She raised hers, as well.

"To . . . new friends," he said. He hadn't known how much he needed someone like Amy in his life until tonight. She was special.

A warm smile tilted her lips. "To new friends," she said, a gleam in her eyes as she touched her glass against his and took a sip.

"Good?"

She nodded. "Excellent. Now, you were saying that everyone in your family needs something from you. Care to elaborate beyond Ben?"

He lifted his fork and tasted his meal. "Mmm. Care to compliment the cook first?"

Laughing, she took a bite and paused.

And paused. And paused so long he nearly fell off the edge of his chair waiting for her opinion.

"This is unbelievably good!" she said at last with a smile on her face that bordered on orgasmic.

All he could imagine was putting that same expression on her face in a more intimate setting. But somehow, he managed to clear his throat and continue their discussion. "Thank you," he said, ridiculously thrilled that he'd pleased her palate.

He loved to cook and often did so to relieve tension when he had home games or just to help himself relax during the off-season. And he'd needed one helluva a lot of relaxing lately.

"Well? You were saying about your family?" Amy prodded without shame.

"Anyone ever tell you you're like a pit bull when you get your teeth into something?" he asked. She didn't reply, merely continued eating and waiting, knowing he'd have to answer eventually. "Oh, all right. I'll tell you, but I'll probably put you to sleep with my family saga."

She shook her head. "Try me."

He shrugged. "Mom's an actress, or at least she was until she aged beyond the point where cosmetic surgery enabled her to take youthful roles."

"Would I know of her?" Amy asked.

"Her stage name is Cassandra Lee."

Amy's eyes lit up. "From the movies *Maiden Lane* and *On Sandy Shores*! My mother is a huge fan and took me to her movies all the time when I was growing up!"

"That's her," Roper said. "These days she's too vain to accept the more mature roles, so she's settled into living her life with me supporting her. Not that I mind, since she worked hard to take care of us while I was a kid."

"It must be hard aging in Hollywood."

"There are plenty of better-known actresses who've handled it. Sharon Stone, Meryl Streep, Annette Bening. Mom has truly made *Poor Me* into an art form. But I'm used to it by now."

Amy finished her meal, leaving nothing on her plate. She wasn't one of those women who pushed the food around instead of eating, and that pleased him.

She raised her glass and sipped her champagne. "What about your father? Is he still alive? Mine isn't. He passed away a few months after I started junior high," she said, her tone wistful.

"I'm sorry." He wanted to squeeze her hand, but she didn't seem to want or need sympathy.

She finished her champagne and smiled.

He poured them both another glass. "My father is still alive. He just wasn't ever much of an influence in my life, except for the fact that I inherited my baseball talent from him. Eduardo Montoya. He was a big-time player in his day. And before you ask, Roper was my mother's name before she had it changed."

Amy inclined her head. "I've never heard of him, but that isn't saying much."

He nodded. "It's kind of nice that you don't know the professional me."

She nodded in understanding. He couldn't get over how much he'd revealed to her tonight. Other than with Micki, he never discussed his famous parents with anyone. He didn't need another reason for people to be impressed with something about him that had nothing to do with who he was inside. Amy was different. She was easy to talk to and genuinely interested in him, unlike the usual women he dated, ones who were more interested in his career, status and what he could buy them. Before now, all he'd wanted from his companions was a good time, in bed and out. Yet here was a woman he could talk to. . . .

Unwilling to think about that, he rose and

started to clean up. Amy helped and in the process, they managed to finish the bottle of champagne. Once the plates were in the dishwasher, and the kitchen was sparkling, he finally led Amy into the family room and turned on the big-screen TV to watch the ball drop in Times Square. He'd have offered to take her home, but he was enjoying her company too much and he didn't want to ring in the New Year alone.

She snuggled into the corner of the couch and didn't object when he eased in close beside her. From the way she'd tripped once on her way into the den and giggled a few times over a joke he hadn't made, Roper knew the champagne had gone to her head.

She was adorable to watch, and he liked having her in his home. Another first.

She narrowed her gaze at the TV screen depicting Times Square. "I can't believe all those people are standing outside in that freezing-cold weather. It was awful when we were there and it wasn't by choice!" She shivered at the memory, giving him just the excuse he needed.

"Spoken like a true Florida girl." Roper pulled her close at the same time the countdown to the New Year began.

"Know what I was doing last year at this time?" Amy asked him, her eyes wide, her face close to his.

"What?"

"Breaking up a fight between two men who wanted to kiss Aunt Darla first once the ball dropped," she murmured. "It's been ages since I spent New Year's with someone my own age."

"Oh, yeah? And when was the last time you were kissed?" he asked, staring at her moist lips.

"Way too long," she said as her eyes fluttered closed.

He knew she had to be slightly tipsy, because he couldn't imagine her letting her guard down this easily otherwise. Still, she'd seemed willing enough earlier in the evening before they were interrupted by the telephone.

He had every intention of taking that next step with her now.

Amy's stomach fluttered as she waited, delicious ripples of anticipation licking at her from deep inside. Roper's eyes darkened and he lowered his head, slowly dragging out the anticipation until finally his mouth came down on hers.

The initial touch set off more sparks. Spiraling whirlpools of desire started slowly and built larger, filling her from inside out.

His kiss was silky smooth, the stuff of sensual dreams as he drew his mouth back and forth over hers and lulled her into a hazy stupor of wanting. She lifted her hands and wrapped her arms around his neck, pulling him closer, something he seemed to appreciate because he slid his tongue over the seam of her lips, teasing her back and forth until she opened her mouth and let him inside.

Her tongue tangled with his, matching every fantasy she'd ever had of him and providing even more. He ran his thumbs over her cheek, gently caressing her face while he ravished her mouth. She didn't need food, not when she had this. Wanting to taste more of him, she curled her hands into the hair at the nape of his neck, then tilted her head back, giving him better access. He swept his tongue one last time around her mouth, then began a warm, wet trail of kisses down the side of her face, her neck, her throat, until his head came to rest on her chest just above her cleavage.

Her heart pounded and her breasts felt full, her nipples tightening into hardened peaks at the thought of his wicked mouth suckling her hard. Moisture pooled between her legs, dampening her panties as desire pulsed through her body.

"You taste sweet," he said against her skin.

She moaned. The sound tore from deep inside her at the same time the crowds cheered at the dropping of the ball.

"Happy New Year," she said, drunk with happiness.

"Happy New Year." He pulled back, and she tilted her head, smiling at him, expecting him to kiss her again. After all, the first time had been spectacular and he obviously wanted her, too.

Instead, he pushed himself up and rose to his feet.

"Where are you going?" she asked.

"To get you a blanket so I can tuck you in. Much as it kills me, I'm going to be a gentleman."

She started to rise, then decided it was too much effort. She hadn't had alcohol in a long time and the champagne had gone straight to her head. Of course, it could also be his kisses that made her feel light-headed and dizzy.

"Sit tight," he said, a sexy smile lifting his lips. "I'll be right back."

Amy lay her head back against the couch and shut her eyes, waiting for him to return. Maybe she'd be able to pull him down so they could finish what they'd started. Her mind might be hazy, but she was clear on what she wanted.

Amy wanted John Roper.

After hanging up with John, Cassandra Lee opened the screen door to her patio and walked outside into the warm air. Although she had to leave in half an hour for the New Year's party she was attending, she had some things to work out in her mind first. Family things. Personal things. Scary things.

She paced the length of her outdoor pool. Normally the rhythm made by her small heels clicking against the stone provided a soothing sound that helped her think more clearly. But her life was truly overwhelming right now and she found it hard to concentrate.

On the one hand, she had director Harrison Smith pressuring her not just to take the role he'd created for her but to let him back into her life. Her daughter was getting married, and instead of enjoying the planning, Cassandra felt more distant from Sabrina than ever. Her youngest son couldn't find himself and her oldest wouldn't cut the youngest any slack. On top of it all, John was undergoing the worst career crisis of his life and Cassandra didn't know how to help him.

At least he wasn't alone on New Year's.

He'd said he had company, which in John's world could mean a one-night stand, but something in his voice told her otherwise. The annoyance in his tone indicated he hadn't appreciated the interruption. Normally John took her calls without question. Cassandra hoped there was something special about this woman, because her son needed happiness in his life. She just hoped whoever she was, she liked a close-knit family, because that's what they were.

She picked up the phone and dialed her youngest son's cell phone. "Hello, Ben," she said when he answered on the first ring.

"Did you speak to John about the money for the gym?" he asked.

Cassandra sighed. She loved all her children, but truly Ben was the most selfish.

"Happy New Year, darling." Lowering herself onto a cushioned lounge chair, she eased back against the pillow. "Yes, I tried to talk to him, but the timing was wrong. John was busy. He said he had company and I think it was a woman. You know we have to approach your brother at the right time. He's got so much on his mind right now."

"And I don't? I could lose this opportunity," Ben said.

"Not on New Year's Eve, Benjamin." Cassandra didn't want to outright scold him.

After all, he'd never had things quite fall his way, not the way John had. "What if you try talking to your brother yourself?" she asked.

"He hates me, Mom. He never wants to help, and when he does, he blames me when things go wrong. But he can't say no to you. He never could. This is the big thing. I can feel it," Ben said, his tone pleading.

Her heart squeezed tighter in her chest. "I'll talk to him as soon as I can," she promised.

"Thanks. I have to go."

"I love you. Happy New —"

The phone line disconnected before she could finish.

Cassandra sighed. That was Ben. Well, at least she'd reached Sabrina and then Roper, wishing them both Happy New Years and receiving one in return.

She rose and headed inside to change and get ready for the party she was attending. The most mellow one of the year. A ladies-only affair among her closest friends, where she could end the old year the way she planned to start the new.

Avoiding her ex-lover Harrison Smith.

Amy awoke with a slight headache and fuzzy memories of an incredible night with a sweet man she'd once thought was anything but. She was glad she'd been wrong about him. As she stretched, she rolled over, and when she nearly fell face-first off the couch, she suddenly remembered where she'd spent the night.

On Roper's couch.

In Roper's apartment.

After that kiss.

"Oh, my God," she groaned, tossing her arm over her face.

"Good morning," he said in a gruff voice.

She peeked out and saw Roper standing over her with a glass of orange juice in hand. "Hi," she managed to say through the fuzzy cotton taste in her mouth.

Knowing she'd have to face him sometime, she scooted upright, bending her knees in front of her. "Is that for me?" she asked, eyeing the cold juice hopefully.

He nodded. "I figured you'd be up soon." He handed her the glass.

"Fresh squeezed?"

He rolled his eyes. "Now, that's pushing your luck."

She laughed. "I was curious just how far your culinary talent went." She took a sip and then downed the glass in two big gulps. "Mmm. That is so good. I'm sorry I fell asleep." The last thing she remembered was planning his seduction while waiting for him to bring her a blanket.

"Me, too." His intense gaze burned into hers.

She swallowed hard. "I hope it wasn't inconvenient having me stay over."

"Only if you consider me lying awake in my bed knowing you were right in the next room inconvenient." He spoke like a man who'd been a gentleman but who'd definitely had second thoughts.

Thank goodness she couldn't hold her champagne. "You're a good guy, John," she said, calling him by his given name.

"I like when you call me that." His face actually flushed. "As for being a good guy, I'm pretty sure it was a first."

She untangled herself from the blanket he'd covered her with. "I really should be getting home. The daytime doorman will let me in without a problem." She hoped. She got up and folded the covers, leaving them in a neat pile on the couch. "I'll just change and give you back your sister's clothes."

"There's no rush. Why don't you wear them home and I'll get them from you the next time I see you."

Meaning he wanted there to be a next time. So did she. But she had a plan for her life, and while last night she'd gotten carried away in the moment, helped by the alcohol, she had to put the brakes on here and now. Even if he was the guy she'd gotten to know last night and not the showman from the wedding, she needed time and space to get a foothold in her new life before getting involved in a relationship.

But she wasn't going to make an issue out of a magnanimous gesture. "Are you sure your sister won't mind?"

"She hasn't stayed over since getting engaged, and even if she wanted to, there are more clothes in the closet. Trust me, she won't care if you borrow some things." He grinned then, a sexy gesture meant to sway her, and it worked.

"Okay, but I'm going to look pretty ridiculous wearing these sweats and my high heels from last night."

"You'll look cute, not ridiculous." He ran his finger down the bridge of her nose, over the freckles she'd always found embarrassing because they made her look so young. It wasn't the first time he'd done it, and the gesture felt incredibly intimate and sensual.

"Excuse me for a minute, okay?" she said, slipping by him so she could head for the bathroom before she got caught up in how delicious he looked wearing low-slung, unbuttoned jeans and no shirt.

His hair had been messed either from

sleep or from running a hand through it in place of a comb or brush. First thing in the morning he looked endearingly sexy, and she'd have to convince herself not to notice if she wanted to get out of here quickly, with a minimum of fuss. She was determined to make her morning-after-nothing-happened escape, thank you very much.

"Amy, are you okay in there?" Roper knocked on the bathroom door, startling her back to reality.

"Fine! I'll be out in a sec." She brushed her teeth with minty toothpaste and one finger before drawing a deep breath and heading out to face him again.

He'd slipped on a royal-blue Renegades sweatshirt and a pair of Nike sneakers.

No less handsome, she thought, holding back a frustrated frown.

He grabbed his keys from the bowl by the door.

"Where are you going?" she asked.

He narrowed his gaze. "Where do you think? I'm taking you home."

She shook her head. "I'll be fine. It's broad daylight now."

"And I'll feel better knowing that your doorman is willing to let you inside the apartment without your key." His tone left no room for argument. Neither did the fact that he picked up a garment bag in which he'd obviously hung her outfit. He handed her shoes to her and waited while she slipped them on.

"I feel silly," she muttered as she followed him into the hall.

"Adorable," he corrected her. Placing one hand on her back, he led her to the elevator. A moment later, the door opened and they stepped inside.

People joined them at various floors, leaving no time for conversation, and Amy was relieved. She tried not to feel as if she was sneaking out of a man's apartment in last night's clothes, but she wasn't a pro at this. It didn't matter that she hadn't slept with him, she was embarrassed, anyway. She couldn't help but feel people were looking at her — and him — and staring.

Because John was famous in this city and was certainly well known in his own apartment building, Amy figured it wasn't her imagination, nor was she being paranoid. By the time the elevator came to a halt on the ground level, she practically ran toward the revolving doors.

Roper watched Amy teeter on those silly heels, which made her look both sexy and cute at the same time. He wanted to yell out and tell her they could take his car instead of a cab, but he figured that would call even more attention to her, something she obviously didn't want.

He could understand her need to escape. She wasn't used to strangers gawking at her the way he was. Since most women — heck, *all* the women he'd dated up until now — *liked* the fact that being with him put them in the spotlight, this was but another facet of her personality that made Amy unique. And special.

Ironically he was more convinced than ever that he'd done the right thing by not having sex with her last night. Now she would appreciate his sense of decency. No matter how hard it had been and how much sleep it had cost him.

Instead of following her through the revolving doors, he hit the handicapped automatic door and caught up with her outside on the sidewalk.

Just in time for the paparazzi to greet them with flashing lightbulbs and microphones shoved into their faces.

Roper fended off the vultures by answering their questions about who had spent the night in his apartment with deliberately chatty nonanswers, giving Amy time to escape.

From the corner of his eye, he saw her flag and get into a yellow cab before the press could stop her. He still held on to her clothes but decided not to worry about that now. No matter how hard he prodded, nobody in the group of reporters was willing to divulge their source or tell him why they'd chosen this morning to stake him out. It made no sense. Despite his recent notoriety, he was small-time news for a New Year's Day morning.

Eventually he returned to his apartment, which felt emptier somehow without Amy in it, and he spent the day watching Bowl games with some teammates who showed up uninvited. He was grateful for the company and even ordered pizza as a show of goodwill. He might have cooked to impress Amy, but the guys could damn well eat takeout.

He called her to apologize and to make sure she'd gotten home okay, but her voice recording picked up. He didn't know whether she was deliberately not answering the phone or if she had plans for the day. He left a message along with his number.

She never returned his call, which left him feeling surprisingly bummed out.

He awoke the next day, a Tuesday, feeling as if he'd never slept at all. Not a good sign.

He'd hoped the coming year would be kinder than the last.

He had a meeting with Micki scheduled at the Hot Zone offices that morning — at her request. He figured he could pump her for information about Amy then. Roper hadn't wanted to bother her yesterday, because he knew how rare her time with her husband and daughter actually was. After his New Year's Day incident with the press, Roper could understand the appeal of solitude.

"Maybe I ought to buy myself an island," he muttered. "Oh, that's right, I can't. I'm frigging cash poor and tapped out." Okay, he knew that was an exaggeration.

He'd made damn good investments with his money and had prepared for the future from day one of his first big contract. He never wanted to be one of those athletes who pissed away their money and were left with nothing to show for it after their successful career was over. But his family was spending cash like water and he was the spout. He had no choice but to keep an eye on things — in case his career ended sooner than planned. He rubbed his shoulder and hoped the rehab and physical therapy would do the trick.

He finished his cappuccino, brewed in a

state-of-the-art machine he'd bought last year, and decided he couldn't wait to meet with Micki later this morning. He picked up his cell phone, needing to talk to his best friend now.

Roper wanted nothing more than some basic information on how to win Amy over. Who better than Micki, who'd rented Amy her apartment, to fill him in?

Roper already figured a girl like Amy might be intimidated by his status and celebrity. Last night he'd questioned the wisdom of getting involved with her once he'd discovered she was living and working in New York. One evening in her company had shown him how different she was from the other women he'd dated. He could no longer just walk away. He was determined to show her he was worth the hassle that came along with him, because he realized they could have a good time together.

And Roper believed in good times. Man, he could use some. . . .

The woman looked spooked, he thought, watching as she ducked into the nearest cab, running from the paparazzi he'd notified. She wore sweats, a sweatshirt and high heels. A ridiculous combination, he thought. Just as ridiculous as the fact that her outfit from last night still dangled from Roper's hands. He snickered. It's about time Roper looked ridiculous.

He intended to make sure the media continued to know where Roper was and when, keeping him in the news, maintaining the negative press.

Shoving his hands into his jacket pockets, he turned and walked down the street, away from the luxury building. He had no doubt the swarm of paparazzi would continue to circle and create trouble for John Roper.

CHAPTER FOUR

New Year's Day in a new town was a bummer, Amy thought, staring at the walls of her small apartment. She could pass the day alone, cooped up inside, or she could brave the cold and hit the department stores. She'd already gone shopping with Sophie and Annabelle for a new work wardrobe, but she still needed heavy sweaters and clothes for the change in climate. Even if shopping hadn't been a necessity, keeping busy was. Anything to stop her from thinking about John Roper and the media circus that was a part of his life.

She could fall hard for the man, that much she knew. Never mind that he had one hot body and he'd singed her with kisses that left her wanting more. He was sensitive and he cared for his family, he cooked, for goodness' sake, and he'd decorated his own apartment. Yet what should be a perfect start to a possible relationship wasn't.

Everything about John Roper and his life was detrimental to her goals and needs.

She'd grown up with a father who instilled in her the need to make a difference in the world, and her short career as a social worker had been a sure way of doing just that. She understood she was idealizing her dad, but even her mother always spoke of what a good man he'd been. Make your father proud, Amy. She'd tried.

She'd failed.

She'd been let go from her job as a social worker for the state because her mother's antics, captured in the paper with Amy by her side, contradicted the necessary level of decorum her boss insisted went with her job. Instead of looking for other employment, she'd moved back home and taken the position of social director at her mom and aunt's retirement community to watch over them. Surely her father had been nodding in approval over that move.

Her dad had been a stabilizing influence in Rose Stone's life, but after he died, she'd gotten more wild. Uncle Spencer had never tried to control his sisters. They were extremely close to him, as was Amy, but he believed in letting people make their own mistakes. Besides, considering he lived in New York, Amy knew there wasn't much he could do even if he'd tried. So Amy had stepped in, taking over where her father had left off. She could be stern when she needed to be, and she'd had things in Fort Lauderdale well in hand.

She'd bailed her mother and aunt out of the local jail more times than she could count for being a public nuisance. From raucous parties to turning the water in the fountain in the local mall pink in honor of Breast Cancer Awareness Month, Amy's mother and aunt had indulged in an array of bad behavior.

The only reason none of the arrests had resulted in anything more serious than a warning, a fine or community service was because their local judge had a crush on Aunt Darla and Rose baked for the police officers, allowing them to avoid the greasy doughnut shops during their downtime. Amy wasn't a complete stick-in-the-mud and she did find her relatives amusing at times, but she'd always had to be the rational one, the savior. Like Roper, she was the responsible caretaker of the group.

But she had the chance now to make a career for herself even if it wasn't a world-changing job. She needed to make herself, her mother and, by extension, her late father, proud.

Amy sighed and shook her head. She hated being the center of attention, which was why she was so thrilled to be working at the Hot Zone. She'd be the person behind the celebrity. Even if she wanted to give a relationship or even an affair with Roper a chance, his lifestyle demanded anyone in his personal sphere succumb to the media attention. And that was something she wasn't willing to be a part of, especially in the big way his life demanded.

She'd just have to push her intense feelings for the man aside in favor of focusing on work and creating a life for herself here in New York.

With one last glance at the answering machine holding his phone number and the recording of his husky voice asking her to call him, she grabbed her purse and headed for the stores instead.

The day after New Year's, Amy sat in the conference room of the Hot Zone offices. All seats around the table were filled and she fidgeted in her seat, ready to begin.

Yank cleared his throat. "The weekly meeting of the Hot Zone and Athletes Only will now come to order." He slammed his gavel down on the table, missing the rubber padding made to cushion the blow. The wooden hammer hit the conference table and Amy felt the vibrations rippling throughout her body. She jumped up from her seat, then discovered she was the only one who had. Micki, Annabelle, Sophie, Lola and even her uncle Spencer had already slid their chairs back, away from the table in anticipation of Yank's move.

Amy's cheeks burned as she lowered herself slowly back into her chair.

"Sorry. We should have warned you he has no aim." Micki, tanned from her time on the island, resettled herself in her chair and the rest of the group did the same.

"And he doesn't care that he's scarring an expensive table," Sophie added.

"Stop talkin' about me like I'm not in the room," Yank muttered. "I'm the one in charge. The meeting's been called to order. As you all can see even if I can't, we have a new member of the team. Amy, we're happy to have you."

"Thank you," Amy said, touched.

"No thanks necessary," Annabelle said.

"Besides, change is good." Lola patted Yank's hand.

"Even if it means I'm getting older and blinder?" he asked.

"Even then," Lola said softly.

"Amen," Uncle Spencer said, probably

because he was aging along with his friend, something Amy preferred not to think about too long or too hard.

She remained silent instead, sensing it was the wrong time to interrupt. Even the three sisters remained quiet, letting Yank be comforted by his wife.

Of course the silence didn't last long. "Well, what are you waiting for?" Yank asked, all bluster once more. "First order of business. Michelle?" he asked, calling Micki by her given name.

The first half hour of the meeting consisted of a run-through of current clients, assignments and status updates, along with banter most often begun or finished off by Yank. Amy found the dynamic interesting, considering the family-run business operated smoothly despite it all.

"Now, on to the new assignments," Yank said.

"Amy, we have your first client all lined up," Micki said. "After Spencer came to us with the idea of hiring you, one of the things that impressed us most was your organizational ability. After all, you've spent the past few years single-handedly running the activities at a retirement community where the older residents are cantankerous at worst and difficult at best."

Amy couldn't hold back a laugh. "That's a better description than any I could have come up with."

"Hey, are you picking on us old folks?" Yank asked.

Uncle Spencer rolled his eyes. "It takes one to know one."

"Look who's talking," Yank said to his best friend.

Annabelle rose from her seat. "Grow up, both of you! Micki, go on."

Sophie and Lola applauded while Annabelle reseated herself.

"Okay, as I was saying, when this assignment came in, we immediately chose you because of your ability to micromanage."

"I'm grateful for your faith in me." Amy rubbed her hands together, the idea of digging into her new job exciting her. "So tell me more."

Micki nodded. "We have a client, a baseball player, who is having serious career issues and who needs to focus completely on both the game and on *his* life. Unfortunately he has family complications that are distracting him."

Amy shook her head. "If I didn't know better, I'd think you were talking about John Roper," she said, without really meaning it.

But every last person at the table turned

their gaze her way.

Oh, no, Amy thought. Not Roper. Somehow she managed not to say the words aloud. She couldn't. Whoever the client was, Amy had no choice but to accept him with a smile. It was her first day, her first assignment, and she could not afford to act like a prima donna.

"So it *is* John Roper?" Amy asked.

All heads at the table nodded.

"Okay, then." She pasted on her brightest smile. "At least it's someone I already know." Thank goodness nobody at the table knew just how well she'd almost come to know Roper.

"That's what we thought," Micki said, obviously pleased with the business pairing.

"Although, if you aren't comfortable . . ." Sophie's voice trailed off, her offer clear. The other woman obviously sensed now, as she'd indicated at the party the other night, that Amy's history with Roper might make it uncomfortable for her to work with him.

Amy shook her head. "It's fine. I'm fine." Nobody at the table knew she'd spent the night at Roper's place New Year's Eve.

A knock sounded on the conference-room door and her uncle Spencer's secretary, Frannie, walked in. "I'm sorry for interrupting but I have news that can't wait."

"Come on in and let's hear it," Annabelle said, gesturing with her hands. "Something juicy, I hope?"

Micki leaned over and whispered to Amy. "Frannie gets the morning papers and fills us in with anything we need to know about our clients that the press got their teeth into first."

"Got it," Amy said, nodding.

"You, my dear, have *arrived.*" Frannie strode over to Amy, taking her by complete surprise. "Photograph and articles."

"Excuse me?" Amy asked, confused.

"Page Six in the *New York Post*!" Frannie exclaimed.

"Get out! What are you holding back?" Annabelle asked Amy. At the same time, Micki snatched the paper from Frannie's hands and began riffling through it.

The other woman, Amy noticed, had a second copy beneath her arm.

"What is on Page Six?" Amy finally managed to ask.

"Only the premier source of celebrity gossip in New York City," Lola pointed out, her voice calm in the midst of the sisters' excitement.

Amy thought she might throw up. "Celebrity?" A sick feeling settled in the pit of her stomach as the memory of the flashing cameras outside Roper's apartment came back to her, more vivid than ever.

"Liz Smith and Cindy Addams's columns are featured there," Sophie said. "What does it say about Amy?"

"Quit keepin' it to yourself," Yank ordered.

Their curiosity piqued, everyone seemed oblivious to Amy's anxiety. Everyone except her uncle Spencer, who glanced at her through worried eyes.

Micki began to read aloud. "What troubled Renegades player needs a distraction from his problematic moves on the field? On New Year's Eve, hottie John Roper forgot his troubles with a lady friend who is surprisingly not of the garden-variety sexpots he normally dates. Who is she and is it serious? Considering this photo was taken outside Roper's apartment building on New Year's Day and the woman was wearing very comfortable clothes, *anything* is possible. Stay tuned."

At least they hadn't mentioned her by name, Amy thought.

"Anything else?" Annabelle asked.

She wanted more?

"The *Daily News* picked up the piece and ran with it." Frannie pushed her glasses farther up on her nose and began to read. " 'John Roper is numbing his pain in the arms of a woman. Amy Stone, a Florida transplant and the newest member of the Hot Zone team, was caught sneaking out of his apartment building New Year's Day wearing nothing more than sweats and high heels from their aborted soiree at the Hot Zone the night before. A new year, a new relationship and maybe a *renewed* career. I say, "Go for it, Johnny!" ' "

Yank snickered.

Amy winced. She'd been trying to forget the incident, going so far as to give up on the outfit she'd left with him. Thanks to the New York press, she was big-time news. She might even have outdone her mother and aunt, and that was saying something.

"What's the original source?" Sophie asked.

"Gawkerstalker.com." Frannie offered her copy of the paper to Amy.

She shook her head.

"Even though we didn't invite the press to the party, I'm guessing someone saw Roper outside the office after the fire alarm went off and called it in. Either they were followed back to Roper's apartment or they found the information on the Web site and staked out his building hoping for a story."

"Well, they got one," Amy muttered. "What is gawkerstalker.com?" she asked.

103

"A celebrity-sighting Web site. People e-mail, text message or call in celebrity sightings," Micki explained.

"You're kidding. I didn't know there was such a thing."

"Celebs are big news, and in New York, athletes are prime targets, too. In fact, there's one more mention," Frannie said.

"Let's get it over with, please," Amy said, resigned.

The older woman cleared her throat and silence settled over the room. "We're not the only ones who keep up with Page Six. Frank Buckley picked up the story, too."

"Buckley is Roper's number-one nemesis," her uncle explained.

Frannie nodded. "I downloaded his comments from his Web site. He says, 'Premier sports agents Spencer Atkins and Yank Morgan may have one helluva time unloading Roper to any team this off-season, and not just because of his poor playing skills. But if his New Year's Eve activities are any indication, Roper's only interested in one kind of game.' "

"Poor playing skills, my ass," Spencer said, jumping up from the table. "The man still had a batting average of 290, thirty-five home runs and 121 RBIs, even with his problems. He's got a no-trade clause and he's not going anywhere," he said, then lowered himself back into his seat.

That was her uncle, Amy thought. Yank might bluster but Spencer spoke when he had something deliberate and calculated to say. She wondered what he'd have to say to her. Then again, considering his hands-off approach to her mother, maybe he'd forgo the lecture.

Sophie spoke, calming the room. "I suggest we all settle down and discuss things calmly and rationally."

Lola grabbed the gavel before Yank could second the motion with a smashing blow.

"Does anyone else have anything to add?" Sophie asked.

Yank rose to his feet again, and for the first time Amy realized his brightly patterned shirt clashed with his brown pants. He must have fought Lola on helping him, she thought. Pride was a valued commodity and Amy could understand holding on to it at any cost.

Right now hers was in shreds.

"Uncle Yank, it's your turn," Sophie said, obviously having taken control of the meeting.

Amy wondered if she did the firing. The memory of losing her social-worker job was still clear in her mind.

"I don't like none of this," he said, shaking his head.

Here it comes, Amy thought, nausea rolling through her.

"There's no reason for the reporter who wrote that article to give me second billing to that yahoo," Yank grumbled, pointing at Spencer. "Athletes Only's a Morgan Atkins production. Not vice versa."

"Sit down and shut up," Lola said, grabbing his arm and pulling him back into his seat. "This isn't about you and your mammoth ego."

"No, it's about me and I want to apologize to all of you," Amy said. "I know I've humiliated this firm by getting involved with a client. If you want to let me go, I completely understand."

Without warning, Yank burst out laughing. "What's to apologize for? You didn't do anything different from any of my other girls."

All three sisters nodded in agreement.

"Amy," Micki said, walking over and placing an arm around Amy's shoulder. "You didn't cause trouble for the firm. In fact, you single-handedly changed public opinion about John Roper."

"How so?" she asked, now thoroughly confused by their reaction.

"I've been trying to get Roper to act up again and take the spotlight off the World Series disaster. You did it without even trying! And the paper is right. You're nothing like the bimbos he usually hangs out with, which lets people see him in a new light. A more respected light, even." Micki's grin said more than her words ever could about how she felt about the situation.

There were murmurs of agreement from around the table.

Amy narrowed her gaze, confounded by the entire morning. She didn't understand New York celebrity at all, but she'd better get a handle on it and fast because her job depended on just that.

"Amy, your client is waiting for you in your office."

She blinked, the pronouncement taking her off guard. "You still want me to work with Roper?"

"Of course! You're still perfect for the job," Micki assured her.

"Uncle Spencer?" Amy glanced at her uncle, needing his affirmation more than ever.

He nodded. "You're our girl," he said with confidence.

Her heart filled, thanks to their support, but pounded hard in her chest with the knowledge that she'd been firmly placed in Roper's universe. Still, no matter how difficult she'd find keeping her distance from the man on a personal level, compartmentalizing was what she did best.

She had no doubt she could handle the job of organizing his life. She only hoped she could handle John Roper.

After the meeting adjourned, Micki followed her uncle to the break room. Refusing help, he'd had his assistant bring Noodle to him and let the dog bark and woof her way to where the food was located before Micki took charge and led them both to his office. They sat side by side on the comfortable couch he'd had since she was a little girl who'd come to live with him when her parents died. Unlike her sisters, she'd follow him around, and even insisted he bring her to work. This place had always been in her heart.

"Well, well, well," Uncle Yank said. "Exciting morning."

Micki nodded. "Poor Amy. She doesn't understand New York and what it means to be an athlete here."

Micki herself had been baptized by fire into the New York PR world. Micki felt awful about the unplanned coverage, but if

Amy was going to survive here, she'd have to weather storms like this. Especially if she was going to get involved with Roper. The man was a media magnet.

Not that Micki knew the extent of their relationship. Roper hadn't mentioned that Amy had spent the night at his place New Year's Eve, but Micki understood why. Roper was nothing if not a gentleman.

She turned to her uncle. "Roper never mentioned the papers when he stopped by early this morning, so I'm sure he hasn't seen the articles yet." Because he'd been solely focused on Amy, Micki thought.

"He probably figured a bigger story would hit and make him old news before the photos were ever published," Yank said.

"Probably." Micki stood and paced the office, taking in the awards on the walls and photographs of her uncle and famous athletes he'd represented over the years — including one of Roper the day he'd signed his multimillion-dollar contract with the Renegades. "I feel bad that Amy's upset, but you have to admit that the media talking about Roper's love life and not his career is exactly what he needs right now."

Yank snickered. "The boy needs more than that. But you're right. It's a good start. I knew you'd come around to my way of thinkin'."

Her uncle was referring to his notion of setting up Roper and Amy. After he'd decided on that course, he'd gone to Micki for help. But having been on the receiving end of her uncle's matchmaking schemes, Micki had refused, despite the fact that she believed the two would make a great couple. Micki wanted nothing more than to see her best friend settled and happy just as she was with Damian.

But she wouldn't meddle. "I didn't come around to your way of thinking. I just happen to think assigning Amy to Roper works for the business." That it would work for them personally, as well, was a bonus. Or so Micki told herself when she'd paired them as a business team — the idea occurring to her just this morning while Roper was questioning her about Amy Stone, his interest clear.

Her uncle laughed. "Either way, the result's the same. They're together. Nature can do the rest."

Amy walked into her office only to find it empty. She returned to check back with Kelly, the receptionist she shared with one of the other publicists. "Good morning again," Amy said.

Before she could ask, the woman handed her a stack of pink message notes. "These are for you," Kelly said with a smile.

Amy narrowed her gaze. "I don't know many people in town and this is my first day. What gives?"

"You're experiencing your fifteen minutes of fame. The papers want to interview you. Mind if I give you a suggestion?" the other woman asked.

"I'm all ears," Amy said, wanting any help she could get.

Kelly leaned closer, her bangs falling over her eyes as she leaned in, and whispered, "Ignore them."

Amy blinked. "That's it? That's the magic formula?"

"That and praying for some other athlete to make a scene or screw up so he replaces you and Roper in the headlines." Kelly nodded sagely.

"Got it. Speaking of Roper, did he —"

"Leave a message? Yes, he did. Here." She handed Amy a white envelope with her name written on the front. "He was waiting patiently until he got an urgent phone call. Then he asked for paper to leave you a note and rushed out." Apparently her new secretary was the epitome of efficiency.

Amy was grateful something was going

right today. "Thank you, Kelly."

"That's my job. Oh, you have a lunch date at 1:00 p.m. today at Sparks. It's a steak house on Forty-Sixth between Second and Third. Since that's prime lunch hour and we're farther uptown, you might want to give yourself some time to get there. Would you prefer cab, car or subway?" Kelly asked, pen in hand, ready to tackle anything.

Florida girl that she was, Amy wasn't ready to take on the NYC subway system just yet. "I'll just go down and grab a cab."

Kelly rolled her pen between her palms. "No, never mind, that won't work. You might not get one at that hour. I'll make sure a car is waiting." She placed her hand on the phone, obviously ready to do just that.

"It seems like an extravagance to take a car for lunch," Amy said.

"We bill it to the client. It's fine, really. SOP," Kelly said.

"SOP?"

"Standard operating procedure."

Amy smiled. "Got it. It looks as if you have everything covered except for one thing."

"What's that?" Kelly glanced up at her, surprised.

"Who am I meeting for lunch?"

Kelly tapped her head with her hands. "I didn't mention that? Roper. It's all in the note he left. Since he couldn't have his business meeting with you due to a family emergency, he said he wanted to take you for lunch and do it there."

"Aah." Family emergency. Amy glanced at her watch. At 11:00 a.m. in the morning. Apparently Roper needed her even more than she realized.

"Take a paper and pen to lunch," Kelly said. "Make notes so you don't forget anything. Not that I'm suggesting you're forgetful, but if it were *me* having a business lunch with that perfect specimen, I'm sure I wouldn't remember anything he said. And I'm pretty on-the-ball," Kelly said, laughing.

Amy grinned. "That you are, and something tells me I'm going to need your expertise during this transition period."

"Did anyone tell you that Rachel, the other publicist I work for, is out on maternity leave? I'm all yours for the next three months."

And Kelly seemed eager to help, for which Amy was grateful. "That's even more good news."

"Do you need me to join you at lunch?" Kelly asked hopefully. "I could hold Roper's hand. I mean, I could hold *your* hand." Her eyes twinkled with mischief and Amy chuckled.

"I think I can handle it," Amy said.

Those words were becoming her mantra.

"You're definitely lucky. The man is one hot property," Kelly said, returning her focus to her ringing phone.

Amy remembered his lips on hers and merely nodded in agreement. Hot property. Yep, Roper was definitely that and more. Keeping her mind on *business* during lunch was going to be *very* difficult.

Roper arrived at Sparks a few minutes early and the maître d' led him to his favorite table, a private one in the corner where he and Amy wouldn't be disturbed by prying eyes. It was bad enough his sister had called crying, begging him to meet her at her apartment. She'd been beyond upset. He couldn't understand the reason for her hysteria, but he'd scrawled an apology note for Amy all the same and headed to the SoHo loft she shared with her fiancé, Kevin. There he discovered the breakdown had been caused by a distraught message from their mother, threatening to come to New York and take over the wedding plans if Sabrina didn't start returning her calls.

Roper could understand his sister not wanting their mother in control of her life. Even more, he could relate to Sabrina's fear of having Her Highness show up on their doorstep. Roper adored his mother, but he loved the fact that she lived in L.A. even more. She still managed to do her share of driving him crazy, but at least it was from a distance. Still, as much as he understood Sabrina's feelings, he wished she'd called Kevin home from work for sympathy instead of him.

She'd pulled him away from Amy. Roper hadn't known Amy was working at the Hot Zone. In fact, the more he thought about his night with her, the more he realized he'd been the one to reveal things about his family and his life while she'd listened, not giving away much about herself at all.

He was glad. For one thing, she remained a mystery he could unravel at his leisure. For another, if he'd known she would end up in his life in such a big way, he'd probably have had second thoughts about getting involved. This way, he was already hooked and he wanted her too much to back out now.

He owed his best friend for assigning Amy as his handler, although he hadn't thought he really needed one. Then again, he did need someone to organize his life, lightening his load so he could concentrate on recovering enough to make it to spring training in February. Micki had made the right call by assigning him Amy. A win-win situation, just the way he liked it.

Not knowing whether she liked red wine or white, he decided on champagne. He thought twice about splurging on Dom Pérignon, then decided his bank account could take the hit. Amy was worth it. The champagne on ice was waiting for her when she joined him at the table.

He wasn't surprised, when his cell phone rang, to find his mother was on the other end. "Good morning," he said, refusing to let his good mood dissipate.

"Hi, darling, how are you?"

"Not bad, considering I spent the morning calming Sabrina down. Do you think you could let her plan her own wedding?" He didn't hold out much hope he'd get through to her, but it couldn't hurt to try.

"What daughter doesn't really want her mother involved in the most important day of her life?" his mother asked.

He leaned back in his seat. "She wants you involved, not taking over."

"I'm just making helpful suggestions." She sniffed. "It's my only daughter's wedding.

116

Can't you just talk to her and explain I love her and want what's best?"

"What's best is what makes Sabrina and Kevin happy." He looked up and saw Amy at the front of the restaurant, handing her coat to the check girl. "I have to go, my lunch date's here."

"Not that crazy agent of yours?" his mother asked.

She'd met Yank on one of her trips to the city. There'd never been two different people placed on this planet, he thought, laughing. "No, with Amy Stone."

"Your Page Six girl!"

He winced. "I didn't know you read the *New York Post* in L.A."

Her light laugh traveled through the phone line. "Darling, you rushed me off the phone New Year's Eve and Ben sent me the *Post.* I put two and two together. You should have told me you were in a new relationship. Where are you taking her?" she asked.

He rolled his eyes and raised a hand, waving at Amy as she approached. "I'm at Sparks. On business. Bye, Mom. Love you." He snapped his phone shut and rose to greet Amy.

"Hi, there," he said, taking in her business attire and trying not to drool at the sight.

She wore a cream-colored pantsuit that

accentuated her tanned skin, and though she'd clipped her hair back, soft curls framed her face, giving her a tailored yet sexy look. Micki had mentioned that Annabelle had taken Amy shopping for a New York work wardrobe and he applauded both women's taste. On Amy, the pantsuit looked feminine, especially when paired with pointy-toed shoes peeking out beneath the hem of the slacks. Beneath the tailored suit jacket, instead of a blouse she wore a V-necked three-button vest cut low enough to tempt and dazzle, but covered enough to be appropriate for work. Business casual and chic — Amy had made the transition from Florida native to New Yorker in no time.

And even dressed for the office, she managed to turn him on.

CHAPTER FIVE

Amy walked through Sparks, the steak house chosen by Roper for their lunch, and found herself taken in by the old-boy charm of the establishment. She appreciated the decor and she tried to focus on that — on anything except the man watching her intently as she approached.

Roper rose as she came closer and waited until she was seated and they were alone before settling back in. "I'm glad you could join me," he said, his voice warm and welcoming.

"I'm glad, too." She placed her napkin on her lap and took a second to cover her stomach with her hand, hoping to ease the butterflies inside, made worse because the car ride had taken longer than it should have. The vice president was in town, roads were closed and *gridlock* was the word of the day. "I'm sorry I'm late. The traffic was horrendous."

"Not a problem. It gave me time to relax a little first." He glanced down and pulled his phone from a holder at his waist. "Excuse me. Phone call." He answered, had a quick conversation that sounded much like the one she'd heard New Year's Eve with his mother, before meeting her gaze once more. "Sorry, that was my sister," he said, placing his phone on the table.

"No problem." She clasped her hands together, thinking that his family most definitely *was* his problem.

"Where was I? Oh, yes. I'm glad you're here and I ordered us champagne." He inclined his head to the side of the table, and for the first time she noticed the ice bucket and the bottle chilling inside.

Memories of New Year's Eve rose quickly and vividly in her mind before she could shut them out. But she couldn't concentrate on business if she was busy remembering how soft and moist his lips had felt on hers or how the intoxicating scent of his cologne had wrapped around her, enveloping her in heat.

She cleared her throat. "It's a working lunch," she reminded him, hating that she sounded stiff, but knowing it was necessary.

"And we will work. But first —" he treated her to a sexy smile "— I'd like to toast our new relationship."

"Relationship?" The word came out more like a squeak.

"Working relationship." A teasing sparkle lit his gaze. "Isn't that why we're here?"

She exhaled hard. "I'd love to toast. I just can't promise to drink."

"Still recovering from New Year's?" he asked.

She shook her head. "I'm over it. I mean —"

"I understand what you meant." He laughed and leaned forward in his seat. "And if you'd just relax around me, I won't even ask why you haven't returned any of my calls."

Her cheeks grew uncomfortably hot. "I needed to distance my work and my personal relationships."

"Which I might have understood if you'd called me back and explained. Or if you'd told me you were working at the Hot Zone to begin with." He gestured to the waiter, who began to unwrap, uncork and pour the champagne.

"The subject of where I was working never came up. But I admit not returning your phone calls was a little cowardly of me. I'm sorry."

"And I'm sorry about the reporters and

the articles in today's paper." His normally easygoing smile disappeared, replaced by obvious regret. "I have no idea how they zeroed in on us after New Year's and I certainly never thought they'd make us newsworthy. I took a private booth back here, so hopefully we're safe from prying eyes."

His cell phone buzzed suddenly, shaking on the table and breaking the connection subtly flowing between them. Although he'd set the phone to vibrate, the intrusion was just as noticeable.

Shooting her an apologetic glance, he picked up the phone. This time, however, his tone was different, brittle even. "Bad time. I'm busy. I'll call you later." He disconnected the call and placed the phone back on the table.

She met his gaze. "Your brother."

He nodded. "You're astute."

"I just remembered what you told me the other night. Where does he live?"

"Nowhere permanent. Right now he's staying with a friend not too far from here."

"So all three of you are in the city."

He nodded. "We love our mother, but distance seems to work best for all of us," he said, laughing.

"Speaking of your mother, I suppose she's

going to call next?" she asked.

He groaned. "Probably, but I'd rather not think about her right now. So back to New Year's . . . I'm sorry for the press showing up like that. If I'd known, I'd have taken you out the back or used my car so they never would have gotten a shot of you in the first place."

"Apparently I need to get used to the New York media. According to the rest of the office, the articles about us did you a favor by directing everybody's attention to your personal life instead of your career." She raised an eyebrow, curious about his view on their joint minutes of fame.

He burst out laughing, a response she didn't expect.

"That's rich," he said. "Eight months ago, those same Hot Zone people wanted my personal life out of the papers. Now they're applauding the coverage." Without warning, he reached over and placed his hand over hers.

The heat was immediate and intense.

"But you don't deserve the publicity." His voice grew low and husky. "So I am sorry."

"I thought, as a publicist, I'd be remaining behind the scenes. But it's fine. Really." She waved away his apology, trying to act in control and, oh, so nonchalant over the incident, which at the moment affected her less than the man himself.

Ever since their first meeting, it didn't take more than a touch to remind her of how easily he could seduce her with a look, a glance or a simple gesture. She'd never had such an immediate connection with a man before and she didn't know how to ignore the sparks that sizzled between them now.

"Okay, then, it looks as if once again we're starting over," he said, pleased. He lifted his hand off of hers and raised his glass.

Relieved he wasn't touching her anymore and disappointed at the same time, she lifted her glass.

"To us," he said simply.

Unable and unwilling to argue, she repeated his words. "To us."

She took a polite sip and placed the champagne back on the table. They looked through the menu, then listened to the daily specials. She ordered a mixed green salad and rainbow trout, he chose oysters on the half shell and prime sirloin steak.

She studied him as he spoke to the waiter. Roper was a man comfortable in his own skin and too handsome in his tan-and-white-striped dress shirt, opened at the throat. He might be suffering personally and professionally, but he hid it well. She guessed his years of dealing with the press had given him a thick skin. Personally, she'd never had one herself. She wasn't surprised he'd ordered steak and opted not to read too much into his choice of appetizer, assuring herself it was only *her* mind that was on aphrodisiacs and sex, not his.

After the waiter walked away, she folded her hands and decided to hit on the reason for their lunch. "I understand you need my services to clear out the clutter in your life so that you can better focus on your career."

He tipped his head and nodded. "That's one way of putting it."

Micki had told her she'd be his handler, but somehow she didn't think he'd appreciate the term, which implied he needed babying. "Well, you'll be happy to know I've given your situation some thought already."

It helped that she'd spent New Year's with him and seen his family dynamics firsthand. The phone calls today had merely cemented her earlier impression. Taking her secretary's advice, she pulled a notepad and pen from her large handbag. "Let's start by listing the things or people in your life causing you to get sidetracked. If we tackle and eliminate them one by one, that will leave your mind clear for baseball."

Roper raised an eyebrow, amused by her

suggestion. "You think you can take on my family and eliminate their issues?"

"If they're the sole source of your distraction, I know I can." Her eyes were on fire with determination.

He pictured Amy, petite in stature but not personality, dealing with his larger-than-life, never-take-no-for-an-answer mother, and he glanced heavenward for strength.

"You start talking. Tell me more about each family member and their main problem, why they need your attention constantly each day. I'll take notes and put together a plan." She raised her pen, ready to write.

No sooner had he chuckled than his cell phone vibrated once more. He glanced at the number, shot Amy a you-were-right look, and felt more certain than ever that not only was Amy outnumbered, but she'd be outmaneuvered in a matter of days.

He spoke quickly, then disconnected the call.

"Third call in . . ." She looked at her watch. "Ten minutes. No wonder you can't find time to get healthy. You're mentally and physically drained by the forces around you."

"*Force* is a good word to describe my mother," he mused.

She held out her hand. "Give it over."

"What?" He hadn't a clue what she was talking about.

"Hand the cell phone over. And the Black-Berry."

"It's a Treo and you may not have either one," he said, shocked by her gall.

She withdrew her hand. "Fine. Then shut them off. Vibrate's not cutting it. You're at a business lunch and common courtesy dictates you keep your mind on business."

He grinned, finally getting it. "Aah, it's my attention you want," he said in a cocky tone. "I can assure you that even if I answer the phone, my thoughts are solely on you, babe."

She rolled her eyes. "Did you forget why we're here? To organize your life. To make sure you learn how to compartmentalize and make baseball your priority again. So it's your choice. Shut them off or hand them over," she insisted, not backing down.

Roper glanced at Amy's fiery brown eyes and determined expression and realized she was deadly serious. Who knew the woman was a ballbuster?

Who knew he'd like that in a woman?

The last female who'd demanded that he put her first had been pushing for a ring. And since he'd been as interested in a commitment with her as he'd been in the blond highlights his hairdresser had been trying to talk him into, he'd bought her a diamond bracelet goodbye gift and broken things off.

"Well? Choose one or I'm walking away from this assignment." And in case he wasn't sure she meant business, she turned and reached for her purse hanging from the back of her chair.

Damn, she was cute when she was being bossy.

He shocked himself by turning both his phone and Treo off, pushing them to the side of the table and focusing completely, solely on her. "I'm all yours."

"Good. That's how it should be." She swallowed hard, obviously not as at ease around him as she wanted him to believe.

Their attraction was something neither could ignore. He could let her have the upper hand when it came to their professional relationship, but he had no doubt that sexually, he was in control.

And he intended to make use of the upper hand. When the time was right.

"Let's hear your game plan."

The waitress served their appetizers, and while they ate, she outlined her goals. "You have three family members pulling you at all hours of the day. You need to set limits.

But first, let's tackle each one of them. Your mother. What is the main reason she's been calling you?" Amy asked. She put a forkful of salad into her mouth, then licked a crumble of blue cheese off her bottom lip with her tongue, wreaking havoc with his attention.

He stared at her moist lips, moving as she delicately chewed her food.

She met his gaze. Obviously embarrassed, she cleared her throat. "Your mother?" she reminded him.

"Right." He paused to suck an oyster from its shell. The food might be considered an aphrodisiac, but Amy supplied all the arousal power he needed. "Other than asking me to lend Ben money?" Which he was sure she would have done again on the phone today if he'd given her more time. "My mother needs a job of her own. Her lifestyle is killing my bank account. And she's bored. She misses acting, not that she's willing to admit as much."

"Hollywood won't hire her because of all the roles she already turned down over the years?" Amy guessed.

He laughed. "Hell, no. Harrison Smith — he's a big-time director — sent her a script for a television pilot over three months ago that was tailor-made for her. He even offered her more money than she deserves at this point in her career."

He shook his head in disbelief. "She said no, but apparently he's waiting for her to change her mind. For some reason, the man only wants Cassandra Lee for the role and has been pursuing her relentlessly."

Amy nodded in understanding. "That's because she's good," Amy said. "What will it take to convince her?"

He shrugged. "She won't change her mind. First, she thinks television is beneath her. But more important, my mother refuses to play the role of a grandmother, no matter how elegant, dignified or perfect the role may be. She thinks spending thousands in plastic surgery and Botox justify her desire to be cast as an ingenue." He shook his head in disgust and frustration. "Sad thing is, she's been saying it to herself for so long, she believes it."

He glanced at Amy, looking for a glimmer of understanding. Heaven only knew why he needed it from her when he'd never wanted it from anyone else. At least she was too busy jotting down notes to realize.

"So tell me more about your brother."

The busboy had cleared their plates, and the waitress set their lunches in front of them. Talking about his family had killed his appetite. "Ben needs a job and a life."

"I've been there," she said with more compassion than he'd afforded his brother lately. "I lived at home for so long it became too comfortable. Maybe that's what's going on with Ben. He just needs the right incentive to get him moving again."

Roper had thought the same thing.

"Does he have any job options? I don't mean investments, but legitimate employment opportunities that you know of?"

Roper took a long sip of water. "His head is so far in the clouds, he wouldn't know an opportunity if it was handed to him. I've offered to make some calls and see if there are any openings as a high school baseball coach in a decent community. He's good enough to teach, he just wasn't solid enough to play pro. Ben won't even consider it."

"When he runs out of money, he'll have no choice. Why don't you give me some leads and I'll see what I can come up with for him."

Roper raised an eyebrow.

"It's my job, remember. Come on."

He rattled off some old ball players he knew were into coaching who might be able to use a guy like Ben. Although he loved his brother, it rankled to have to call in favors knowing Ben wouldn't appreciate the effort and would probably turn down any opportunity Roper uncovered because *he* felt he deserved better.

"Just be prepared. Ben won't make it easy. He'll play the guilt card because I had the father with the talent, while his dad had none. He likes living on pipe dreams of what life owes him, instead of what he could actually do to make it on his own."

Amy jotted down a few more notes. "Delusions of grandeur," she said without glancing up. Her brows were furrowed in concentration and her lips puckered as she wrote. Lips he still wanted to kiss more than he wanted to breathe. But she was working with him now. There would be time.

Neither one of them had eaten much, but he sensed until she finished dissecting his family, she wouldn't be interested in food.

"Are you ready to talk about Sabrina?" she asked.

He leaned back in his chair and stretched. "Sure am. She's the easiest one. My little sister is marrying a great guy. A normal accountant. The wedding is planned for next fall, after my season ends. I'm paying for the big day, but that isn't a problem. I want to pay. She deserves the best. Problem is, she isn't in charge of her own wedding, our mother is. Or at least she wants to be."

"Long distance?"

He nodded.

"Sabrina calls me several times a day with another of Mom's outlandish ideas, things Sabrina doesn't want but Mom thinks are best. Sabrina wants me to mediate, but frankly, I don't want to do any more than write the damn check."

Amy chuckled. "Typical man."

He grinned. "I tune them out when possible, but if I don't answer the phone right away, they hunt me down. Don't get me wrong. I love them but —"

"They need to live their own lives," Amy finished for him. "But they haven't had to since you've always done everything for them." A few more notes and Amy finally put her pen down and met his gaze. "Got it all," she said, then picked up her knife and fork. "God, I'm starving." She dug into her meal with a gusto he'd never seen in a female.

Just watching her renewed his appetite and they finished their meal in comfortable silence. As soon as their waiter placed the check on the table, he placed his hand on the leather folder.

"I've got it," she said, reaching for the billfold at the same time so their fingers met.

He'd always let Micki pay when they went

out for business and he should allow Amy to do the same, especially this first business lunch when he figured she needed to feel in control.

But he let his hand deliberately linger so he could touch her a little longer. "You already talked me into turning off my phone and Treo. Don't add insult to injury by paying the check. My fragile male ego can't handle it."

She laughed. "I don't think your ego has been fragile a day in your life."

"You'd be surprised," he said, sobering. She probably thought the insults from Buckley and the fans rolled off his back. Maybe at one time they would have, but not any longer. He was afraid they were right and he was a washed-up has-been.

Without warning, she slipped her hand from his. "I'll get it next time," she said, leaving him with the distinct impression she did understand the fragile ego thing.

Just as he understood hers. "No, this is business. I don't mind letting the Hot Zone pick up the tab." Before she could get too cocky, he added, "I'll get it on our next date."

She opened her mouth to speak, but he glanced down at the check, ignoring her so she couldn't argue. Because there would be a real date.

She could count on it.

Once the check was paid, he walked her out of the restaurant and onto the street. To his surprise, they'd made it through the meal with only a few stares. No one asked for an autograph or bothered him with stupid questions, like how did it feel to single-handedly blow the series?

He waited as she glanced up the street to locate her driver, then held the car door for her as she climbed inside. He had a physical-therapy appointment downtown so he declined a ride and sent her back uptown alone.

But not before she promised she'd be in touch with a plan to help him reclaim his life. She believed she could fix things for him, and for the first time, he admitted to himself that he needed her to be right.

He'd always been the one taking care of others. No one had ever given much thought to what *he* needed, not because they didn't care, but because they knew he could take care of himself. Even though Amy was only doing what the Hot Zone paid her to do, he appreciated her efforts. He believed she'd do her best, although he had less faith in her ability to get his family under control. It wasn't personal, nor was it a lack of belief in her abilities. He just knew his family, and short of doing their bidding, there was no denying them.

But he was looking forward to seeing Amy try.

He called in the tip about Roper's lunch at Sparks Steak House with the niece of Spencer Atkins. He supposed he ought to feel guilty about causing the guy trouble, but Roper's life was already imploding. There was no reason not to help the process along by placing him squarely in the public eye.

He wouldn't want people to forget about Roper or his part in destroying the Renegades' chances of winning the World Series. Not when the man was paid more than anyone else on the team to come up with the ultimate post-season win.

Besides, wasn't it time that the high-and-mighty realized how fragile fame and fortune were? Some people worked hard for their talent. Others thought it was their birthright. Roper was one of the entitled. He took what belonged to others without thought or care. Roper would soon learn otherwise.

He hung up his disposable cell phone and tossed it in the trash. Nobody could trace this call. Celebrities and athletes showed up in papers and columns all the time, but he felt better covering his tracks. He wouldn't want anyone to discover his grudge.

Better to just help Roper's fall from grace anonymously and enjoy the spectacle from a distance.

Amy left the restaurant on a euphoric high. She knew what she needed to do to help Roper and she had some ideas already to research and implement. On the way back to her office, she stopped by Micki's and ran the plan by her, receiving a thumbs-up in return. She had her secretary following up on some of the coaching possibilities Roper had mentioned for his brother. She felt certain once each of his needy relatives was squared away, they'd leave Roper in peace, allowing him to get back to what he did best.

All he needed was some organization, some direction and a firm, guiding hand. *Her* firm, guiding hand.

She wished she could share her excitement with someone other than her boss, but she hadn't made any real friends in the city yet. So she fell back on the familiar. She called her mother.

Rose answered on the first ring. "Hi, Mom."

"Amy!" her mother said, clearly excited. "Darla, it's Amy!"

Amy could envision her yelling across the small kitchen even though her aunt was always within whispering distance.

"Your aunt Darla sends her love," her mother said.

"Send mine back," Amy said.

"Darla, Amy sends her love right back," Rose yelled.

Amy smiled, a pang of homesickness hitting her despite the fact that she was exactly where she wanted to be. "How are things down South?"

"Bo-o-o-r-ing. It's been raining nonstop. We've seen all the movies playing in theaters. Twice." Her mother let out a long-suffering sigh. "How are things with you?"

"Pretty great." Amy knew better than to tell her mother anything specific about John Roper or she'd be on the next flight out to matchmake. "I have my first client and things are really working out for me here."

"No need to thank me. I knew I was doing the right thing throwing you out of here," her mother said smugly.

"Need I remind you I left on my own?"

"And I must tell you, your replacement is fantastic," her mother said, ignoring her. "Better than fantastic. She's organized daily bingo — for *money.*"

Amy winced. Clearly the new director didn't know what she was up against. "There's too much cheating going on to use real prizes." Amy had kept the prizes small and manageable, so nobody would win a jackpot at someone else's expense.

"You're telling me. Marilyn Hornsby stole my card right out from under me and won a jackpot of one hundred and one dollars, the weasel," Rose said.

Her mother went on about the new director and the goings-on in the community. Amy missed them, but she definitely had more of a challenge here. And she couldn't help feeling a sense of peace that came from not being in the center of her mother's world. "I've really got to get back to work now," she explained.

Rose cleared her throat. "I understand. Just make sure your uncle Spencer isn't working you to death or I'll have to have a talk with him."

"Stay out of it," Amy ordered.

"Are you sure?" her mother asked.

"Quite sure. I came here to get a life, not to have you meddle — I mean — interfere in mine. I know you mean well, but no thank you."

"Fine." Her mother sniffed.

Amy grinned. "Stay out of trouble and don't give the new director a reason to quit," Amy warned.

"As if I can possibly cause any trouble. It's boring here, I tell you. She's running the place like a military base," Rose whined.

Amy laughed. "I thought she was wonderful."

"Wonderfully uptight," her mother muttered, the truth coming out.

Amy wasn't surprised her mother had fibbed at first so Amy didn't feel bad for leaving. Or maybe so she would. Knowing her mother, Rose figured if Amy thought the new director was so perfect, she'd get jealous and run home. She wouldn't put anything past her mother.

"Have you met any nice men?" Rose asked.

"No one in particular." She crossed her fingers as she lied.

Another drawn-out sigh sounded over the phone line. "Leave it to my daughter not to meet men when she works for a sports agency loaded with hotties. Rich hotties."

Amy pinched the bridge of her nose. Definitely time to hang up. "My secretary's calling me. I have to go. I love you, Mom. And I miss you."

"I love you, too. And we miss you. Don't

we miss Amy, Darla?"

"We both miss you," Rose said, blowing a loud, smacking kiss through the phone.

Grinning, Amy hung up, and with her mood light, she went back to figuring out how to change John Roper's life.

After Roper left Amy, he headed straight for the physical therapist's. Taking her cue, he kept his cell phone and his Treo off, and sure enough, got through his physical-therapy appointment uninterrupted. He even fit a short gym session into the day. Amy's solution worked well for him so far.

But by the time he arrived back home, there were no less than half a dozen messages on his answering machine, most of them from his mother. Roper thanked God she lived long-distance or else his life would be more of a hell than it was now. In her messages, his mother managed to hit all of his buttons and he called her back immediately, feeling guilty for taking an entire afternoon to himself.

That's what he got for jumping into the role of man of the family too early in life. His parents' affair had been hot, heavy and had petered out just as fast as it had started, leaving his mother pregnant in an era when women didn't have kids out of wedlock. The beautiful starlet had turned to a man she'd thought would save her. Another impulsive decision, leading to the birth of his siblings. Ben and Sabrina's father soon tired of living with his famous wife and took off, leaving Cassandra with three kids. Though Roper had been young, he'd taken charge. The family had come to rely on him, and he had been the decision-maker and fixer of everyone's problems ever since.

He called his mother back and left a message both at her home and on her phone, hoping that would buy him some peace until morning.

Then he headed for a hot shower. As he stripped and flipped the water on hot, his thoughts turned to Amy, and he changed the temperature to icy cold instead. He wished that the effect she had on his body was all he liked about Amy, but in the short time he'd known her, he'd learned there was so much more. The take-charge attitude he hadn't expected, the understanding of his relationship with his family, her pure determination to succeed in her new job that he could see in her eyes.

Eyes that made him crazy with desire.

He finished showering, dried himself and fell into bed, exhausted.

What seemed like moments later, he woke

to the sound of his doorbell ringing. His doorman had a list of approved people to let up, so his uninvited guest had to be someone he knew. A glance at the clock told him he'd crashed all night. It was morning.

He reached for the nearest pair of jeans lying on a chair and made his way to the door. Without coffee, he wasn't ready to see anyone.

He glanced through the peephole and let out a groan. He especially wasn't ready to deal with the woman standing impatiently on the other side. Cassandra Lee had arrived.

CHAPTER SIX

No sooner had Roper opened his door than his mother barged right in. "Darling!" She presented her cheek for a kiss, which he dutifully gave.

Then he stepped back and looked at her linen pants and blouse, obviously wrinkled from travel. "Did you tell me you were coming and I forgot?" he asked, knowing he'd done no such thing.

She narrowed her gaze. "Don't play games with me, John. You didn't answer your phone, you didn't return my e-mail or text messages, so I'm here." She waved her hands around expressively, ending by cupping his cheek in her hand. "I was worried about you."

He narrowed his gaze, which didn't take much since he was still half-asleep. But mentally, he was now wide-awake. That his mother loved him was fact. That she might have been concerned about his silence also might be true. But no way would she fly across the country just because he hadn't picked up his cell phone.

"What's really going on?" he asked.

"I don't know what you mean. But I do need coffee." She headed for the kitchen, leaving him no choice but to follow after her. "I took the red-eye and I'm exhausted," she said, speaking with dramatic effect as she always did.

She blamed her original drama coach. Roper blamed her love of drama.

She made herself at home in his kitchen, looking through cabinets in her search for caffeine. Finally he took pity on her and opened the correct canister, removed the beans and ground them. Maybe once she had her coffee she'd tell him why she was really here.

Out of habit, he switched on the radio and Buckley the Bastard's voice sounded around him. Though he cringed, he believed in dealing with life as it came. He needed to know what was being said about him if he was to deal with it.

He handed his mother a steaming mug. "So how was your flight?"

"Long." She wrapped her hand around the cup and sighed. "Then to add insult to injury, the airport lost my bags. Of course they promised they'll deliver them as soon as they find them, but who knows when that will be." His mother paused to take a sip of coffee. "Mmm. You always did have the touch." She lowered herself into the nearest chair, obviously exhausted.

But only one word rang in his ears. "Your *bags?* Plural?"

"Well, yes, bags." She tucked her set blond hair behind one ear, the shoulder-length strands somehow managing to look sophisticated on her and not at all too young despite her best attempt. "How else can I stay indefinitely unless I brought enough clothes? Although New York does have the best stores. Better than L.A., even, and that's saying a lot. I think I'll call my favorite personal shoppers and have them start putting things away for me," she mused.

"What do you mean, you're staying indefinitely?" Roper felt a blinding headache coming on.

She placed her cup down and stared at him as if he were the crazy one. "Darling, your sister is getting married and she needs her mother to help her. And of course, you're going through a career crisis of your own."

"Thanks for reminding me," he muttered.

"Not to worry. Mother's here." She treated

him to her brightest smile.

That's what he was afraid of.

"This just in." Frank Buckley's voice spoke into the silence. "Guess who had lunch at Sparks Steak House yesterday? Nice that our friend John Roper has time for wining and dining his new lady when he should be getting ready for the season." The man waited a deliberate beat. "But that's a high-paid athlete for you. No sense of responsibility. The Buck Stops Here, folks."

"Son of a bitch." Roper bristled at the report and accusation. "Who the hell called it in?" he asked.

"It could have been anyone from a waiter to a patron," his mother said, rising and putting her arm around him. "You know what it's like to be a celebrity. You grew up under a microscope. Let it go."

He twisted his neck from side to side, releasing tension. He wished it was as easy as his mother said. "I just don't like feeling as if my every move is being tracked and scrutinized," he muttered.

"It's part of the life," his mother said.

"The difference between us is that you enjoy it. I just want to play baseball."

His doorbell rang, cutting off whatever his mother might have replied.

He pinched the bridge of his nose. "Who

knows you're here?" Roper asked her, resigned to more company. "Ben? Sabrina? One of your actress friends you charmed the doorman into letting up without my okay?" He saw his privacy going down the drain.

His mother shrugged, her gaze wide-eyed and innocent. "Actually, no one. When I couldn't reach you, I packed and headed straight for the airport."

He headed back to the front door and peered through the viewer, needing advanced warning of the person he'd be dealing with next. One look and his mood lifted. This was someone he didn't want to disappear.

Roper opened the door, welcoming Amy, an addition Roper himself had made to his doorman's list. "Thank God," he said, pulling her inside.

He needed someone on his side when dealing with the steamroller he called his mother.

"Strange welcoming but I'll take it." Her smile broadened, easing his strain.

"Not so strange. You aren't a member of my family, so I'm glad you're here." He shut the door behind her and drank in the sight of her.

Dark denim jeans covered her legs like a

second skin, while a deep indigo top with bell sleeves floated around her, belted at the waist. Only a hint of a lace tank peeked out from beneath the flowing top. Once again she looked work appropriate and yet so damn sexy, he didn't care that his mother was in the other room.

"So what brings you by?" he asked.

"Well, first the doorman asked me to give you this," she said, handing him an oversize envelope with a handwritten scrawl he recognized as belonging to his most persistent fan. And not a fan in love with him, either.

Ever since the end of the series in October, Roper had been receiving letters and packages from a fan who called himself Season Ticket Holder, a not-so-veiled reference to the fact that he expected more results for his money than Roper had provided.

"Thanks for bringing up my mail," he said, not wanting to make a big deal of the letter and draw attention to the fact that he had someone determined to remind him of his failures. He accepted the envelope from Amy and tossed it aside.

"You're welcome. Now, I'm here because I have a plan." Amy's eyes glittered with excitement. "I was up late working on a way to organize your life and give you the time you need. I really think you're going to be impressed."

"Who's at the door?" his mother called, her voice coming closer with every word she spoke.

"Your sister?" Amy whispered.

He shook his head. "Worse."

At that moment, Cassandra Lee joined them in all her dramatic glory. "John, aren't you going to introduce me to your —"

"Mom, this is Amy Stone, Amy this is my mother, Cassandra Lee," he said, cutting her off before she could draw any conclusions about who Amy was. No way was he playing "fill in the blanks" with his mother.

Amy's eyes opened wide. Clearly she hadn't been expecting to find the movie star in the flesh. To Amy's credit, she recovered quickly and stepped forward, her hand extended. "I'm a huge fan," she admitted. "It's wonderful to meet you. John's told me so much about you!"

"All of it good, of course?" his mother said, lightly clasping Amy's hand.

"Is there anything else?" Amy asked, working his mother like a pro. "I had no idea you were coming to town."

"That's because John didn't know, either. I just love surprises and I missed my children." Her gaze darted away from Amy's just enough for Roper to know his mother was lying.

Just enough. Because Cassandra Lee was an accomplished actress, only her son would have caught the slip.

"I'm sure you know John's sister is planning a wedding and she needs my help," his mother continued.

Unfortunately for him, it didn't matter why his mother was here. Only that she'd arrived and planned on staying. Which meant what little peace and quiet he had, which admittedly wasn't much, was now over.

He had one source of salvation and she just happened to have arrived at the right moment. He wondered if Amy could save him from his family or if she just believed she could. He supposed he'd know soon enough.

Amy met John's gaze over his mother's head. He winked at her, but in his eyes, she saw the plea for help. She had to admit being needed by him was seductive, even if it was her job to keep his mother out of his way.

She'd planned on talking to him about his brother, but she could adapt to the unexpected. Surely even a famous actress had to be easier to deal with than the perpetually naked residents she dealt with back in Florida.

"I'm exhausted after traveling all night. Would you mind if we got to know each other later? I need to lie down." Without waiting for a reply, Cassandra started for the guest room down the hall.

"Wait!" Amy strode up to her. "You don't want to stay here, do you? John gets up early in the morning. Wouldn't a hotel suite be more comfortable? You'd have room service day or night, turndown service in the evening and a full staff to make you more comfortable," Amy said, finishing on a winded breath.

Cassandra's eyes lit up at her suggestion. "That's a wonderful idea. John, wherever did you find her?" his mother asked.

Amy glanced at Roper, whose tight smile had turned into a full-fledged grin. A sexy grin, not that she wanted to admit as much.

"I work for the Hot Zone," Amy said.

He walked over and slung a casually draped arm over her shoulder. "Isn't she the best?" Roper asked.

"I must admit she's got more on the ball than the usual women you associate with." Cassandra looked Amy over with practiced ease.

She tried not to fidget under the scrutiny

or imagine how she came up short compared to the other women in Roper's life. A New York makeover could only go so far. . . .

As if sensing her discomfort, Roper pulled her closer. His body aligned with hers, bare chest and all. Heat shot upward as his masculine morning scent wrapped around her, making her tingle.

She swallowed hard, then cleared her throat. "Well, why don't I go make that hotel reservation?"

"Good idea, but not the Ritz Carlton or the Waldorf. I prefer the London NYC. Their staff is my favorite. Book me one of their specialty suites."

"Mother, you do not need twenty-two-hundred square feet of space for a short stay. Book her a Vista Suite."

"A two-bedroom," Cassandra countered.

"Fine," Roper said through clenched teeth.

Obviously this was a vintage performance by his mother.

"Please ask if Chef Gordon Ramsay is in town. If so, invite him to dinner. We're old friends," she said, as if Amy were her assistant.

Amy accepted the direction with a nod, and his mother continued to instruct Amy on her likes and preferences. She wished she had her pen and paper ready.

"When you call, you may tell them who I am, but put the reservation under John's name and ask them not to let *anyone* know I'm there."

Amy nodded. Another celebrity quirk she assumed. One that would get Cassandra Lee the perks due her by virtue of her name but assure her some privacy at the same time.

Desiring anonymity with the media was something Amy could understand. "No problem. Anything else?"

Cassandra shook her head. "No, I'll talk to them when I arrive and make sure I have what I need, but thank you. You're a doll."

Roper squeezed Amy's forearm lightly, which she took as a show of appreciation.

A few phone calls and no less than three interruptions later, Amy had arranged for a Vista Suite that overlooked Central Park with extra-special service to compensate for the fact that the two-bedroom rooms were booked, lucky for Roper. She hired a limousine to pick Cassandra up and drive her over, with a stop at Saks on the way so she could pick up some clothes to tide her over until her suitcases were found.

And thirty minutes after that, Roper's mother was gone in a flurry of air kisses and promises to call after she'd napped and taken a refreshing bath. It was only 10:00 a.m.

Roper collapsed on the couch in the living room, patting the space beside him.

"Your mother is a living, breathing tornado," Amy said, flopping down next to him.

"Welcome to my world. Yet you handled her like a pro." Awe tinged his voice as he tipped his head to one side.

She met his gaze and tried not to read more into the molten stare than gratitude, but it was hard. The problem for Amy was more than attraction. She liked doing things for him. She enjoyed helping him and being successful at it. And she definitely liked it when he looked at her with those bedroom eyes that held promises she just knew he was capable of keeping.

"It's what I'm paid to do," she reminded herself, and him. Too bad she wasn't listening.

"And you did it well."

She didn't miss the sudden drop in his tone. The husky sound had her heart skipping a beat.

"Now, about that date . . ."

The one she'd refused to think about since he'd mentioned it at lunch the day before.

He stretched his arm over the couch, not so subtly reaching her shoulders with his fingertips. She recognized the practiced move for what it was and shot him a knowing look he ignored.

She wished she could do the same with his suggestion they go on a date. "It isn't a good idea to mix business with pleasure," she told him.

"I couldn't agree more."

She grew immediately wary. "You agree with me?"

He nodded. "Of course I do. Business is business. That's what you did for me this morning and that's what we'll discuss in a few minutes. Our date will be personal. We won't mix the two at all."

She rolled her eyes, unable to hold back a laugh. "That's ass-backwards logic." But a damn good attempt at manipulating her into saying yes, she silently admitted.

He chuckled. "I'll pick you up tomorrow night at eight?"

"I don't remember saying yes."

"I don't remember you saying no, either. So tell me, what brings you by?" he said as if that settled that.

But switching subjects gave her time to compose herself. She started filling him in on her plan to manage his life, starting with his brother. She informed him of the progress she'd made in getting Ben interviews at various schools in the northeast, leaving Roper to figure out how he'd approach Ben.

Amy then suggested he win Cassandra over to the idea first. Getting his mother on his side would all but ensure Ben's agreement. But she knew convincing his mother that coaching wasn't beneath her son was the equivalent of convincing Cassandra that television wasn't a step down from the big screen. It was a daunting task and they both knew it.

And all the while they talked business, Roper's invitation lay between them. Knowing she should say no to dinner was one thing. Actually doing it was something else. She had few friends in town, and like it or not, Roper was one of them.

Deep in her heart she knew she'd made her decision. Besides, dinner was harmless. Wasn't it?

Cassandra generously tipped the doorman, who had brought up her many purchases and deposited the bags in the foyer. Shopping usually brought her inner peace, but not today. She was running as fast as she could from L.A. and she wondered how long she could hide the reason from her son.

John always saw through her, more so than any of her other children. She couldn't let him know she was running not just from a role he'd demand she take, but from a man she'd once loved. She'd lived on her own for so long, she was afraid of the pull this man had over her.

All the drama she lived for in acting was suddenly part of her life, and she wasn't ready to face it. Instead she'd decided to go to New York to help her children.

And they needed her, Sabrina and her wedding, Ben and his inability to find himself and John and his career problems. The fact that a big city like New York was the perfect place to hide from Harrison Smith was merely a bonus.

After Amy left, Roper picked up the envelope she'd delivered. Just as he'd thought, his Season Ticket Holder fan had written yet again. This time he went beyond expressing his displeasure with Roper's performance last season. Thanks to the recent spate of news coverage, his fan had another gripe. He said in his computer-generated note, "Instead of spending your money on women and entertainment, I suggest you work harder at digging yourself out of the hole you're in. Otherwise instead of the Hall of Fame, you'll be looking at the Hall of Shame."

Roper groaned and tossed the paper into the garbage. The guy wasn't even original. He was just a pain in the ass.

Roper spent the next two days taking care of his daily workout regimen, then either refereeing his mother and sister or spiriting his mother around Manhattan, during which time she refused to discuss her life in L.A., the role she was avoiding or job possibilities for Ben.

She dismissed a future for her younger son in coaching as squarely as she did the role Harrison Smith wanted her to take. She felt it wasn't fair to make Ben feel any more belittled than he already did with all the failed enterprises behind him. Roper knew better than to argue with a woman who had made avoiding conversations she didn't like an art form.

Instead he tried to call his brother to set up a meeting. He figured a face-to-face discussion might help Ben understand why Roper didn't want to invest more cash in any more get-rich-quick schemes. Then he could pump up his brother's ego by explaining all the good he could do by coaching kids. It wasn't that Ben didn't have baseball talent. He did. He just didn't have major league talent.

Roper had thought Ben would appreciate the chance to plead his case for the gym money, if nothing else. But Roper couldn't reach his brother. Ben had no phone other than his cell, where Roper's number would show up. And since Ben refused to return Roper's calls, it was obvious Ben was avoiding him — which led Roper to believe that his mother had tipped Ben off.

Which left Roper more frustrated than ever.

Amy spent the next two days familiarizing herself with the New York press and media, their names, as well as those of other Hot Zone clients. Roper was her first assignment, but she wanted to show she was on top of things and ready to go at a moment's notice.

She also was learning to check the papers and relevant Web sites each morning, and for the second day in a row, she clicked on Frank Buckley's blog for eSports. Without a doubt, the man had it in for Roper. As she looked back at his daily rantings, each day started off with a line drive aimed directly at the Renegades' center fielder.

Unfortunately yesterday's was the worst,

at least as far as Amy was concerned. She read aloud, " 'Guess who had lunch at Sparks Steak House yesterday?' "

Amy was outraged, and not just because she'd once again been linked romantically with Roper. "The man calls himself a reporter? He ought to check his facts. It was a *business* lunch," she said aloud. And she'd rather any attention she received be for acting as his publicist rather than as his girlfriend.

A knock startled her, and she glanced up from the papers on her desk to see Annabelle standing in the doorway, an amused smile on her face.

"You heard me talking to myself?"

The other woman nodded. "Want some advice?"

"Gladly."

"You can ignore the rantings or you can send a professional letter correcting him. My vote would be to ignore it. I wish I could say that it would make it go away, but at least it'll keep you calm. Mind if I come in and say hi?" she asked.

Amy waved her in. "Of course not. I could use the break." Amy put her pen down and pushed her chair back so she could relax. "You're right. I'm going to ignore it. I wonder how Roper does."

Annabelle seated herself in a chair across from the desk and smoothed her short skirt over her legs. "Frankly, I doubt he does ignore it, which is another reason why he's so stressed."

Amy nodded, knowing the other woman was right. "So how's your daughter?" Amy asked.

"Delicious. She is the sweetest thing." Annabelle's expression softened at the thought of her little girl. "I don't have pictures on me, but they're in my purse and on my desk. Stop by later and I'll show them to you," she said like a proud mother.

Amy smiled. "I can't wait to see them."

"What about you? How have your first few days been?" Annabelle asked.

"Oh, a little like trial by fire," Amy said, only partially joking. "Between the newspaper incident the first day and Roper's mother showing up unexpectedly yesterday, I have my hands full. Short of getting him out of town —" No sooner had she said the words than she realized she had the solution. "That's it!"

"What's it?" Annabelle leaned forward in her seat.

Amy bit down on her bottom lip, wondering if her idea was pushing it. "Well, I realize Roper's family issues can't be solved

162

overnight, but spring training is around the corner. He's got to do something — and I just realized taking him out of town is the key. Getting him away from his family to a place where he can work out, where he can do his physical therapy and focus solely on getting his game back is exactly what he needs." She glanced at the woman across from her. "What do you think?"

"I think it's brilliant. Of course, who knows how Roper will feel, but he's dedicated enough to his career to like the notion." Annabelle nodded. "Yep, the more I think about it, the better I like it. And I have the perfect place for him to escape to."

Amy grabbed her pen and a fresh piece of paper. "Where?"

"Vaughn's place in Greenlawn," she said of her husband's lodge.

Amy had heard about the Upstate New York retreat from her uncle Spencer. Next to his wife and daughter, the place was Vaughn's pride and joy. "Tell me some more."

"Well, during the summer it's a camp for underprivileged kids, but during the winter it serves as a retreat. The price tag is high, but that's because he wants to attract a clientele who will help him fund the summer camp for the kids."

"That's such a wonderful thing," Amy said.

"That's Vaughn. He just gets what these kids need." Annabelle's pride in her husband was unmistakable as her blue eyes softened. "But for guests like Roper, there are rooms and suites. Each has a fireplace. There are a variety of restaurants for meals, room service for privacy and a state-of-the-art gym. And it's about an hour and a half from the city, which can be a hassle if you need a physical therapist to travel there, but since Vaughn's football buddies make use of the place, we've managed to locate a really good P.T. nearby. I'm telling you, it has everything you need."

Amy's mind was reeling with the possibilities. "It sounds as if it does."

"The best part is the people who can afford it understand the idea of privacy. Nobody will bother Roper at all." Annabelle spoke with animation in her voice, her hands waving in the air as her excitement grew.

"Will it be booked now? It *is* a winter resort. . . ."

Annabelle shook her head. "Yes and no. Yes, it's booked, but that doesn't mean there isn't room for Roper. The Hot Zone reserves a suite each year for clients or family members who need the break. No one's using it now that I know of."

Wow. Roper could escape, and while he was preparing mentally and physically for the season, Amy could help him with anything his family needed here in the city. She liked the idea. A lot.

After jotting down the name of the lodge and its location, Amy glanced up. "Sounds perfect. The only question is whether I can convince Roper to leave without telling his family exactly where he's going." And seeing how Cassandra had reacted when he'd ignored a phone call, Amy knew she could be courting disaster. "There's another issue, too." A big one, Amy thought.

"What is it? I'm sure we can figure out a solution."

"Money. Although Roper doesn't discuss it much, Yank told me to keep his expenses low because his family isn't only soaking up his time, they're a drain on his cash flow, as well. He's hardly broke, but what's liquid goes fast. And if his rehab doesn't go as planned, he'll take a big hit. I don't know if he'll agree to spend money on the lodge when he has a gorgeous Manhattan apartment sitting empty."

"Hmm." Annabelle's forehead wrinkled in thought. "Well, the Hot Zone has already

165

paid for the season. And he is our client . . ."
she said. "Don't worry. I'll clear it with
Uncle Yank."

Annabelle rose and Amy stood to walk her
out. "Thanks for stopping by. Talking to you
helped me flesh some things out," Amy said.

Annabelle grinned. "My pleasure. That's
what we do around here, help one another
any way we can. Remember that and feel
free to knock on my door anytime."

"I'll do that," Amy said.

Annabelle paused. "You work on Roper
and let me know when he wants to go."

Amy nodded. She couldn't possibly com-
mit to a time frame yet. Coming up with
the idea had been the easy part. Convincing
Roper to take her up on spending the rest
of his off-season at Vaughn's lodge in
Greenlawn would be her greatest challenge.

CHAPTER SEVEN

The rest of the day passed quickly and too soon, and Amy had to head home and get ready for her dinner with Roper. He picked her up as planned and drove her in his Porsche to a small restaurant called Leto's in Little Italy.

He'd taken over an entire restaurant where his friend was the owner and chef, ensuring their privacy. When she'd questioned the expense, he'd assured her his friend owed him a favor. Then he'd gone on to regale her with amusing tales of his baseball exploits and time on the road. She'd engaged him with her crazier stories about the residents at her mother's retirement community and the fun she'd had trying to keep them out of jail.

Roper at his most charming left Amy without any defenses to resist. Nobody had ever gone to such lengths to impress her before. It wasn't the fact that he'd arranged to shut down an entire restaurant that struck a chord with her, but the fact that he cared enough about her desire for privacy to bother. She forgot her resolve to keep her distance. During dinner, he covered her hand with his and she let him, enjoying the contact. She promised herself she'd turn the discussion to business and her idea for him to go into seclusion, but instead, she let herself be swept away by his charm, and not once did the subject of work come up.

In short, she allowed the impulsive part of her nature, the part she'd inherited from her mother and her aunt, to overrule her common sense. Amy didn't like denying herself the things she enjoyed, and though she'd spent years in Florida smothering those yearnings, it had been easy when she was away from people her own age, away from temptation.

And John Roper was a temptation she couldn't ignore.

Once dinner and dessert ended and they were settled back in his car, he lay an arm over the back of her seat. "So, my place or yours?" he asked, staring at her with those sexy, mesmerizing eyes.

She knew what she ought to say, just as she knew she couldn't. She wasn't ready to end their time together. She'd been alone for too many nights, and he made her feel too good to cut the evening short now.

"My place," she answered before she could change her mind.

Roper didn't expect anything to happen between himself and Amy. He didn't. She'd made her feelings perfectly clear, yet he couldn't help wanting her, desiring her, needing her.

He'd never clicked with a woman the way he connected with Amy. From the food they had in common to her understanding of his family and the on-the-road lifestyle he lived as a ballplayer, there had never been a lull in their conversation. Normally women's eyes glazed over when he talked about his time on the field. Locker-room stories only interested them if he mentioned famous names. Not Amy. She tried to get a grip on who his friends were and who he merely tolerated. She talked about her time in Florida with a self-deprecating humor he appreciated.

He already knew he had a good friend in Amy, something he valued. She'd seamlessly stepped into his life and had taken over where Micki had left off. As much as he loved his longtime friend, she now had a husband, a daughter and a life that kept her busy. Roper understood the changes, but he was grateful to have Amy to fill the void. Grateful enough that he didn't want to screw things up and lose her before their friendship had time to take hold. Yet by the time she let them into her apartment, his desire was becoming hard to control.

He'd talked her into dinner by respecting the fine line she drew between work and pleasure. As much as he desired to kiss her, hold her, feel her body around his, he'd have to let things progress without pushing too hard too fast. Somehow.

"Coffee?" Her soft voice broke into his thoughts.

He nodded. "That would be great."

"Make yourself at home while I go make us some." She gestured to the small couch with a sweep of her hand. "I should warn you, though, it won't be freshly ground," she said as she disappeared into her kitchen.

"I'll manage," he said, laughing.

She peeked out from behind the dividing wall. "Good, because otherwise I wouldn't be able to invite you back."

He was just glad she wanted him here.

She disappeared back into the small kitchen area.

While waiting for her to finish making their coffee, he glanced around, seeing the personal touches and changes Amy had put on the apartment. Over the plain white wooden slatted blinds, Amy had put up new ruffled curtains that gave the place a womanly feel. She'd added plants on the windowsills and photographs of palm trees, of pink and yellow homes and southern landscapes on the walls. So feminine. So Amy.

"Coffee is served," she said, returning with two white mugs. "I remembered you ordered yours with a little milk, no sugar at the restaurant, so that's the way I made it. But if you want to add anything, just let me know." She placed both mugs on coasters on a glass table in front of the couch.

"Thanks. I'm sure it's perfect."

He sat beside her on the sofa, keenly aware of her sweet scent. "I love the changes you made to the apartment," he said, reminding himself to take things slow. "Especially the curtains."

She smiled in appreciation. "They're homemade."

"That makes it even nicer." He took a sip of the too-strong, practically burnt coffee and somehow managed not to wince.

"Well?" She rocked back and forth in her seat, eager for his approval.

"Delicious." He even managed to keep a straight face. Insulting her coffee wouldn't exactly endear him to her. "So how do you like living in New York?" he asked.

"It's different. The pace is faster, the expectations higher, but somehow I'm loving it." Her eyes glittered with an excitement he found arousing.

She'd kicked off her black pumps. Her simple black dress was casual and not intentionally seductive. She wore just enough makeup to accent her pretty features, but not enough to disguise her freckles or tan.

At a glance she was so Floridian — laidback and at ease — but inside, he knew she had definite strength of character. He admired the adventurous spirit it took to pick up her life and move to a new city. This strong woman drew him to her and he found it difficult not to put his coffee cup down and pull her into his arms, showing her just how much he desired her.

"I'm glad you're happy here. It's better than being homesick." He leaned back and lay one arm over the couch cushion, feigning relaxing though his body was strung tight.

She nodded. "True. I miss my family and the warm weather, but this change was way overdue."

"So how did you end up working at the

retirement community in the first place?" he asked, taking advantage of the opening to learn more about her.

She placed her coffee mug on the table and he followed her lead.

"Let's see. I didn't start that way. I graduated college with a degree in social work. I took a job working for the state. It was heartbreaking and difficult, but I was making a difference in the world."

"So what happened?"

"My mother happened. My boss was extremely conservative. All he cared about was propriety and how our behavior reflected the office and the work we did."

"Which shouldn't be an issue for you. You're the epitome of propriety." But obviously her mother wasn't.

Amy curled her legs beneath her and the hem of her dress slipped higher, creeping up her thighs.

His mouth grew dry. His fingers itched to slip his hand beneath the short dress and touch her bare skin in an intimate caress.

"Propriety isn't easy to come by in a family like mine," she said, obviously unaware of the direction of his thoughts.

Amy was exactly what he saw. She was real and she appealed to him on a gut level. One that forced his imagination to go into overdrive. He wondered what she wore beneath the dress and drew a long, steadying breath.

"My mother and my aunt have this tendency to get themselves arrested for things like indecent exposure and being a public nuisance."

He couldn't suppress a grin. "I'm sorry. I know I shouldn't laugh, but it's funny."

She shook her head. "Not to the man who hired me. Or to his very proper boss."

"Go on." He squeezed her hand, encouraging her to tell him the rest. "I promise I won't laugh."

"Don't make a promise you can't keep." She smiled, surprising him. "Mom got a part-time job at a wig store in town. Not just any wig store but one specializing in wigs for cancer patients. She took it on herself to advertise during the annual Halloween Parade." Amy paused, picked up her mug and took a sip of her vile coffee, keeping him in suspense.

Not wanting her to question him about his drink, he took a sip from his mug, too.

"Anyway, Mom dressed up as Lady Godiva wearing nothing but a long wig and a sign with the shop's name around her neck."

He nearly spit out his coffee in shock.

"Oh, God."

Her own mouth twitched with humor over the situation. "The police called me to come get her. I bailed her out, but she'd already gotten the press she wanted, including a photograph of her wearing the sign on the front page of the paper with me walking beside her on her way home from jail."

"Let me guess. Your boss lacked a sense of humor?"

She nodded. "I was damned immediately. Guilt by association. That's when I decided somebody needed to keep an eye on my mother and keep her in check. Since my father died, she'd become even more outrageous. So I moved back home. Uncle Spencer had just bought land with some real-estate partners and they were developing a seniors' community. I stepped right in and took over."

He shook his head. "You have some very interesting relatives."

"Coming from you, that's quite a statement," she said, laughing.

"Good point." He glanced down at their hands. He still held hers and she hadn't pulled away. "I take it this is why you hate being on the receiving end of publicity?"

Amy nodded. "It's part of the reason." She didn't know how to further explain, but she tried. "My dad was nothing like my mom. From the time I was little, he taught me the importance of making a difference. He was a lawyer who specialized in family law and he did his part to make the world a better place."

He squeezed her hand lightly and she appreciated the gesture. She smiled, and one look into his eyes told her his understanding wasn't an act. He got what she was saying.

What she couldn't explain to him, what she didn't want to even admit to herself, was that her fear of the press went deeper. Being fired from her first job just for being photographed beside her naked mother reinforced her belief that her mother's wildness was a trait she had to suppress — in her parent and in herself. Because a secret part of Amy admired her mother's brazenness. That same part sometimes yearned to be set free so she could jump in pools on a whim and openly enjoy life without fear.

She had more of her mother in her than she cared to admit. Amy had gotten drunk at college and joined her best friend in streaking outside the boys' dorm. When she'd woken up the next morning, she had a fuzzy recollection of a wild night, but nothing more — until the football players whistled at her the next day. "Nice ass, Amy!" they'd called, and the memory of what she'd done came flooding back. It wasn't the first time she'd done something crazy. But she always tried to make it the last. And by attempting to temper her mother's antics, she managed to control her own.

During her years at the retirement community, she hadn't exactly excelled at keeping her mother in check — but short of enforced confinement, not even her father had been able to do that. What Amy had accomplished, however, was to turn her uncle's retirement home into a successful establishment, and she'd proved to herself that working behind the scenes was her forte.

"Hey." Roper reached out and brushed a strand of hair off her face.

She trembled at his touch, her body immediately responding.

"Not everybody's cut out for my kind of life. Hell, sometimes I'm not cut out for my kind of life," he said, chuckling.

"Poor baby." She spoke lightly, but she was feeling anything but casual toward him at the moment.

He understood her feelings. He cared. And from the moment she'd met him, she'd wanted this. Wanted to be alone with him and see where things went.

Maybe it was that damned wild side and maybe this yearning for Roper was real. She didn't know, but when she looked into his intense eyes filled with desire for her alone, everything inside her told her to go for it.

Her heart pounded hard, echoing in her ears. The tension had been building between them all night, and sharing her past, her fears, herself, only intensified the connection.

She wondered if he'd make the first move or if she'd just throw caution to the wind and kiss him first. It was a tie. They met in the middle, lips lightly touching at the same time he wrapped his hand around the back of her neck, locking her in place.

She wasn't going anywhere but liked the pressure of his palm pressing her ever closer, deepening the kiss. Fireworks went off inside her brain while sizzling heat seared her body inside out. She was lost in the moment while he seemed to grow frenzied. His hands threaded upward through her hair, while she grasped his shoulders and dug her nails into him, needing more with each passing second.

With shaking hands, she moved to his shirt, working on the buttons, opening one at a time, making sure her fingers grazed his chest. "Did I ever mention that I like how you're always so nicely dressed?" she managed to ask him.

He lifted his head and smiled. "No, but I'm glad you noticed."

She laughed softly. "I noticed everything about you. Of course, it's hard for a woman who's used to running around in shorts and flip-flops to compete with you. I changed at least fifteen times tonight," she said, embarrassed at the admission.

His eyes grew darker, hotter, if possible. "I've never seen you looking anything but perfect," he said as he brought his hands around to the back of her dress.

Her nipples tightened even more than they already were, puckering hard as he slowly undid her zipper, lowering it until he reached the small of her back.

"I'd like to see Florida through your eyes," he said in a husky voice. "And I'd love to be with you when you're running around in those skimpy little shorts and tank tops."

She licked her damp lips. "I don't recall mentioning that my shorts were skimpy or that I wore tank tops."

"It's my imagination. Let it get carried away, will you?" He splayed his hands across her back and sucked in a shallow breath.

"No bra." He closed his eyes and counted to ten, all the while skimming his hand up and down her bare back. "I'm glad I didn't know about this before now."

"Honestly, this dress didn't call for one."

"Honestly, I'm glad." He pulled the dress down over her shoulders, releasing her breasts.

She tried not to squirm or show her embarrassment as he stared at her full breasts, tight nipples and overall bare top half.

He leaned his head back against the couch and groaned. "Amy, you are so gorgeous."

She shook her head. "I've seen the women you've been with, so let's not go there, okay? If I wasn't so far gone with wanting you, I'd be more self-conscious. Let's not give me time to get there." She glanced away as she spoke.

It wasn't that she didn't think she measured up as much as she knew how hard the women in his circles must work to keep up appearances, cosmetic and otherwise. She was just an everyday woman with an everyday body. It was a reality she understood. How could she not mention the obvious?

He shook his head. "Listen," he said in a serious voice. "Considering I'm here with you, and you can feel how much I want you, I think we're clear on what looking at you does for me." He covered her breasts with his palms and she forgot all sense of embarrassment.

Heck, she nearly passed out from the glorious sensation of his warm palms and hot touch. And when he slowly, gently, cupped their weight, palming her flesh, she writhed, squeezing her thighs together, letting small waves of pleasure build higher.

A soft moan escaped her throat and he reacted immediately, lowering his head and pulling her nipple into his mouth. She whimpered. He merely suckled her harder, using his tongue to lick and his teeth to lightly graze her flesh. Nerve endings on fire, unable to control herself, she rocked her hips from side to side, desire and longing building inside her. And when she couldn't take the sensations he evoked any more, he seemed to know and transferred his attention to her other breast, giving it equal loving attention.

Bells went off in her head and it took some time before she realized it was a cell phone and not ecstasy causing the sound.

Hers? His? She wasn't sure, but reality, which had been far away, dawned slowly. It wasn't her phone.

"John?" she asked, calling for his attention.

He didn't respond.

"John?" She curled her fingers into his shoulders.

"What?"

"Your cell phone," she said, pushing him away.

He blinked and raised his head, his eyes glazed. "Ignore it," he said, leaning closer, obviously intending to kiss her again.

But she wasn't lost in the moment anymore. Nor was she so far gone she wasn't aware of what she was doing. She shook her head and scrambled to her feet. "No, it might be important."

He raised an eyebrow. "The woman who insisted I shut my cell phone off when I'm with you now wants me to answer it?" he asked in disbelief.

She rose and began to work her dress back up over her shoulders. They'd moved too fast and she needed space. "Get the phone, okay?" she asked, hoping he'd take the hint and give her a minute.

He ran a hand over his eyes and groaned. "It's stopped ringing."

"Then listen to your voice mail."

Obviously she'd made her point, because he stood. His shirt hung open, a reminder of how close she'd been to heaven.

He walked up behind her and reached for her dress. She flinched, but when he ignored her reaction and merely did up the zipper, she felt badly. "I'm sorry. This was just . . . I got carried away." She hoped he understood, because she didn't want an argument.

Roper stared at Amy. They'd been hot and heavy until his damned phone ruined the moment. He had no choice but to be a gentleman and respect her wishes. Talking could come later.

He grabbed for his phone and dialed his voice mail.

For once it wasn't his family interrupting. One of his teammates wanted to meet for drinks. Roper had no desire to leave Amy or to hang with the guys, but the damage here had been done.

"Anything important?" Amy asked, as she turned to face him.

He shook his head. "Nothing that can't wait."

"Well, at least it isn't an emergency." She ran a hand through her hair, trying to fix the strands he'd messed with his fingers.

"Amy —"

"It's getting late," she said.

Obviously she wasn't going to let him talk

about *them,* which was quite a contradiction to her planner personality. She liked things discussed and analyzed as long as *she* wasn't the one under the microscope.

He flexed and unflexed his fingers, grasping for calm. He was frustrated. But getting angry at her withdrawal wasn't going to get him anywhere. He forced himself to remember she'd given him insight into her past, and maybe he could work with that, given time.

"You're right. I should get going." Maybe he would meet his teammate for a drink. He was definitely too wired to sleep.

She walked him to the door. He met her gaze, and in her eyes he saw vulnerability. He lost his anger in an instant.

"Listen, I'm supposed to meet my mother at my sister's apartment tomorrow. Some sort of wedding-planning talk that is bound to turn into World War III. Join me and you'll get a firsthand view of the situation we're dealing with. Maybe you can offer some ideas about how to keep me out of it." And this way he could keep Amy with him while he figured out how to best handle her fear.

"I'll come tomorrow and see what advice I can offer."

"Good. See you at nine?" he asked as he

opened the door.

She nodded. "And, John?"

He turned, placing an arm on the door frame. "Yes?"

"Thanks for dinner. I had a really nice time."

He smiled. "Me, too." On impulse, he leaned in and placed a kiss on her cheek. He lingered for a moment, inhaling her scent to remember in his dreams later that night. "See you in the morning." At which point he hoped to have figured out how to breach her defenses again.

Because now that he'd had a taste of her, there was no way in hell he was going to let her walk away.

Amy's hand shook as she locked the door behind Roper and headed for her bedroom, the events of the night fresh and vivid in her mind. How in the world had she let things go so far?

She knew the answer to that.

Roper. He was the reason she'd gotten so carried away. One minute they'd been talking and getting to know each other better and the next he'd looked at her with those golden-green eyes and she'd melted into him like a snowflake in July. Pathetic, that's what she was. She couldn't even keep the resolution she'd made to herself the day before.

She pulled an old T-shirt from her drawer and awkwardly unzipped her dress, remembering how sensual it had felt when Roper had undressed her, his strong fingers skimming her back. She shivered at the memory, her nipples puckering into hard knots.

She let out a frustrated sigh. She'd told herself going into the date that she needed a friend, but she'd lied to herself. She'd agreed to go to dinner because she didn't want to turn him down. She liked him too much and wanted him too badly.

They hadn't discussed business and she hadn't wanted to ruin their time together by bringing up the lodge. Instead she'd put herself and her needs before the job.

Her mistake had been in thinking she could resist his charm. That she could deny her desire for him just because it was the smart thing to do. It was time for her to put her priorities back in order.

He was a client. Her relationship with him was professional. And her first order of business tomorrow would be to convince him to head upstate for some R and R — Rehab and Running away from his family.

In other words, she needed to be hands-on when it came to her job, not when it came to John Roper.

Roper picked Amy up the next morning with a game plan. It wasn't solid and it had more than a few holes, but it was a start. Every plan had a goal and his was to sway Amy into thinking there was nothing wrong with them picking up where they left off. She didn't like the fact that he attracted the media and he didn't blame her. But there was nothing wrong with a discreet affair between two people who were extremely interested in each other.

The first step in convincing her was to keep them together. He picked her up with lattes from Starbucks for both of them, a grin on his face and an attitude that let her know he wasn't holding a grudge over her turning cold on him the night before.

Once they were settled in the car, she turned to him. "Before we get going, I need to talk to you about a few things."

He raised an eyebrow. "What is it?" She sounded serious but not panicked, which he took to mean she was about to hit him with a professional, not personal, matter.

"I should have brought these things up sooner but I was distracted." Her cheeks flushed and her gaze darted from his, leaving no doubt just what that distraction had been. She drew a deep breath. "Anyway, the first thing I want to talk about is the media. I read Buckley's blog."

He leaned his head back against the seat. "That's a surefire way to ruin my morning. What about it?"

"Well, we were spotted at lunch. You didn't mention it to me but I'm sure you know."

Yeah, he knew. He gripped the top of the steering wheel with both hands. "I didn't think you needed another reason to avoid me."

"That's personal. Professionally, I'm the person you're supposed to go to on things like this. So if our friendship or relationship or whatever you want to call it is going to hinder our professional relationship, then we have a problem. I can turn you over to another publicist —"

"No."

Losing daily access to her was the last thing he wanted. "You're right. I should have told you right away about the blog. But you have to realize that I'm his target right now. Buckley's going to keep hitting on me until he finds someone else."

She pursed her pink-glossed lips and nodded slowly. "Which begs the question. *Why* are you his target? There are other things going on at the moment. Basketball brawls. Hockey suspensions. Why you? Why now?"

He swallowed hard and decided to white-wash the truth. "I, um, *dated* his ex-girlfriend. She's now his wife."

She narrowed her gaze. "So it's jealousy."

"Insanity is more like it," he muttered.

"Well, whatever the reason, that's twice in one week you were spotted out and about without any promotion ahead of time." She leaned forward, giving him a view into her soft blouse and the cleavage he'd tasted last night. "Is that kind of coverage normal?" she asked.

He cleared his throat and tried to focus. "No, it's not."

"So how does the press just happen to know where you are?" she asked, persistent in her curiosity.

"Don't know. Don't care." Actually, he did care. A lot.

He just couldn't change it.

"Well, you need to start to pay attention. Who knows your schedule and routine? Who do you speak to and mention your comings and goings?"

"As in you think someone close to me is reporting to Buckley?" he asked in disbelief.

"Not just Buckley. Gawkerstalker.com knows where you are, too, way too often to ignore them. Someone is phoning in information."

He frowned. She was new to this business and to his life. She didn't know his inner circle as well as he did. Nobody would deliberately sabotage him. "Maybe it's just a coincidence. Someone might have recognized me and decided to leak the information. It happens all the time."

She drew a deep breath. "Fine. Just pay attention in the future. That's all I ask."

He conceded with a jerk of his head, then glanced at the dashboard clock. "We need to get going." He turned and reached for the handle, but her hand on his shoulder stopped him.

"There's something else I need to run by you," she said.

He turned back her way. From her serious expression, he wasn't going to like this subject, either. "What is it?" he asked, resigned.

"What's your biggest priority at the moment?"

He let out a laugh. "Come on, you know the answer to that. My career. The upcoming season."

"Then why not act like it? Why aren't you at the gym this morning instead of playing mediator between your mother and your sister?"

He sat up straighter in his seat, his shoulders stiffening. "Not that I need to answer to you, but I'm going to the gym later today." He resented being put on the defensive just because he cared for his family. "Right now they need me. They're my responsibility and I won't turn my back on them."

She ran a hand through her hair, her frustration obvious. "They're adults, despite how they act. They should be able to look after themselves." She paused, then reached out and placed her hand on his arm. "You have a good heart, John, but if you don't start putting yourself first and get your shoulder healed and strong, they won't have you to turn to financially, now will they? Not with a lot of your future money tied to playing time and performance?" she asked softly.

If it was anyone else asking the question, he'd turn on them in a heartbeat. But he knew Amy had his best interest in mind by pushing him to face things he'd deliberately been ignoring.

"How do you know this?" He spoke through clenched teeth.

"Yank thought I should be filled in. So I'd

know how important this assignment was," she admitted.

He hated that Amy was privy to his secrets. "So it was just business."

"Exactly." She inclined her head. "And in that vein, so is my suggestion. Are you aware of the fact that Annabelle's husband owns a lodge in Upstate New York? A town called Greenlawn?"

He folded his arms across his chest. "What about it?"

"The Hot Zone has a suite available and I think it would be a good idea if you went into seclusion there until spring training."

Nothing could have surprised him more. He was speechless.

"They have a full-scale gym and trainers and there's a physical therapist in town who caters to the athletes who stay there. You'd have no distractions, no family complications. You could focus totally on rehab and getting yourself in shape for the season," she said, her hands waving rapidly as she described her vision.

He shook his head. "Won't work."

"Why not?"

"Because my family will have no problem calling me upstate with their problems. Hell, they'd drive up in a heartbeat."

Her brown eyes glittered with anticipation. "Not if they don't know where you are. All you need to do is tell them that you're on a business trip of sorts. We'll sneak you out of town and I'll put out any fires here."

Her enthusiasm for the idea would have been infectious if not for the fact that there was no way in hell it would ever work. "I appreciate the thought. But I have a responsibility to my family. I've been the one they turned to from the day my stepfather took off. They need me. I can get strong and juggle them at the same time. It'll be fine," he assured her.

She shook her head and shot him an I-don't-believe-you look. "Just promise me we'll revisit the subject when things get too intense?"

He shrugged. A promise to revisit wasn't the same as a promise to leave town, but it would keep Amy satisfied. "If things get out of hand, I'll rethink things. Feel better?"

"I would if I believed you," she said, laughing. "But that's okay. I'm not finished trying."

CHAPTER EIGHT

Amy followed Roper down the hallway to his sister's apartment. "I'm not sure I'll ever get used to the musty smell in these places," she said. The odor assaulted her every time she stepped off an elevator in Manhattan. Considering she'd practically grown up outdoors, she wondered if she ever would.

"I hear you. When I'm on the road, the thing I appreciate most is the fresh air and the wide-open spaces."

She blinked, surprised he noticed it, too. "Really? I'd think you were a city man, Mr. Metro," she said, laughing.

He turned toward her. "I see you've been reading my old press."

She shrugged. "It's my job to keep up on where you've been so I can help you with where you're going." In truth, she'd enjoyed digging through the old interviews and articles on Roper, learning more about his public persona and how different his personal, private one was.

"You could ask me," he said, stepping closer. "Where you're concerned, I'm an open book."

She inhaled and his scent immediately replaced everything else around her. Her heart rate accelerated as she finally let herself take notice of *him*. His pressed khakis, the sprinkling of hair peeking out of the unbuttoned space on his shirt. The desire to back him against the wall and feel his hard body against her was almost overwhelming.

Without warning, the door behind them opened and Sabrina stepped into the hall. "John, thank God you're here. You have to do something about Mom," she whispered.

Amy breathed out, releasing the tension but not the desire pulsing inside her.

He closed his eyes for a brief moment, obviously composing himself before turning to face his sister. "Can anyone stop a tornado?" he asked. "How did you know I was here? I didn't even get a chance to knock," he said, shooting Amy a look of regret.

Why? Had he been about to act on the chemistry that drew them to each other, even when minutes before they'd been at odds on how to handle his career and family? If so, what would she have done?

Before Amy could formulate an answer that satisfied herself, Sabrina grabbed her brother's hand and yanked him into the apartment.

With the quick instincts of a ballplayer, he encircled his arm around Amy's wrist, so she ended up dragged along with him.

Once inside, Sabrina glanced over Roper's shoulder at Amy. "Hi, again." She obviously remembered Amy from the New Year's party.

"Hi." Amy lifted her hand in a partial wave. "I hope you don't mind that I'm here."

"The more backup the better," the other woman said, sounding pained.

Having met Cassandra, Amy understood.

Apparently so did Roper, because he walked over to his sister and wrapped an arm around her shoulder. "Breathe in and out," he instructed.

Sabrina shut her eyes and complied.

"Better?" he asked a few seconds later.

She nodded.

"Good. Now, let's deal with her together. Come," he said, in a reassuring tone.

Sabrina visibly relaxed.

Amy marveled at the calming effect Roper had on his sister, but then, when she let him, he had his own unique effect on her, as well.

They walked a few steps into the next room, where Cassandra sat beside Kevin, a pen and pad in hand. "So let's go over your guest list," Cassandra said.

"Hi, Mom, Kevin. How's it going?" Roper asked, making his presence known.

"It's going," the other man said. With his dark hair and dark eyes, Kevin was good-looking in a studious way. His rimless, fashionable glasses added to his attractiveness.

Of course, in Amy's eyes, he didn't compare with her jock Roper, but she could definitely see his appeal. *Her jock?* She caught herself and blinked.

"Kevin, I'd like you to meet Amy Stone. Amy, my soon-to-be brother-in-law, Kevin Reynolds," Roper said, interrupting her thoughts.

Kevin stood and shook Amy's hand. "A pleasure to meet you. And now that you're here to handle your mother," he said to Roper, "I'm going to take the dog for a walk." He paused to kiss Sabrina's cheek before heading for the door.

Cassandra merely laughed. "You know I'll be here to finish up later," she said to Kevin.

"Wait," Sabrina said, running after him

but not before giving their mother a frustrated glare. "We don't have a dog!"

Amy turned her unexpected laugh into a cough. "Hello, Miss Lee, it's nice to see you again."

Cassandra looked up, appearing more rested than she had earlier. "Please call me Cassandra. It's lovely to see you again," the other woman said, but her voice sounded uncertain. She was obviously confused by Amy's presence. She settled her glance on her son. "John, we were discussing wedding plans."

"It looked as if you were torturing Kevin," Roper said.

He was too far away for Amy to nudge him in the ribs, so she settled for a warning look instead.

His mother ignored his comment. "Did you know they haven't chosen a reception hall yet? They can't pick a place unless we know the number of guests on the list and what the venue can hold. I already have one hundred of my own —"

Roper nearly choked. Even Amy's head started to pound. She couldn't believe how the actress bulldozed her way into everyone else's life. No wonder Roper was concerned about finances.

"Didn't you hear us say we wanted a small

wedding?" Sabrina asked as she rejoined them in the living room.

"Is Kevin okay?" Roper asked.

Sabrina nodded. "He's fine. He just needed some fresh air. Mother, did you hear me? We want a small, intimate affair."

Cassandra waved her hand back and forth in the air. "No, that's what you think now. But when you look back, you'll realize you wanted a big wedding, so that's what we're going to make sure you have."

Sabrina looked at Roper with big, pleading eyes.

For the first time, Amy realized exactly why he felt so strongly about not abandoning them to go to Vaughn's lodge. Each member of his family needed him for their own reasons. But they would take and take until there was nothing left — and that included cash. And it wasn't as if anybody was actually in the wrong. They were just needy. Roper had fallen into the caretaker role and now they all expected it of him, at his own expense.

Roper stepped between his mother and sister. "Mom, look, it's their wedding. I think they can make their own decisions."

Cassandra tipped her head in her elegant way. "And you know this because you've been married before?" she asked him with sweet sarcasm. "*I* know best."

"Because your big wedding and subsequent divorce make you an expert?" Roper asked.

"Argh!" Sabrina stormed out, heading to what Amy assumed was her bedroom.

Cassandra placed her pad and pen on the table, rose and strode to the window, all without meeting Roper's gaze.

Amy couldn't imagine the stress these kinds of confrontations put on him. Watching the commotion today, Amy was even more certain now. All the reasons he didn't want to go to the lodge were the exact same reasons he needed to go so badly. So he could take care of himself for once and let his family learn to stand on their own.

Amy walked over and put her hand on Roper's shoulder for support. He surprised her by covering it with his own.

"Weddings are stressful," Amy said. "Perhaps there's a way you all can sit down and talk and really hear one another," she suggested.

Cassandra swirled around. "I never did find out what exactly you are to my son. You mentioned working for the Hot Zone, his public relations firm?"

"Officially Amy's my go-to person at the Hot Zone." Roper jumped in and spoke for her, something Amy didn't want or need him to do.

"You see, Cassandra, the Hot Zone felt that given Roper's current situation, he could use someone to help keep him on track with his physical therapy before the start of the season," Amy said, eager to speak for herself.

"Sort of like a handler," Cassandra said.

Amy nodded. "Exactly."

His mother studied Amy for a long while, enough to make her uncomfortable. But she held her ground and refused to fidget even though Cassandra didn't hide her blatant attempt to take stock. "So you're here with him today because he needs help handling his family?" Hurt suffused Cassandra's tone.

Amy's heart constricted. She didn't want wounded feelings. "I'm just here for support," she said, deliberately backing off.

She saw Roper's dilemma so clearly now. His aging mother was unsure of her place in Hollywood and in her children's lives. It wasn't Amy's place to butt in. She could guide Roper, but she couldn't tell his family what to do. She realized that now.

Amy turned to Roper. "Don't you have an appointment with the doctor and then with the physical therapist today?"

He glanced at his watch. Surprise at how

fast the morning had gone registered on his face. "I do, but my family needs me right now. I'll call Aaron and reschedule."

She might as well start *handling* him now. "No, you won't. Your shoulder might heal on its own, but you won't get your strength back without hard work."

"Amy's right, John," his mother said, shocking Amy.

If the stunned look on Roper's face was any indication, he agreed.

"I'm tired. I've upset your sister and obviously overstayed my welcome. I'm going to go back to the hotel. First I'll go talk to Sabrina and make peace. We can pick up the wedding talk another time. I still say they'll regret a small wedding later." With a wave, his mother headed in the direction Sabrina had gone, leaving Roper and Amy alone.

Roper leaned against the wall and let out a low groan. "She gave in," he said, relieved.

"For now. And only because I backed off first," Amy said.

"You are amazing." She'd been astute enough to realize that his mother might perceive her as a threat. Roper shot her a look filled with admiration and gratitude.

She shrugged. "Years of experience at the retirement community, I guess. I just sensed she needed to feel in control of things."

"Well, it worked." Roper knew another reason why Amy had been able to get his mother to step aside for today, at least — because his mother was astute enough to sense there was more to Roper's relationship with Amy than business. She'd said as much on the phone after meeting Amy at the apartment the other day. Cassandra thought her son had a thing for Amy, which worked to Amy's benefit because his mother played nice to Roper's girlfriends.

She had spelled out her reasons to him the one and only time he'd brought a girlfriend with him to L.A. The woman hadn't had nearly Amy's intelligence and she'd grated on his mother's nerves, but Cassandra had been the gracious hostess, giving in to all the other woman's requests — to go shopping on Rodeo Drive, to tour Paramount Studios — all because, as she'd told Roper later, she knew he'd grow tired of her quickly.

And he had. He always did. The women he met and dated up until now didn't have enough substance to make him want them in his life long term.

"Time for the doctor," Amy said.

He rolled his eyes at her bossy tone. He wanted to tell her that she wasn't in charge. That he could make his own decisions. That he was the man.

Until he realized that if she hadn't been here, he would have canceled his appointment. She'd done her job, keeping him on schedule. Damn, but he liked her take-charge personality.

"Amy, do you want to join us for a late lunch this afternoon?" Sabrina called out as she and his mother walked back into the room.

Amy paused, then said, "Love to." She shot him a satisfied grin.

Knowing Amy, she figured keeping his mother and sister busy would enable him to work uninterrupted.

She was right.

But he'd have the last laugh. Because while he was going to his appointments, she'd be getting grilled by his inquisitive family.

He ought to tell her, then decided against it. Amy could handle herself.

"Can we talk before you take off?" Amy asked.

He nodded and she walked him to the door.

"Ready to rethink the lodge?" she asked.

He shook his head. "So far you've got things well under control. When you don't, we'll talk." He threw down the gauntlet, knowing she'd work doubly hard to prove she could corral his family.

No escape necessary, or so he hoped.

"Promise?"

He nodded.

"Say it."

"I promise." He couldn't hold back his grin.

"I'm going to hold you to that," she said, pointing at him for emphasis.

"I wouldn't expect anything less of you." He grabbed her finger long enough to stop her and glanced at her satisfied smile.

He could think of just one way to wipe the smug grin off her face. He leaned forward, brushing a long, lingering kiss over her lips before turning around and walking out. Leaving them both wanting more.

Roper walked out of the office of the team's orthopedist, the best in the city, and barely felt the cold winter air. He'd gone from a euphoric high, leaving Amy with a stunned expression after that kiss, to this. He'd just gotten the results of an MRI he'd had taken last week and the news wasn't good. Despite his workouts and physical therapy, his strength wasn't returning as quickly as he'd hoped. The MRI didn't show anything that would impede his progress, but the doctor

also said that sometimes healing didn't oc-
cur at the pace a patient wanted. He'd have
to listen to his body or risk further damage.

The doctor was warning him. Spring
training might start late for him.

Or not at all.

Roper had seen many players who never
bounced back after surgery, and in his case,
he wasn't coming off a stellar season to start
with.

Mentally he'd needed good news today.
Promising news. He hadn't gotten it.

"A delay ought to go over well with the
already-pissed-off fans," he muttered, kicking uselessly at an empty coffee cup litter-
ing the sidewalk. On the city streets, nobody
spared him a second glance.

Someone talking to himself wasn't unusual
here. He was just lucky there were no
reporters around to let the world know he
was losing it.

At least, since he'd seen the team doctor,
he didn't have to call his coach. The doc
would do it for him, which took one load
off his shoulders. Roper had a couple of
hours before his physical-therapy appointment, so he headed home to unwind.

As he passed the front desk with a wave
to Stan, the doorman, called him back.

"What's up?" Roper asked Stan, who'd

been on the day shift ever since Roper had bought the place two years ago.

"Another delivery for you." He held out a box with a familiar scrawl.

"The guy doesn't give up," Stan said, lifting his cap and scratching the top of his head.

Roper began to shrug, and the immediate soreness reminded him of his already shitty day. "He's a Renegades fanatic who doesn't think I'm earning my keep. At the moment he's got a valid point."

Stan frowned. "Maybe if he showed you some support, you'd get your groove back faster."

Roper appreciated the man's backing. "Thanks. Not much I can do but ignore it." Still, the thought of how much he'd disappointed the fans, his teammates and himself gnawed at his gut.

"I still don't like that he knows where you live."

Roper forced a laugh. He didn't like it much himself, but again, there wasn't anything he could do about it. "Half of New York City knows where I live. It's not a national secret. But I appreciate your concern."

"Yeah, well, it just doesn't sit right. I mean, the guy doesn't try to hide what he's doing. He just sends you things that don't fit in the mailboxes and have to come through me. You need to get these things screened."

He waved at an older woman passing by. "Afternoon, Mrs. Davis," he said.

"Hello, Stanley." She smiled warmly and kept walking.

"Anyway, I don't like it," he said, turning his attention back to Roper.

"It's his way of getting my attention." As if Roper could or would ignore the upset-fan letters still trickling into the stadium addressed to him.

"Why don't you open it down here? That way I can get rid of it for you afterward," Stan offered.

Roper recognized his curiosity but also his point. Who wanted more reminders of his shitty season hanging around his apartment? "Why not?"

Stan pulled a box cutter from beneath the desk. "Do you want the honors?"

Roper shook his head. "You can have them."

Stan neatly slit the box and opened the flaps, then Roper took over. He reached inside and pulled out a Ziploc bag, sealed shut.

For good reason. The contents defied description.

Roper looked, blinked and stared again. "Holy —"

"What the hell?" Stan asked, narrowing his gaze and staring at the bag in disbelief. "Is that what I think it is?"

Roper held the bag with two fingers, keeping it far away from him. "It sure is, Stan. It's a bag of shit." Probably dog shit.

And written on the bag in permanent marker were the words *You Stink.*

Roper's stomach roiled in a combination of nausea and humiliation.

"The nerve of some people. You get on upstairs and take it easy. I'll get rid of this." Stan pulled the bag from Roper's hand, stuffed it in the box and stormed away, heading for the back of the lobby where the trash was located.

Appreciating Stan's discretion, Roper nodded. Shaken, he headed farther into the building and took the elevator upstairs. He'd just reached the kitchen and lowered himself into the nearest chair when his cell phone rang.

He pulled it out of his pocket, glanced down and groaned, answering it despite knowing better. "Hi, Mom," he said, hearing the exhaustion in his voice.

"Hello, darling. What's wrong? You sound

down. What happened at the doctor's?"

"Just some frustrating news," he admitted. "I'm not getting better as fast as I'd hoped." He didn't even think of upsetting her with the news about his recent package in the mail.

"What's up?" he asked, for the first time almost grateful for his family to focus on.

His mother paused. "Are you sure you're okay?"

"Yes."

"I'm calling about Ben. I visited with him after lunch and I'm horrified by where he's living. Did you know he's crashing on a friend's couch? He gave up his apartment because he couldn't pay the rent." Her voice rose in panic. "I had no idea things were so bad. He never told me."

Obviously Ben had managed to lie about where he was living until faced with his mother in the flesh.

Roper massaged the back of his suddenly stiff neck. "Mom, Ben's a big boy. There are any number of jobs he could take that would bring in a weekly salary so he could keep an apartment. He chooses not to apply for them. Just like he chooses to ignore my phone calls or discuss potential coaching jobs."

Just like his mother chose not to take acting roles she believed were beneath her. The difference was that Ben had lost enough of Roper's money that Roper no longer felt obligated to help his brother.

"You never did understand how frustrating it is for Ben to live in your shadow," she said.

Roper let out an angry groan. "I'll tell you about frustrating. I just had a doctor's appointment where I learned that despite all the work I've done in the past few months, my shoulder isn't strong enough for spring training. I've been killing myself and it just doesn't matter. So I can't summon much pity for Ben at the moment. He's brought his problems on himself."

A long pause followed, which Roper took to mean his mother finally understood how serious he was about not wanting to discuss Ben. "Is there anything I can do for *you?*" she asked, her voice softening.

"No, thanks. I'll be fine. I want to grab something to eat before my P.T. appointment, so I need to get going."

"Okay. But just one more thing? I have a situation," she said.

Roper narrowed his gaze. Did it ever end? "What kind of situation?"

"It seems that Harrison Smith followed me to New York. In fact, he's staying in the same hotel. He wants me to take that role I told you about and he's being very persistent. He sent me roses. Not real roses, mind you, but mink roses. Flowers made from fur. They are simply gorgeous. But that's not the point."

"What is?"

"He insists on having dinner tonight and I can't deal with him alone. It's getting harder and harder to resist him."

"So don't." Roper exhaled hard. "A meaty role would be good for you. Why don't you just take the part?"

"Darling, I couldn't do that. Just do me a favor and join us for dinner tonight. I'll be forever grateful."

"Ask Sabrina and Kevin."

"I did, but they have one of Kevin's business dinners. I need you, darling."

"No —"

"And bring that delightful young woman, Amy, with you."

"Delightful young woman?" Just what had happened at lunch, anyway? She hadn't said.

"Well, yes. We got to know each other earlier and she's a joy. I'd love for her to join us at dinner."

He'd love to see Amy, too, but not at a family dinner with a Hollywood director. "Mom, I've had a rough day and it's not over yet. I'm not in the mood for a long dinner."

"Good! We'll make it short. Better for me."

He glanced heavenward. She wasn't listening. If he didn't show up, he'd never hear the end of it. Maybe having dinner out would be better than eating alone in his apartment, thinking about his recent package in the mail or the doctor's report. Besides, he knew when he'd been beat.

At least there was a silver lining. His day had sucked. He deserved a break. And he needed to see Amy.

"Where and when?" he asked.

She mentioned Kelly's, a small, casual restaurant he'd been to a couple of times. "Oh, listen, that's my call-waiting," his mother said. "Your brother's on the other line. I'll see you tonight at seven."

Roper nodded, hung up, then called Amy.

After spending the day with his family already, he wouldn't have been surprised if she'd said no to dinner. But surprisingly, she agreed to join them. She even said she'd meet him at his apartment because he'd just be getting back from the physical therapist — where, after today's news, he realized he'd have to put in one hundred and fifty percent. He needed to focus on his career, not his family. And not on the beautiful

woman who'd agreed to be his salvation at
dinner tonight.

CHAPTER NINE

Amy waited in the kitchen for Roper to finish dressing. She hadn't planned on seeing him again today, but he'd sounded so down, she couldn't resist coming along to dinner tonight to make sure he was okay. And considering his mood when he'd answered the door, she was glad she'd agreed. She'd watched his mother in action this morning and again at lunch and realized how wearing the woman was on those around her. Cassandra Lee expected the world to fall at her feet. No doubt she'd become used to it in the heyday of her career. And then afterward Roper had ensured she always had everything she needed, Amy thought.

But who made sure Roper had everything he needed? she wondered.

The sound of footsteps drew her attention, and she glanced up to see Roper join her wearing a pair of black jeans and a light blue Burberry shirt. Amy wasn't into designer clothes. But the Jordan sisters were trying to change that, and thanks to them, Amy recognized the classic plaid. She had to admit, she liked that she could hold her own with Roper, a man who was always immaculately groomed, no matter what his mood.

"You look good," Amy said, the words out before she could stop them. A heated blush rushed to her cheeks.

His gaze bore into hers. "Thank you. You're looking pretty hot yourself."

She blushed deeper.

"We have a few minutes before we have to leave. Can I get you something to drink? Water? Perrier?" A smile tugged at his lips. "You see? I heard you when you said you didn't want to drink around me."

"Those weren't my exact words," she muttered. She'd only said no to a drink last time. But he'd read her mind. Which probably meant he understood her reasons. He was hard to resist when she was sober. Give her a drink and she'd succumb to his charm in an instant. "No, thank you. I'll wait until we get to the restaurant."

"Okay, then. Let me just straighten up and we'll head on over. With a little luck, Mom and Harrison Smith will be early, too, and we can get this meal over with," he said, sounding even more preoccupied than usual.

"Why do I have the feeling that you're worried about more than spending the evening with your mother?"

He shrugged, eyeing her as if deciding whether or not to talk. "I'm just sick of hearing from disgruntled fans. They're entitled to their feelings, but it would be easier if I didn't have to deal with it at home, too."

She narrowed her gaze. "So why do you? Doesn't your mail go to the stadium or directly to us at the Hot Zone?" She was pretty sure the stadium mail was automatically forwarded to the Hot Zone, protecting him from unwanted correspondence.

It was just another service the Hot Zone offered to their clients. Long ago, Micki had made sure that someone screened all clients' fan mail before being passed on to those athletes who wanted to see it. The rest was answered by someone at the PR firm with a signed photo or as directed by each client.

"Most of my mail goes the standard route. But even though I'm unlisted, it's not too hard to find out where someone in the public eye lives. This guy's been sending me stuff all season."

"At your home?" she asked.

217

He nodded. "You brought up a letter the other day," he admitted. "But that wasn't the worst of it." He twisted his head from side to side, obviously aggravated.

She propped her hands on her hips. "I think you need to elaborate."

He groaned. "Besides the standard letters, I've gotten a bobblehead doll with a knife in its shoulder. And then today's *package* was something else."

"A knife in its shoulder?" she asked, her voice rising. "And it was a bobblehead doll of *you?*"

"Calm down." He stepped toward her, placing a hand on her arm.

Not likely, she thought, a chill sweeping through her body. "What was in today's package?" she asked.

"Forget it. It's just some crazy fan. Fanatical. Get it? It comes with the territory of playing in the majors and getting the big bucks."

She raised an eyebrow at him in question. Did he really think he could gloss over this? "Oh, no. You aren't getting away with avoiding my question. What was in the package?"

He lowered his hand from her arm and met her gaze. "Dog shit with a note saying *You Stink.* At least I think it was from a dog," he muttered, not wanting to contemplate that thought too deeply.

She winced, both nauseated and horrified at the same time. "You have got to be kidding me! That is the most disgusting, scary thing I've ever heard. This guy is nuts!"

"It's a fan, remember? Just let it go."

"I remember Uncle Spencer telling me about the time a tennis player was stabbed during a championship match. You can't brush this off. Did you report it to the police?"

He rolled his eyes. "Now, that would be overreacting."

She scowled at him. "Then did you mention it to someone at the Hot Zone? Did you tell Yank about the bobblehead? Of course not," she answered for him.

"Since you already know the answer, why should I bother answering the question?" he said, laughing at her.

She wasn't fooled at his attempt to change the subject. "First thing tomorrow I'm going to have all your mail forwarded to the Hot Zone. We'll make sure you get your bills and things that are safe as soon as possible."

He inclined his head. "Not a problem."

She blinked, startled by his easy agreement. "Oh."

"I'm not a glutton for punishment. I should have done that from the beginning.

It's more of a mental drain than any kind of real threat. But thank you. Good idea."

"You're welcome." She exhaled hard.

"So how about we just go to dinner?" he asked.

"Sounds like a plan." Dinner wasn't the only thing on her agenda.

Now there was more than just his family eating away at him. He also had this nutty fan whose so-called gifts were just sick, and getting worse. Amy didn't want them to get dangerous. At this point, she was more sure than ever that she had to get Roper out of town.

With or without his consent.

Considering Ben had deigned to show up, dinner had been surprisingly pleasant, Roper thought. There had been no talk of the televised pilot his mother kept turning down or Roper's career skid. Instead Harrison Smith had led the discussion, getting to know Roper, Amy and Ben, and essentially ignoring the diva at the table. By the end of the meal, Cassandra was sulking, proving to Roper that the man had his mother wrapped around his finger. She claimed not to want the attention, but she didn't want to be ignored, either.

Roper silently applauded the man's ability

to get under his mother's skin. No man had done that during Roper's lifetime.

Harrison was busy with the waiter, placing his dessert order. "The lady and I will both have crème brûlée," he said, placing his hand over Cassandra's.

Cassandra slid her hand from his. "I'd prefer the tropical sorbet. I have to watch my waistline," she said, becoming animated for the first time all evening.

Harrison snorted. "She'll have crème brûlée." He placed his hand behind her chair and leaned closer. "Are you really going to avoid your favorite dessert just to spite me?"

Cassandra sniffed but didn't reply.

"Remember when we couldn't afford more than one dessert and we shared it once a week back in film school?" the other man asked.

"You two knew each other in film school?" What rock was he living under? Roper wondered. And what else was his mother hiding?

"Mom, you're holding out on us," Ben said. "Did you and the director here have a thing going on back then?" he asked, chuckling.

"Maybe she doesn't want to share personal information at the table," Roper said to his sibling.

The waiter conspicuously cleared his throat. "Would anyone else like to order something?"

"I'll have a decaf cappuccino," Amy replied quickly, probably to kill the oncoming argument between the brothers.

"Espresso," Roper added.

"Regular coffee," Ben said.

"And two crème brûlées?" the waiter asked, double-checking with Harrison and Cassandra as he collected the small menus.

To Roper's surprise, his mother nodded. "That's fine," she said with an obviously forced sigh.

She'd caved in to the director. It didn't matter that the subject was something as insignificant as dessert. Cassandra had given in. Now that he'd witnessed her relationship with Harrison Smith firsthand, Roper knew why his mother was running scared.

The man didn't cater to Cassandra's prima donna whims and he didn't put up with her nonsense. He also knew her a lot better and perhaps more intimately than anybody had guessed. Just because Ben had asked his tacky question at the wrong time didn't mean he was wrong. Something deeper than an argument over a role was going on between these two.

With the waiter gone, Ben leaned forward, elbows on the table. "So you two have a history?"

"Your mother didn't tell you?" Harrison asked.

Cassandra visibly squirmed in her seat.

Ben shook his head. "No, Mom's been holding out."

Roper opted to add his thoughts. "Frankly, I thought you wanted her for the role in your pilot because of her past body of work," Roper said.

"That's one reason. Your mother is talented. But we also go way back to our days as struggling artists. Remember, Cassie?"

Roper nearly choked on his water.

"Cassandra," she corrected him, her haughty tone returning.

"Cassie!" Ben laughed loudly. "That's really something else." He grinned, enjoying his mother's discomfort.

Roper wasn't. He was confused by the interaction and worried about his mother's ability to handle Harrison. On the other hand, Harrison dealt with his mother extremely well. Roper was beginning to like and appreciate the man for that reason alone.

He glanced at Amy. She sat beside him and had remained quiet for most of the meal, watching the dynamics around the table much as Roper had. But that didn't mean he hadn't been intensely aware of her the entire time. She smelled delicious, her perfume a subtle but constant reminder of the always simmering attraction between them.

"It's not Cassie, Benjamin, and you know it," Cassandra finally said. "So behave."

Harrison grinned. "She's always been Cassie to me." His cell phone rang, and after checking it, he glanced up. "Would you excuse me for a minute? It's my daughter and she wouldn't call if it weren't important."

Roper nodded. He'd appreciate a minute or two with his mother without the other man's imposing presence.

"Well, well," Ben said, catching his mother's wandering gaze. "You've been keeping secrets."

"Not really. We knew each other back in the day. So what?"

"So the man remembers what your favorite dessert is. That's not something a woman takes lightly," Amy finally spoke, telling Roper his observation was on target.

Cassandra waved her hand in the air. "He has a good memory."

"Okay, *Cassie,* whatever you say." Ben

finished off his drink.

Roper would never give Ben credit, but his brother had a point. Nobody had ever called his mother by such an intimate shortening of her name. Never.

His mother flushed deep.

This meal was actually turning out to be fun, as well as enlightening, Roper thought. "Okay, you two obviously had a fling and he's obviously interested again. That's not a big deal. He seems like a decent-enough guy. So the real issue is why you're fighting him so hard."

"That's obvious," Amy said when his mother remained silent. "It's because he's so intense. The man has the looks of Sean Connery, the charisma of Jack Nicholson and the persistence of a pit bull. Overwhelming." She fanned herself with her hand.

Cassandra met Amy's gaze and an unfathomable understanding flashed between the two women. Something Roper didn't for the life of him understand. "Females," he muttered.

"Just cut your mother some slack," Amy said, placing her hand on his arm. "It's obvious she needs time to adjust to Harrison's pursuit."

"Exactly," his mother said, folding her

225

arms across her chest. "Cut me some slack, John." She turned to her other son. "You, too, Benjamin. Stop enjoying this so much. You're both encouraging Harrison. And that is something I do not need, want or appreciate."

Roper saw his opportunity and grabbed it. "If I back off, will you consider the role Harrison is offering?" He believed in a good quid pro quo and he'd just offered his mother a very fair exchange.

She opened her mouth to answer just as Harrison returned.

Taking pity on her, Roper didn't push her to decide now. But he'd definitely be discussing it with her again later.

"I'm sorry about that," Harrison said, taking his seat once more.

"Is everything okay with your daughter?" Amy asked.

He nodded. "She's in the middle of an ugly divorce and she needed my opinion on something."

"I'm sorry," Cassandra said. "That can't be easy for her." Her compassionate tone took Roper off guard.

"It isn't. She's an MBA and earns more than her husband, whom she supported while he tried to make a living screenwriting. Now he's asking for a divorce, alimony,

226

full custody and child support. The man isn't worthy of my daughter," he said, fired up on his child's behalf. He cleared his throat. "But thank you for caring." Harrison placed his hand over Cassandra's, sending her into another frenzy of unsettled movement.

It was all Roper could do not to laugh, watching his normally composed mother fidget and fuss under a man's attention.

Half an hour later, they'd finished coffee and dessert. When Roper asked for a check, he discovered that while taking his phone call, Harrison had apparently also made arrangements to pay the entire bill. Roper thanked the man. He wasn't all that bothered, since he had the definite feeling there would be plenty of opportunities for Roper to return the favor.

Harrison didn't strike him as a man who gave up easily.

They made their way to the street. Roper held on to Amy's hand, not wanting her to hail a cab and disappear before he had a chance to talk to her alone.

But he managed to catch up to his brother when they reached the sidewalk. "Hang out for a few minutes, I want to discuss something important with you, okay?" he asked.

Ben didn't reply.

"It's good news for you, so chill," Roper muttered.

"Thank you for a lovely dinner," Amy said to the director, probably to distract everyone's attention from Roper and Ben.

"My pleasure. I've been wanting to meet the people who are close to Cassie. Perhaps next time Sabrina and Kevin can join us, as well," he said.

"Sabrina will definitely want to check things out for herself," Ben said.

Cassandra flipped her pashmina scarf around her shoulders. "I think Harrison will be back in L.A. long before we can arrange everyone's schedules," she said.

"You think wrong," Harrison said. "I've freed myself up for the foreseeable future. Nothing is more important to me than you." His voice grew deep, making Roper shift uncomfortably on the sidewalk.

Beside him, Amy squeezed his hand, seeming to understand.

"You mean, convincing me to take the role of someone's mother and *grandmother.* On TV." Cassandra straightened her shoulders in a haughty display, but beneath the pride, Roper saw the fear.

He suddenly understood. His beautiful mother was afraid that if she took the role, she'd be acknowledging her own mortality.

Harrison stepped forward and clasped her hand in his. "I meant what I said, Cassie. Nothing is more important to me than *you.*"

The two stared at each other, the silence only broken by the honking of a car horn and the screeching of tires.

"Should we leave them alone?" Amy whispered.

Ben shrugged. "Seems like it."

Roper was about to agree when his mother's voice rose higher. "Like I'm going to believe you aren't sweet-talking me in order to get me to take this godforsaken part. I'm nobody's fool," she said, before stepping into the street to hail a cab.

Before anybody could react, a yellow car pulled up and Cassandra Lee placed herself inside. And then she was gone.

Harrison turned to Roper, Amy and Ben, completely unflustered. "So happy to meet you," he said. "We'll have to do it again sometime."

Ben inserted himself between Roper and the director. "I'd be happy to. There's a script idea I've been toying with. A ballplayer who couldn't make it in the minors due to a tragic past."

Harrison nodded, listening politely. "Call me and we'll talk," he said to Ben.

"Will do." Ben then took off down the

street, his wave telling Roper exactly what he could do with his request.

Harrison turned back to Roper. "It was good to meet you, too," he said, extending his hand.

Roper inclined his head and shook the other man's hand. "She's a complicated woman," he said of his mother.

"Always was." Harrison's smile spoke of deep understanding for Cassandra's ways.

"Are you really here indefinitely?" Roper asked.

Harrison nodded. "As long as it takes," he said, then turned to Amy. "A pleasure." He lifted her hand for a kiss.

"Same here," she said, her cheeks pink.

He turned and strode down the street, hands in his leather jacket pockets, whistling as he walked.

"Hmm." Roper stared after the man, at a loss for words. "Nothing about tonight was what I expected."

"I bet not. Your brother is a character," she said.

"He was too pushy with Harrison, too crude with Mom and too eager to get away from me." He glanced at the dark sky thickened with clouds. "Frustrating," he muttered. "So what did you think of Harrison Smith?"

"A very interesting man," Amy said, her eyes sparkling with intrigue. "I know I've only recently met your mother, but I can't imagine anybody flustering her the way Harrison does." Amy rubbed her hands together briskly.

She obviously still wasn't used to the cold. "I've known her forever and I've never seen anything like it, either." He flagged an empty taxi.

The cab slowed to a stop in front of them. Roper held the door open so Amy could slide inside before joining her. She gave her address to the driver and Roper, exhausted from his day, decided not to argue.

"Does it bother you? That he's so obviously interested?" Amy asked.

Roper didn't have to think about his answer. He shook his head. "Not as long as the man's feelings are real and he isn't using her reaction to him as a means to get her to take the role."

The role, as well as the man, really had to be right for Cassandra Lee. Roper would have to do some digging into the director's past and make sure he was good enough for Roper's mother.

"Well, he seems genuine," Amy said.

"Says the woman who was ready to fall at his feet," Roper said, laughing.

She playfully smacked his shoulder. "I was not. I could see your mother's dilemma clearly, that's all. Harrison is a charming man."

"A mix of Sean Connery and Jack Nicholson and a pit bull. Is that what you like in a guy? A bulldozer?" Roper asked.

"That's an interesting question." Amy leaned her head back and glanced at him. "I haven't thought about it, really. I think it's all about chemistry and whether, like you said, the man is the real thing. The rest should come naturally." Her voice dropped lower, thicker, making him think she was referring to them.

Or maybe that's just what he wanted to believe.

Inside his pocket, his cell phone rang, interrupting the dark intimacy of the back of the cab, and Roper groaned. He pulled it out of his pocket. "What is it?" he asked.

"Now do you understand why I can't take the role or be alone with him?" His mother didn't bother to say hello first. "He wants to have lunch tomorrow to discuss the part. I need you there."

Her voice was loud enough for Amy to hear, and she groaned, too.

Roper rolled his eyes. By the time his mother let him interrupt her long enough

232

to say he'd discuss lunch with her later tonight, the taxi had pulled up to Amy's building. While he was hanging up the phone, she'd thanked him and promised to call him from the office tomorrow to discuss mail forwarding among other things.

He'd planned to walk her in and kiss her good-night. He'd have settled for just kissing her right there in the cab.

Instead, the opportunity to segue into any kind of a kiss was lost. He slammed his hand onto the torn leather backseat in frustration, then gave the cabbie his address.

The life of an orphan suddenly seemed appealing, he thought wryly.

After last night, Amy realized she needed a new plan of action for Roper, and by the late afternoon, she had one in place.

Still, as she sat at her desk, she couldn't help but take one last look at the daily papers. The *Post* lay on top of the pile. Metro Jock Receives Major Shock. The article went on to discuss the frustrating news Roper had received from his doctor and how unconfirmed rumors had him pushing back his start date to weeks after the start of spring training.

She called her secretary on the intercom. "Kelly?"

"Yes?"

"Do me a favor? Please pull all the most recent sightings and blurbs about Roper on the Internet, TV and radio and make sure I have copies before I leave?" She wanted to take a look at where Roper had been when he was sighted and ask him to think about whom he'd spoken to each time. She needed to see if there was a connection or common denominator. Clearly someone was out to punish Roper. But whether it was Buckley or the crazy fan or someone in his personal circle, she had no idea.

"How the hell do they find out about these things?" Amy asked in frustration.

"Good question. I don't got an answer, either," Yank Morgan said as he entered her office without knocking, cane in hand, fluffy dog at his side.

"Hi, Yank."

"Hi, girlie. How are you doin'?"

"Fine if not for these." She ran her hand over the stack of newspapers. "Did you see that Frank Buckley's been picked up by satellite radio with a corresponding TV deal? He won't just be seen and heard in New York. The whole country will get to experience the foul man."

Yank nodded. "Lola read it to me this morning. Don't fret about what you can't

234

change and change what you can. That's
what I always say. In other words, forget
about Buckley the Bastard."

"I would if the media would let me." She
flipped over the paper that had Buckley's
deal on the back and picked up the *Daily
News.* It, too, had a blurb about Roper's
life. "Which metro jock was spotted with
his lady of the moment and his famous
actress mother at an intimate family dinner
at Kelly's restaurant? Could wedding bells
be in the picture for either couple?"

"Argh!" She threw this edition into the
trash.

"You must've just read the one about dinner. How was it anyway? I've been meaning
to tell Lola I want to eat there one day
soon."

Amy appreciated the subject change.
"Delicious. You'll enjoy it," she promised
him. "So are we all set?"

"You're ready to go. Our boy thinks you're
picking him up for a business lunch with
me. The limo knows to head straight up to
the lodge. Dealing with the fallout is up to
you." Yank let out a loud laugh that startled
Noodle from where she'd plopped onto the
floor.

"I can handle it," she said, repeating her
new mantra, the one she'd adopted for

maneuvering in the Hot Zone world. After all, she could think of many times she'd taken a hard stand with her mother, going so far as to lock her in her own home, just to keep her out of trouble.

"Of course you can. I just came by to wish you luck," Yank said. He turned, whistled and walked out, dog toddling after him.

Amy gave a silent prayer for success.

Between the stress of Roper's injury and therapy, the constant fan backlash, his mother's daily drama and the tracking of his every movement in the paper, Amy knew she was doing the right thing.

She just knew Roper would never see it the same way.

Cassandra definitely needed a new plan of action to avoid Harrison. Running from L.A. hadn't helped. He'd followed her. She didn't know how much longer she could continue to convince John to act as a buffer and she knew better than to include Ben again. Harrison had told her Ben wanted to discuss a script with him. Her son was shameless and would use whoever crossed his path. She understood she wasn't blame-less in how Ben had turned out. She'd babied him for too long. But she understood him, too, and she couldn't just cut him off, which was why she kept turning to her oldest son to help.

But who was going to help her with her director? The man was persistent in the extreme. He wanted her to return to L.A. with him as a couple and he wanted her to take that role. Television. Could she hold her head up in Hollywood after such a huge step down?

Cassandra didn't know what she feared more, the role he wanted her to play on screen or the part he wanted to play in her life.

CHAPTER TEN

Roper glanced out the tinted window of the car Amy had hired to pick him up and take them for lunch. He still didn't understand why he couldn't have just met her and Yank at the restaurant for this sudden meeting, but she'd insisted. Now, as he sat beside her, she remained eerily quiet.

"What restaurant are we going to, anyway?" he asked.

She shrugged. "I'm new in the city and I'm bad with names. I can't remember," she murmured. Her gaze strayed out the window and she drummed her fingertips on the hard leather armrest beneath the window.

Taking her cue, he sat in silence, watching as the scenery changed from the luxury shops on Madison Avenue to more eclectic scenery as they made their way farther north.

It wasn't until the driver turned right onto 102nd Street and merged onto FDR Drive that he spoke up. "We're leaving the city?"

"Looks that way." She didn't meet his gaze.

His gut churned with anxiety. He braced his hand on the seat in front of him and leaned forward so the driver would know he was talking to him. "Excuse me, but where are we headed?"

"Upstate," he said.

"Upstate." Roper placed his hand on Amy's jeans-clad thigh.

Faded-jeans-clad thigh, he realized now. Warm, tight yet supple. He shook off those thoughts, reminding himself he was annoyed. He looked her over, from the top of her ponytailed hair to the bottom of her Converse sneakers. Her outfit wasn't exactly business casual.

"Dammit, Amy. Don't make me guess." Because he didn't like the direction his thoughts were going.

She turned toward him, her knees nudging against him as she moved. "We're going to the lodge, and before you blow up at me, hear me out."

He stiffened in shock. "What gives you the right to kidnap me and take me somewhere I explicitly told you I did not want to go?" His anger simmered on low boil. If he'd been with anyone but Amy, he'd have lost it by now.

She straightened her shoulders and met his gaze head-on. Now that he'd been clued in, she was no longer hesitant around him, but was the determined Amy he'd grown to admire.

"Correct me if I'm wrong here, but you have a goal. You want to be ready for spring training as close to the beginning as possible, right?"

He inclined his head, unwilling to give her more than that for the moment.

"In order to get ready, you need not just to be physically ready, but mentally ready." Her eyes blazed with certainty.

When he didn't reply, she nudged his leg with hers. "Well?"

"Right," he muttered.

"Well, as far as I can see, you're far from being ready either way. If you stay in the city with your mother pulling you into her problems every five minutes, and your sister needing help planning her wedding, and your couch-potato brother hanging over your head and shit arriving at your door — and I mean that literally, as well as figuratively — you'll never have five free minutes to focus on *you*." She poked him in the chest as she spoke.

He shifted in his seat, finding it difficult

to argue the point, yet unwilling to concede to her tactics. "So you took it on yourself to bring me to a place where I could get tough for the season."

"Yes."

"Care to tell me where you get off manipulating me?"

"I'm paid to make sure you're ready. Both Yank and Micki agreed we had no choice."

His cell phone rang and he grabbed it from his pants pocket.

"Who is it?" Amy asked before he could take the call.

He glanced at the screen. "My brother."

Taking him off guard, Amy reached out and swiped the phone from his hand. In an instant, she opened the window and threw the device into thin air.

"What the hell?"

Amy's heart raced a mile a minute. She truly couldn't blame him for being angry. But with the act of throwing his phone out, her heart pumped faster and more furiously in her chest. She'd scared herself while his face flushed red with anger.

"The Hot Zone will replace it," she said, repeating what Micki had told her last night when she'd called to support Amy and her plan.

They agreed that given the chance, Roper

would use his phone to call and check on his family or let them know where he was. Both women were convinced, though, that once he had the opportunity to unwind and he saw how focused he could be on his career, he'd willingly go along with their plan.

"I don't believe this." He ran a hand through his hair.

"Believe it." Amy turned back toward the window, intending to ignore him.

Reverse psychology. She couldn't think of another way to work around Roper's anger. She curled her hands into fists and looked out the window, not really seeing the passing scenery.

"What's going to stop me from picking up a phone at the lodge and calling someone to come get me?" he asked.

"Nothing except your own common sense. I'm counting on the fact that you want to get healthy enough that you'll give this experiment a chance. See what relaxing without pressure does for your frame of mind."

He'd soon discover that his suite had been stripped of a telephone and the staff had been instructed not to give him access to either the house phone or anyone's personal cell phone. He could definitely find a way to leave or call home if he was downright determined, but it wouldn't be easy. And Amy hoped that by the time he found the means, he'd no longer have the desire.

She drew a deep, calming breath. "I'm betting that after a few days, you'll be thanking me for this."

"Not likely," he muttered.

"You don't need to worry about your family," she reassured him. "Micki is making herself personally available to them for any emergencies. You trust Micki to handle them, don't you?"

He didn't reply. Instead he shifted in the seat beside her and exhaled hard. Reverse psychology, Amy reminded herself, pushing aside the gnawing guilt.

Then she followed his lead and ignored him for the rest of the long car ride upstate.

A woman who introduced herself as Lisa, the assistant manager, escorted Roper to his private suite. He wasn't surprised to see he had a dresser and closet full of his favorite brand of workout clothes, T-shirts and a note assuring him anything else he needed would be provided by the concierge — whom he had to walk downstairs to reach since he had no phone in his room.

The suite had a fully stocked kitchen,

including a refrigerator and pantry, along with a set of dishes and utensils for him to use. A quick glance told him the coffeemaker was state-of-the-art and his favorite flavored beans were sitting beside the appliance along with a note.

Relax and enjoy. You need it and so does your career. Courtesy of Athletes Only and the Hot Zone.

On the nightstand, there was a list of restaurants on the premises, a room service card and a printed schedule of activities specifically put together for him. From the daily physical-therapy appointment to the orthopedist on call if there were any problems, to the gym hours and scheduled masseuse, every one of his needs had been taken care of. Despite the fact that it was already past lunchtime, even today had been booked. He had a full afternoon of rehab and relaxation waiting for him.

Obviously he could find someone with a cell phone or grab a ride to town and use a phone, but something stopped him. Maybe it was the niggling feeling in the back of his mind that Amy had a point.

Though at the moment he was loathe to give Amy credit for anything.

Amy left her suitcase open on the bed and

pulled out a swimsuit. She hadn't had a real swim since leaving Florida, not that she considered an over-chlorinated indoor pool the equivalent of what she was used to, but she'd have to make do. She had a lot of frustration and, yes, guilt, to work out and she knew no better way than a swim.

She changed and headed for the spa and gym area where the pool was located, deciding to leave her captive to his own devices for a while. And since it was winter, and most of the guests were skiing, she had the pool to herself.

She dove in and swam laps, taking the length of the pool with the crawl stroke she'd perfected as a teenager living down south. She made her way through the water, up one end and back down the other, over and over until exhaustion threatened to overwhelm her. Satisfied she'd burned calories, as well as nervous, excess energy, she drew herself up and out of the pool.

But she wasn't ready to head back to her room just yet, so she settled on a chair and relaxed, planning to wander the area and get familiar with the other amenities before going back up to shower and face Roper's anger over dinner.

As it turned out, he didn't show up for the reservation she'd booked at one of the lodge's most exclusive restaurants, nor did she see him for the next three days. She kept track of him via the staff and by checking up on him with the physical therapist and others around the resort, so she knew he hadn't escaped her so-called prison. She caught glimpses of him wandering the grounds or working out in the gym, but she left him to his own devices, grateful he hadn't attempted to borrow a phone or hitch a ride home.

She had to admit she was impressed. Even if she was growing increasingly upset and frustrated by his refusal to talk to her at all.

Three days had passed since Roper arrived at the lodge. He'd relaxed for the first time in ages, though it had taken a while. He had no idea unwinding from the reality of life could take so long or be so difficult. Hell, he hadn't even realized how physically and emotionally taxed he'd been until his first massage.

At first, being out of touch from his family had been difficult. He'd worried constantly about his mother and how she was dealing with Harrison Smith. He wondered how many expenses she'd incurred without his sister's permission in planning the huge wedding. He didn't worry much about Ben, since without money, his brother was unlikely to get into too much trouble.

After a while, though, a funny thing happened. He stopped thinking about his family's problems and he started focusing on himself. Not on the negative things, like not returning in time for spring training, but on what he could do to work harder and smarter in order to get back to the game he loved. Without his time being divided, he started to get into the routine set up for him, and he began to see how distracted he'd been before. How much he'd needed this escape.

How right Amy had been.

At first he'd deliberately avoided her, missing planned meals out of spite, wanting to make a point that he might have chosen to stay here but he was still in charge. He justified his actions by telling himself that he was just doing as she'd instructed, thinking only of himself for a change. Which he was. Yet he'd catch her watching him through the gym windows or eating with some of the guests she'd obviously met during her time there. He knew she was giving him space just as he knew he was being childish by avoiding her.

He waited for her at lunch at her normal time. When she didn't show up, he asked

Lisa about her. The woman told him Amy wasn't feeling well. She was laid up with a cold and said she'd be in her room if he needed anything. He didn't *need* anything, he was just starting to miss her.

Hell, he'd missed her from the minute he'd shut her out. But if she wasn't feeling well, he doubted she'd want to see him, so he had chicken soup sent to her room with a *Feel Better* note that he signed himself.

The next day, she was still out of commission. When he called, she told him that she felt awful and didn't want to give him her cold, so it was better he not stop by. He sent the doctor over instead, but respected her wishes and stayed away. Her cold lasted another three days.

In the meantime, he worked out, relaxed and fell into bed exhausted at night, earlier than he was used to. He woke each day feeling refreshed and ready to start over again. And he began to sense that his body was responding to routine, consistency and *lack of stress*.

Everything was progressing well. The only thing missing was Amy, and he figured by tomorrow, she'd either come out or he was barging in. After this past week, he'd come to the definite realization that if he was going to remain here next door to the woman

248

he wanted more with each passing day, he was damn well going to do something about it.

His scheduled routine was finished for the day and he eased his aching body into the warm, bubbling water of the hot tub, soaking and unwinding. Every time he began to wonder how his family was doing or what their reactions were to not being able to reach him on demand, he pushed the thought out of his mind. He'd become an expert at it, and with each passing day, the guilt lessened. Amy was right — he trusted Micki to handle them. If a true emergency had cropped up, he'd have heard. He closed his eyes, tipped his head back and thought about absolutely nothing.

Much too soon, a female voice broke into his blessed silence.

"Mind if I join you?" she asked.

He forced his heavy eyelids open to see a gorgeous woman in a tiny string bikini sinking into the tub as if his answer was a foregone conclusion. Since he didn't own the rights to its usage, he supposed it was.

Her chocolate-brown hair screamed perfect dye job and her wide smile indicated perfection. Celebritylike perfection. Everything about her seemed familiar, but he couldn't place her name.

"John Roper, pleased to meet you." He extended his hand in greeting.

She grabbed it for a surprisingly strong shake. "Hannah Gregory," she said.

He snapped his fingers in the air. " 'Lies Lost,' " he said, suddenly remembering her Top 40 hit. "I'm a fan."

Her smile grew wider. "Thanks. Since I have three brothers and I was born and raised in New York, I'm a die-hard Renegades fan. Nice to meet you, too," she said. Leaning back, she let herself grow more comfortable in the water.

He waited for a negative comment on his season, but it never came.

"So what are you doing here at the lodge?" he asked.

"The band wanted to get away, so here I am." She waved one arm in the air. "They went skiing. Brr," she said, her distaste for the outdoor sport obvious. "How about you? What brings you to Greenlawn?"

He contemplated how to phrase his kidnapping diplomatically. "R and R," he finally said, opting for discretion.

"That seems to be what this place is known for."

"So I hear."

She began to hum, a pleasant sound that didn't disturb him, and he shut his eyes once more.

After a few minutes, her voice once again broke the silence. "Listen, the boys and I are having a small get-together in our suite tonight. Why don't you join us?" she asked. "They'd love to meet you. Especially Mike, my drummer. He's also a fan."

Roper opened his eyes to see she wasn't even looking at him. In fact, her eyes were shut and she was enjoying the bubbling water. Clearly she wasn't flirting with him, just extending an invitation. One he appreciated, since he was ready for some human companionship here in Greenlawn.

He was surprised to realize that he was relieved the beautiful Hannah wasn't showing any interest. Though there might have been a time when her perky breasts and pretty face, all probably molded by a plastic surgeon, might have appealed to him, it was the lightly freckled Floridian who held his interest now. Despite the fact that she'd tricked him into coming up here.

Damn Amy, even out of sight she wasn't out of mind. She had obviously spoiled him for anyone else, which only served to convince him he had to act on his desire.

And what better way to break the ice after a week of not speaking than at a small party? "Sure. I'd love to come," he told Hannah.

It wasn't as if he had someplace else to be tonight. He was on his own in this little slice of seclusion.

"Great." She still didn't open her eyes. "I'm catering food up to my room. That's why we love this place. We can really keep to ourselves."

He nodded. That suited his purposes just fine. He glanced up at the ceiling, then asked Hannah the question circling in his head. "Mind if I bring a friend tonight?"

She shook her head. "Not at all. The more the merrier." She rattled off her suite number, then began to chat with him about the season in a way that told him she was one of the minority — an understanding fan who knew even a million-dollar player could have a bad stretch.

By the time he climbed out of the water, he realized that despite Hannah's celebrity, she was as down-to-earth as they came. She even reminded him of Amy.

He wrapped a towel around his waist and ran his fingers through his hair. "I'll see you around eight?" he asked.

Hannah, who'd also come out of the tub and had begun to dry herself off, nodded. "Come earlier if you can't find anything to keep yourself occupied," she said.

"I might just do that."

"Do what?" a familiar female voice asked.

He jerked around to see Amy staring at them. He wondered what she'd overheard, and worse, what she thought was going on between them.

"Hey, there," he said to Amy, trying not to look or feel guilty when he had no reason.

"Hi." Amy lifted one hand in an awkward wave. The other pulled tighter on the towel that covered her one-piece bathing suit. "I didn't mean to interrupt. I just thought a sauna would be a great way to finish off this awful cold. And it's through there. The sauna, I mean." Her gaze darted from Roper to Hannah, then back again. She took a step back, and then another one, clearly intending to escape.

"Don't go." Her obvious discomfort tugged at something inside him and he wanted to reassure her. "Hannah was just inviting us to a party tonight. Hannah Gregory, meet Amy Stone. Amy, Hannah is —"

"I know who Hannah is," Amy said, extending her hand. "Nice to meet you. I love your music," she said with genuine warmth.

More warmth than she was shooting his way at the moment.

Hannah beamed at the compliment, suddenly looking even younger than she really was. Given the frosty look Amy turned his way, and considering she had walked in on the tail end of their conversation, it was obvious she thought the events at her cousin's wedding were repeating themselves. She believed she'd witnessed John Roper picking up a woman while he had another one waiting in the wings, hell, while she was upstairs sick.

Apparently Amy didn't know him as well as she thought she did. It was time he enlightened her as to the man he really was.

He looked forward to the challenge and to ending the night exactly where he belonged. In Amy's bed.

Back in her room, as Amy showered to get ready for Hannah's party, she knew there was no way she could compete with a music pop star who was gorgeous, impeccably groomed and much more worldly than Amy could ever be. Again, it wasn't that she lacked self-esteem, she just understood what it took to keep up in Roper and Hannah's world. They exuded star quality without effort, and as young as Hannah was, Amy had no doubt she'd had plastic surgery of some sort to keep that perfect body and face. So Amy wasn't even going to put herself in that league. As her mother had taught her, she should always just be herself.

Still, Amy was human and she couldn't help but wonder what Roper had thought when he'd turned from Hannah in her itsy-bitsy teenie-weenie bikini to face Amy in her Speedo one-piece racing suit.

It shouldn't matter.

But it did.

Just like she shouldn't be personally interested in Roper.

But she was.

And that truth had been driven home to her when she'd heard the sound of Roper's deep, familiar laugh coming from the whirlpool and she'd walked in on him making time with a gorgeous woman who, true to form, hung on his every word.

Amy knew she ought to have expected it, but since she hadn't talked to him in a week and their last real encounter had been an argument, she hadn't been able to laugh it off. Instead, unwanted and unbidden jealousy had swamped her and remained with her, even now.

Four days with a respiratory virus had nearly killed her, and Amy had dragged herself out of bed for the first time in days to take a sauna and visit the outside world. She hadn't expected to run into Roper, and she sure as heck thought she'd look better the first time she did. But her nose was still red, her eyes sunken and tired-looking and her choice of bathing suit wasn't exactly sexy.

She stepped out of the shower and towel-dried her hair, then used a diffuser to air-dry the curls. The one benefit to being in New York was the lack of constant humidity, but there was no getting away from the fact that she wasn't a model-thin, glossy-haired starlet. She picked clothes that suited her, but at times like these it was hard to remember that she liked herself just fine.

Drawing a deep breath, she headed over to the room number where Hannah was staying. She'd told Roper she'd meet him there, knowing she'd need time to pull herself together before seeing him again.

Voices, laughter and soft music sounded from inside. Amy knocked once and the door eased open, so she let herself inside. She took in the small group of people, immediately noticing they were dressed as casually as she was in her jeans and a loose-fitting cotton long-sleeved T-shirt. One hurdle over, she managed to relax.

Then she zeroed in on Roper sitting beside Hannah, along with a bunch of other guys who joked and talked while she strummed on her guitar. Although he was laughing and enjoying himself with the guys, Roper didn't look particularly hung up on the pretty musician. In fact, he seemed more mellow and relaxed than she'd ever seen him.

A sudden sense of peace settled over Amy as she realized she'd done the right thing by bringing him here. At that moment, he seemed to sense her presence. He turned her way, his gaze locking on hers. A welcoming smile eased the corners of his mouth upward in a grin that told her he was genuinely happy to see her.

She walked over and joined the group.

"Hi, there," Roper said, light sparkling in his eyes.

"Hi," Amy said, not wanting to interrupt the ongoing conversation.

"Join us," Hannah said.

"We're just listening to Hannah and her favorite relaxing music," one of the guys said.

The other woman rolled her eyes. "They are not. They're being guys, making crude jokes and basically ignoring me," Hannah said.

"Who's this pretty lady?" A big, dark-haired, tattooed guy asked. His easy laugh was at odds with his rougher appearance, and Amy could tell he was a teddy bear in wolf's clothing.

"I'm so bad at names." Hannah blushed. "But I remember your first name. It's Amy. Amy . . . ?"

"Stone," Roper said, rising and stepping over to join Amy, placing a protective, possessive arm around her shoulders. "Amy Stone, meet Mike Morris, the drummer."

"Hey, don't forget about us," another of the group said.

Amy glanced over. Two identical faces, both blond-haired men, stared back at her.

"Joe and John Glover, Amy Stone." Hannah gestured between all involved. "You can see how rough it is. I'm surrounded by guys all the time. I'm glad to have another girl here." She placed her guitar beside her and jumped up. "Me and the guys, we tour together all the time, but sometimes it gets a bit much, if you know what I mean."

Amy laughed, glancing at the men she found herself suddenly surrounded by. "I can imagine."

"Don't listen to her," Mike said. "She loves us." His gaze caught Hannah's for a brief second before he quickly glanced back at the other guys.

"Like a brother, baby." She made a face at her drummer, but the stare and the connection lasted long enough to tell Amy there was something between them. Something they both fought to deny.

Hannah turned to Amy. "Come on, let's get to know each other," Hannah said, pulling her away from Roper and to the far side of the room.

She handed Amy a can of Coke and grabbed one for herself, another thing that surprised Amy. No drugs or alcohol. Everyone here seemed high on just hanging out and enjoying life.

"So how do you know Roper?" Hannah asked Amy.

"I work for his PR firm."

"Publicist?" Hannah asked, drinking her Coke directly from the can.

Amy nodded. "But on this assignment, I'm more like his handler."

Hannah nodded. "I'm ducking my handler-manager at the moment," she said, sounding way too wise for her years.

Amy was intrigued. "Mind if I ask why?"

Hannah strode to the window and looked out. Amy joined her, struck by the beauty of the falling snow. White and full flakes dropped against the backdrop of the inky night sky. So different from Florida and yet so magnificent it took her breath away.

Hannah sighed. "My manager likes to keep me in the headlines even when I don't have a CD currently out. You know the expression, no publicity is bad publicity? Well she lives by that mantra and frankly it exhausts me."

"How so?" Amy wanted a point of comparison for Roper's life. The two sounded similar.

"I can't go out for dinner without the press finding out about it. If I call a guy friend just because I need a shoulder to cry on, the next thing I know I'm reading about how we're an item. I know this sounds selfish considering how fortunate I've been, but I need some downtime and it's been hard to get it lately." She glanced around the room at the guys in the band. "They understand and feel the same way. So we came up here without telling her where we are."

Amy placed her soda can down, unopened. "Boy, we all have a lot in common." She didn't know why she thought she could trust Hannah, but she did. Something about the sincerity she sensed in the other woman's demeanor and personality spoke to Amy. "I basically dragged Roper up here kicking and screaming for the same reasons. Nobody knows where he is and I really need to keep it that way."

Hannah turned toward Amy, her eyes full of understanding. "He's had it rough lately, hasn't he?"

"He has. Much more than he deserves. I want him to have time to regroup without personal issues pulling at him. Every day he gets here is a bonus as far as I'm concerned."

"He won't be outed by any of us, that I can promise you." Hannah crossed her heart.

Amy glanced across the room and her gaze met Roper's. He held the stare for a long moment before he winked and turned his attention back to whatever Mike was saying.

They hadn't had a real conversation since the car ride up here one week ago. Her cold had sidelined her, but watching him now, maybe it was for the best. He'd had a chance to come to grips with what she'd done and why. He'd needed to be here and he understood that now.

Amy refocused on Hannah, realizing Roper's emotional health depended on everyone's discretion, but apparently Hannah felt the same way. "I believe you'll keep his location secret."

"I will. We're in seclusion, too." Hannah leaned closer. "You care about him, don't you?"

"Of course I do. He's my client and this is

my first big assignment. I can't afford to have him dissatisfied with the end result."

Hannah rolled her eyes. "I wasn't talking about liking him as a client. I saw the way you were looking at him. Not just now, which was pretty intense, but earlier at the pool. You didn't like finding him hanging out with me."

"I . . ." Amy opened her mouth, then shut it again. She thought about denying the other woman's words but what was the point. "Was it that obvious?" Amy asked.

Hannah nodded. "I'm afraid so."

"It wasn't personal." Amy raised her hands to her hot cheeks, embarrassed at being found out. And here she thought she'd managed to seem professional.

"I know that." Hannah waved a hand, dismissing Amy's concerns. "Want to know how I know? I mean, can I share a secret so you'll understand?"

"Absolutely," Amy said.

"I figured it out because I have the same problem with Mike." She tipped her head toward the drummer, who still stood talking to Roper. "I'm head over heels," she said with a sigh. "We spend so much time together on the road, we know each other really well. I know he finds me attractive. I see how he looks at me, but he won't act on it."

"Why not?" Amy shot a covert look at the big man who looked as if he could handle himself with this or any woman.

"He says he doesn't want to screw with the chemistry of the band if something goes wrong. But that isn't it." Hannah shook her hair out of her face. "It's the age thing. There's ten years between us. That's an issue for him, not me. Age and Big Mama."

"Who?" Amy tried not to laugh at the name.

"My mother," Hannah said, wrinkling her nose. "And the band's manager I was telling you about earlier. I think Mike's afraid of her," Hannah whispered. "Not that he'd ever admit it."

Amy understood Hannah's situation. She wouldn't exactly say she was head over heels for Roper, at least, not yet, but the damn attraction was there and strong. But she didn't want it to interfere with her doing her job. She didn't want her private life to become public, either. Still, she couldn't deny how much she desired him or the fact that the feelings weren't going away.

Maybe she just ought to sleep with him, get it out of her system and be done with it, she thought wryly.

And then she wondered why not.

Although the idea had come to her suddenly, the yearning between them had been building since they'd met at the wedding and the feeling had only grown stronger since they'd begun working together. She swallowed hard and glanced his way. She took in his strong presence, his sexy body, his handsome face, and suddenly she couldn't think of anything else.

"What do you think?" Hannah asked her, drawing Amy's attention back to their conversation.

"About what?" She'd obviously missed everything the other woman had just said.

Hannah rolled her eyes, obviously realizing what Amy was preoccupied with. "I said I was thinking of just seducing Mike. Slipping into his bed and daring him to throw me out." She laughed, but Amy could see Hannah was serious.

"Not a bad idea," Amy said, wondering if she could pull off such a stunt herself.

"That's what I've been telling myself. We're here, we're alone except for the twins — but they don't care about anything except their music — and there's no Big Mama to interrupt." Hannah's eyes flashed with anticipation.

"I like it," Amy said, her mind already

wondering how she'd manage it herself.

"As for Big Mama, I've thought about hiring another manager and cutting out the nepotism, but she really means well. She's pushed and pushed and helped us get where we are. But honestly, she needs to back off sometimes. And if things work out between me and Mike, her interference would be a make-or-break point between us." Hannah nodded decisively.

Amy knew Hannah meant what she was saying, but as she knew from watching Roper deal with his family, it was one thing to talk a tough game, another to execute it against a well-meaning but interfering parent. "You need to be blunt and tell her to let you live your life."

Hannah sighed. "She thinks it's her job to direct my life. Tell me, is it possible to prevent a steamroller from doing its job?"

"I wish I knew," Amy said, thinking of Cassandra Lee.

Amy had spoken with Micki earlier and Cassandra had given her hell for sequestering her son and refusing to discuss his whereabouts. Micki had assured Cassandra that Roper was fine and taking care of himself for a change. She'd offered the woman anything she needed from advice to reservations. She just wouldn't give Cassandra the one thing she wanted. Her son's current address.

Amy looked into Hannah's eyes and said, "Just remember it's your life. If you don't take control of it, everyone else will."

"Sound advice," Roper said, coming up behind them.

"It is. It just isn't easy," Hannah murmured. "I should go talk to Mike. We're supposed to go over some things for this summer's upcoming concert. We'll talk later," she said to Amy.

Hannah worked her way over to her band and, with great finesse and a lot of sex appeal that included swaying hips and a full pout, managed to extricate Mike from the rest of the guys.

Impressive, Amy thought.

And when Roper strode over and cornered her, she hoped she had the nerve to act as boldly as Hannah had. What a difference a week made. Now Roper glanced at Amy with a devilish grin, all evidence of his anger at being tricked gone. So when he turned his sex appeal her way, it wasn't hard to believe in herself and her ability to act on her feelings.

Because Amy was finished fighting the attraction between them.

CHAPTER ELEVEN

Roper studied Amy, her tight jeans and sexy loose-fitting top, and realized she fit right in here. The woman who'd been uncomfortable earlier in her one-piece bathing suit was gone. In her place was the siren who called to him day and night, in his dreams and when they were wide-awake. Like now.

She shoved her hands into her pants pockets. "So have you calmed down?" she asked.

As if he hadn't had a reason to be upset with her, he thought wryly. He wasn't fooled by her attempt to put the onus on him. But he didn't mind it, either.

He leaned against the wall, just plain enjoying her. "You mean, have I forgiven you for dragging me up here against my will?" He was teasing. He just wasn't sure whether or not she knew it yet.

She stepped closer until they were inches apart. Her scent, strawberry shampoo and pure woman, overtook his thoughts and all he could concentrate on was taking her in his arms and kissing her senseless — with no cell phone, Treo or family member interrupting them.

"I was looking out for you." She met his gaze with those huge brown eyes that broke down his defenses.

Not that he had any left when it came to her. "I know that now." He treated her to a slow, easy, genuine smile meant to relax her and put all conflict behind them for good.

She released a puff of air, her relief that he was no longer angry evident. "So what made you come around and finally understand?"

"You did." A stray curl fell onto her forehead and he plucked it off with one hand, allowing himself the pleasure of smoothing his palm down her head in a gentle caress. "Deep in your heart, you aren't a manipulative sneaky person. Some time up here alone, no one to bother me, a workout and a whirlpool, and I relaxed enough to remember that."

"Wow. You're complimenting me." The corner of her lips turned up in a cheeky grin. "Not only have you forgiven me but you're pretty mellow."

"And you seem to be enjoying yourself,

too. You must be pretty relaxed yourself."

"I wasn't, but I am now," she said.

He hoped the reason was his forgiveness, but he couldn't be sure and raised an eyebrow in question. "And what's so special about now?"

"Your calmer attitude, for one thing."

"And the other thing?" he asked.

She shrugged, her attitude playful. "Isn't a girl allowed to have secrets?" She bit down on her lower lip.

His gaze followed the movement, his gaze drawn to her sensual mouth. So she was playing coy. Miss All Business was suddenly flirting, he thought, amused. Hmm. Well, he couldn't say he minded.

She was one of the perks of being here. "I took a walk earlier and discovered an amazing place. Want to see?" he asked.

She glanced over at their hostess, who appeared pretty tied up with her drummer. "I don't think they'll miss us," she said, a mischievous glint in her eye.

"Come." He took her hand and together they walked through the lodge's main lobby where people wandered, some alone, some in small groups, while others gathered around the big-screen television at the bar.

"Do you want to stop first and have a drink?" He gestured to two empty stools in a private area.

She shook her head. "I'd rather have all my faculties tonight. Nothing to drink. But thanks, anyway."

He inclined his head and kept walking. Normally he'd think her unwillingness to indulge in alcohol was her way of reminding him they were only business associates, but something was different about her tonight. It wasn't just her light mood or her teasing. It was *her*. She hadn't removed her hand from his grasp and there was a sudden confidence emanating from her he hadn't seen since meeting her at the wedding. Whatever had brought on the change, he was thankful for it. And he had the sudden hope that her unwillingness to drink had more to do with her desire to remember each and every minute between them.

He led her past the gift and sundry shop to a point beyond the restaurants. While working off his frustration earlier, he'd come upon a solarium that was being cleaned. He let himself inside and found himself viewing a winter wonderland beyond the glass. It was a place he'd spent a quiet, contemplative hour.

The door was closed and he knocked once. When no one answered, he pushed it open and led her inside. Instead of turning on the lights, he kept the room dark, and when the door slammed shut behind them, he quietly turned the lock, giving them complete privacy.

"What is this place?" she asked.

"A sunroom," he said. "I asked Lisa and she said it's usually only open during the summer. But when I walked by, a crew was dusting and I peeked inside." He'd looked out the wall-to-wall windows at the snowy landscape beyond and immediately knew he wanted to share the sight with Amy.

She strode to the windows and stared outside. Instead of looking at the scenery, he watched her. Eyes wide, she stared at the frosty view, lit up by outdoor lights and the ski trails in the distance.

"Wow. It's beautiful," she said in awe. "I've never seen snow like this before. I mean, I've seen the dirty slush in the city this winter but nothing like this."

He hadn't realized what she'd missed growing up in Florida. "Then I'm going to have to get you outside to experience the snow for real while we're here."

"Ooh, I'd love that." Her voice dropped to a deeper husky sound that resonated inside him.

He stepped behind her, wrapping his arms around her waist and looking out from over her shoulder. White snow covered the bare branches and stars filled the night sky. Without even realizing it, he eased himself forward so his body pressed more fully against her back. His hands splayed across her stomach, and of its own volition, his penis grew hard and aching. It thrust against his jeans and pressed insistently against her rear end.

She sucked in a deep breath, but she didn't protest or try to escape his hold. Obviously much had changed and he wasn't about to question why.

He rested his chin on her shoulder. "It's beautiful," he said, turning his head slightly and nuzzling his lips against her neck.

"Mmm. Growing up in Florida, I always thought I had it all. Sunshine and beaches, warm weather. But now I know what I was missing. Will you really go outside with me? I want to touch the snow and feel it between my fingertips," she said, her excitement rising.

He was rising, as well.

"I want to make a snow angel like I've seen on TV," she continued.

Her enthusiasm was contagious, and he felt as if he were experiencing the same surge of emotions as Amy — all for the first time. "I'll take you anywhere you want to go," he promised her.

She tipped her head backward. "I believe you," she whispered.

She stared out the windows some more while he continued to nuzzle her neck with his lips, which quickly turned to suckling her soft skin. He couldn't get enough of her taste, her scent, all of her.

He slipped his hands into the waistband of her jeans. She didn't object, so he let his fingertips dip lower until he passed the low band on her panties and brushed the soft hair beneath.

She sucked in a shallow breath, and at the moment, he let his waist jerk forward, seeking relief he knew he wouldn't find just yet. But that didn't mean she couldn't enjoy and he intended for her to do just that.

In the silken silence that surrounded them, he unbuttoned her jeans and lowered the zipper, never once turning her to face him.

"John?" she asked, her voice uncertain.

"We're alone," he reassured her. "I locked the door. Besides, no one comes back here. And with the thick trees out there, no one can see in. It's just us," he promised her. "Isn't that what you wanted for me? Peace and quiet? Time to focus on what's important?"

He let his words settle, let her make of them what she would. He wasn't about to think or dig too deeply into his meaning now. The words had escaped, and right now he meant them.

Before she could back away, he picked up where he'd left off, easing her jeans just low enough on her thighs to give him access, but not too low that she couldn't pull them up and get decent if she wanted.

"Trust me," he whispered in her ear.

"I do." Then, as if to prove it, she shifted and spread her legs slightly, opening for him.

He'd been waiting for this moment, more desperately than even he'd realized, and as he slid his fingers past the triangle of hair and down to her damp heat, desire the likes of which he'd never known swept over him.

A soft moan escaped her lips.

"Do you like that?" he asked, already knowing the answer. Proving his theory, he pressed his forefinger between her dewy folds. Moisture licked at his skin and a rush of heat suffused him from inside out.

If this is what nearly entering her with his finger did to him, heaven help him when they made love. And they would. Soon. But her pleasure came first. He shifted positions and slid his finger inside her.

She shook and trembled, clearly already on the verge.

"I've got you, so don't be afraid to let go." As he spoke, he pushed his fingertip into her, then slowly eased out, making sure his thumb hit on the tight nub of desire with each slide.

She clenched her hot, wet inner walls around him, which only served to increase the friction of his finger's glide. Unable to control his own body's reaction, he began to pump his hips against her back in a steady rhythm.

He had control, but barely.

And then without warning, she turned toward him, releasing his finger from between her legs, taking him off guard. With shaking hands she reached for the zipper on his jeans and pulled them down.

She glanced down and stared. "Commando," she practically stuttered.

He shrugged, then grinned.

Laughing, she wrapped her arms around his neck, but he kissed her first, reveling in the sweet welcome of her mouth. He didn't know how, but he held on to some last shred of sanity, enough to know they had to be fast. The longer they stayed, the more risk of someone wandering back here by accident, as he had this afternoon.

"We should hurry," he said.

Amy nodded. "Please tell me you have protection." She wished she'd asked before she'd acted on impulse and yanked down his pants, no matter how impressive the sight.

But her entire body was on fire, desire pulsing through her and begging for release.

"As a matter of fact, I do." He bent to extricate a condom packet from his pocket.

Though relieved, a part of her wasn't sure how to feel about the fact that he had a condom on hand, ready to go at a moment's notice.

"Amy?" he asked as he took care of the situation.

"Hmm?"

"Wipe the frown off your pretty face and look at how old this thing is." He held up the ripped packet, obviously worn from being carried around in his wallet. "My father knocked up my mother in a day and age when it just wasn't done. I promised myself a long time ago I'd never get caught without one."

The frenzy had momentarily lapsed in favor of deeper, more important talk. She couldn't suppress a smile. How could she be upset with a man like him?

"You're one of a kind," she told him.

He grinned. "You are, too, freckles." He tapped her cheeks.

She ought to be embarrassed, but he said it in a way that made her feel cherished.

"Listen, I'd lift you and be inside of you already but I could never explain reinjuring my shoulder if I did." He grinned, but she couldn't mistake how deep his voice was, how much his need matched her own.

"Good point." She glanced around the dark room, lit only by outdoor lights creeping in. To her right was a covered bar and stools that looked just the right height for what she had in mind.

What the heck? she thought. In for a penny, as the old expression went. She was already tempting fate by letting out the bad girl she always had a hunch was inside her. She pointed to the covered stools.

Next thing she knew, Roper had pulled her over and positioned her on one of them, in the most vulnerable way she could imagine, legs spread wide, waiting, just for him. But she didn't have time to think too long.

Condom on, he pulled her toward him and tilted her back against the chair. His gaze never leaving hers, he thrust into her completely.

Amy saw stars, and not only because it had been so long since she'd had sex. He filled her body in a way that reached up, up through her throat and threatened to make her head and body explode with the perfection of the feeling.

A low groan escaped from his throat and his big body reverberated inside hers. She grabbed on to the seat of the chair and held on tight as he slid out, then thrust deep once more. He repeated the motion, and to Amy's surprise, each time she felt fuller, more intense pressure inside her.

Together they quickly found a rhythm and the pleasure built higher and faster each time his body connected completely with hers.

In.

Out.

In.

With each successive thrust, she felt more of him. Took more of him.

Gave more of herself.

He cupped her face in his hands and kissed her long and hard, branding her even more than his body was doing. His tongue swept through her mouth, taking possession as he took control — gliding out of her body slowly at first, easing back in deep, not stopping to let her catch her breath. As the passion and yearning grew, gentleness gave way to more pressure, deeper thrusts that brought her ever closer to completion. She couldn't do anything more than squeeze her body tight around his and ride out the masterful storm he created.

And just when she didn't think she could take anymore, everything inside her exploded in bright lights and the most intense pleasure she'd ever known. The sensations took her even higher, rocking her world until finally, they subsided in slow, sweet passion.

She opened her heavy eyes and found Roper staring at her, his expression intense. "Are you okay?" he asked, concern in his voice.

"Never better." The pulsing continued throughout her system as she struggled to catch her breath.

"I thought our first time would be in a bed." His gravelly voice told her he hadn't yet completely recovered, either.

"I think I'd have killed you if you stopped to go find one."

She thought about his words and their implications, which summed up the kind of man he was. For so long, she'd been consumed with avoiding anything happening between them. Meanwhile, he'd thought about their first time. He cared about where they made love.

Was it any wonder her feelings for him continued to grow?

He leaned his head back and groaned. "I locked the door, but we shouldn't continue to tempt fate."

She laughed. "Good point."

He slid out of her, his regret at leaving her obvious. After he pulled up his jeans, he gently helped her stand and fix her clothes until there were no telltale signs of dishevelment to give her away.

He then smoothed his hands over her hair and pulled her close for a long kiss before breaking apart once more. "There's a bathroom on the other side of the room. I'll be right back."

While he was gone, she stared out at the landscape, the snow and glittering lights. She was lightheaded and in shock, as much from what she'd done as from the feelings attached to what she'd once considered merely a physical act.

If asked, she'd have said that she cared about the few men who'd come before Roper. Until tonight she'd have been telling the truth. But now, post-Roper, she realized she'd been so naive and ignorant.

There was sex. And there was making love. And though she'd obviously liked the men she'd been with in the past, none had ever induced such a cascading flood of emotion.

She pressed her hands against the cold window and then used her palms to cool her flushed face. But nothing eased the internal heat and nothing stopped the sudden realizations that came next.

She'd never felt this way before. So right, so uninhibited, so free. Only with this man. And that was what she'd feared all along — that the overwhelming desire he fueled in her would overwhelm common sense. That she'd act on instinct and satisfy her desires at the expense of the consequences.

And those consequences in this case were clear. She risked losing her heart to the wrong man. A man whose life meant cameras and public scrutiny. All the things she'd been hiding from in Florida for years.

Roper released the wildness in her she'd repressed for most of her life — the part of her that was so like her mother and aunt, making public spectacles and taking risks. Tonight she and Roper had been in a secluded place with minimal to no risk of being caught bare-assed having sex in front of wall-to-wall windows, she thought.

No press around. This time.

And yet despite it all, she couldn't regret their time together here for that very reason.

It was theirs alone.

When Roper returned from the bathroom he'd sensed Amy's withdrawal, caused no doubt by too much time alone to think about what they'd done. He'd expected regrets and recriminations. A long talk about things between them being a mistake. But she'd surprised him by linking her hand in his for the walk back to their rooms. She might be more subdued, but she hadn't pulled away.

Hannah's party had broken up early, a discovery they'd made when they'd found the twins, Joe and John, drinking at the lobby bar and rolling their eyes at the fact that apparently, Hannah had finally gotten her way with Mike the drummer.

Amy had seemed ridiculously pleased with the tidbit of gossip, which Roper attributed to one of those female things he'd never understand. Who cared what happened between Hannah and her band member? Since the news only served to fully restore Amy's good, playful mood, Roper decided he should not only care but be thankful.

When they reached Amy's room, she unlocked the door and pulled him inside. That was when he got to live out his fantasy of making long, slow love to her in a bed with music playing and lots of time to savor and enjoy.

Which they did, twice before she collapsed on top of him and fell fast asleep. Before he followed, he had time to watch her. She didn't snore, but she made cute little noises while she slept.

Noises, he suddenly noticed, that he didn't hear now.

He reached for her, assuming she'd rolled over to the other side of the king-size bed, but he came up empty. He forced his eyes open and discovered he was alone. A glance at the clock told him it was only 9:00 a.m., and he decided to trust that wherever Amy had gone, she hadn't run far away with morning-after regrets.

He propped one arm behind his head and stared at the ceiling. Thinking back on the night, he knew he'd seen a more adventurous side to Amy than he knew she possessed and he decided he liked it. A lot. The fact that she didn't regret hooking up in the solarium reinforced his notion that she wasn't someone he'd grow bored with too soon. She was good for him professionally and personally, he decided. And for now that was all he needed to know.

As his schedule started at ten, he headed back to his room for a quick shower. Then he stopped by the front desk to make his first request of the concierge. His plan? To fulfill a promise he'd made to Amy and show her all the ways he could make and keep her happy. Not just in bed, although he had to admit they'd gotten off to one helluva start.

Amy had liked waking up next to Roper. She'd liked it too much, so she rose quietly, showered and met up with Hannah at the breakfast buffet. They walked the length of the long table together and Amy filled her plate with at least one of everything.

"I'm starving," she said, the smell of pancakes assaulting her senses.

"Sex will do that to you," Hannah said.

Amy choked. "How do you know what went on?" she asked, praying the other woman hadn't seen or heard anything from the solarium.

Hannah laughed. "Until now, it was only a guess. One based on the fact that I'm beyond ravenous and I know what I was doing all night," she said with a grin.

"So things between you and Mike worked out?" Amy grabbed one last pastry before heading for a small table in the corner of the restaurant.

Hannah followed. "Let's say they're at

least moving forward. The only way they'll be better is if he gets Big Mama's blessing. All he's ever wanted was his career and she can make or break him."

They sat at a table and immediately dug into their food. While she and Hannah ate, they exchanged life stories, Amy about growing up without a father and as the only sane one among two childlike adults. She even revealed her mother's Lady Godiva episode and what it had cost Amy in terms of not just a job, but a life among her peers, something she hadn't been able to realize or put into words until now.

And Hannah described growing up with her mother, who lived her own unfulfilled dreams through her talented daughter. Hence the reason for the other woman becoming her manager and directing Hannah's life, so that music was its only focus.

"You know you have to take control of your mother," Amy said, stabbing her fork into a piece of waffle and talking to Hannah as if she'd known her forever.

Considering they'd already confided in each other about sex and their men, Amy figured the bond was already there. She liked people and talked to them easily. So this friendship with Hannah wasn't a surprise, merely welcome.

She missed having someone to talk to. For years it had been her mother and her aunt, but with Hannah, Amy realized how badly she missed the companionship of someone her own age. A best friend.

"Not only do I know I have to take control, but I plan on doing something about it. Mike is going to kill me, but I intend to call my mother and let her know where we are." Hannah accentuated her decision with a raise of her coffee cup.

Oh, wow. That was a huge step. "What exactly do you plan to do when she gets here?" Amy asked.

"I'm going to tell my mother that she will have to make a choice. Accept my relationship with Mike without any interference or lose not just her place in my life but her position as our manager." Hannah set her cup down and met Amy's gaze, not a hint of uncertainty in her eyes.

"You love him that much," Amy said.

"I do. You don't spend that much time with someone, in the studio, on the road, and not get to know him, the good and the bad, quirks, faults and all. He's worth it to me." She nodded definitively.

"You go, girl," Amy said. She knew what Hannah was risking and yet she approved of her going after what she wanted most in life.

Hannah shook her head, her long ponytail falling over her shoulder. "Yeah, well, enough about me. Once my mother arrives it'll be pure chaos."

"When will that be?" Amy asked.

"I need another few days to savor this time with Mike. Then I'll call Mama. At which point I'm sure I'll be on your doorstep, begging for you to save me from her," Hannah said, half jokingly.

"Can I ask you a silly question?"

Hannah nodded. "Of course."

"I just realized that growing up the way I did and moving into a retirement community left me with few . . . okay, make that *no* real friends my age to speak of. Now I'm getting to know people at work, but I've revealed more to you than to any of them." She glanced at her water, feeling ridiculous. "But what about you? Don't you have a best friend or someone you go to when you need a shoulder? Or advice?" Why would the famous Hannah Gregory confide in Amy?

Hannah laughed. "I can see why you'd want to know, but the truth is I'm more like you than you realize. When I was young, I was tutored so I could take singing jobs, commercials, whatever Mom could line up.

Now I'm in the studio or on the road. I'm with the guys all the time. The people I meet are either other performers, in which case there's jealousy or competition, or they're intimidated by me. I can't relate to them. You're the first woman I've met in ages I'd want to call my friend."

A warm, fuzzy feeling settled around Amy's heart. A friend. Silly as it seemed, she was feeling more and more complete with each passing day.

She wanted to reach across the table and hug Hannah, but the ringing of Amy's cell phone prevented her from acting on impulse. "Excuse me. Just for a second."

"Hello?" The phone number indicated it was Micki even before Amy had answered. "What's wrong?" Amy asked, because they'd agreed Micki wouldn't call and risk Roper being around and getting worked up by information from home. Amy would call her if she needed her.

"What isn't?" Micki asked.

Amy closed her eyes, realizing for the first time just how easily the real world — and Roper's problems — could intrude on her idyllic time here.

CHAPTER TWELVE

"So what's going on?" Amy asked Micki. She held the phone to her ear and mouthed an apology to Hannah.

"Cassandra Lee has camped out at my office and refuses to leave until I tell her where Roper is. I couldn't believe how attached she is to him until I found out the real reason she's parked herself at the Hot Zone." Micki sighed.

"Which has something to do with Harrison Smith?" Not a difficult guess, Amy thought.

"He followed her here and now they are both seated on my couch. Both wearing full-length furs. Cassandra has a matching hat."

"Oh, Lord." Amy held her forehead in her hand. She could just imagine the sight. "Do you have a plan? Short of divulging our whereabouts, I mean."

"As a matter of fact, I do." Micki's laugh let Amy relax a bit. "Uncle Yank is going to take them out to lunch. Or should I say Uncle Yank and his guide dog, Noodle, are going to take them out. Cassandra thinks he's going to explain why we have Roper secluded, which he will. And then I am sure she believes she'll charm him into giving out the phone number."

Micki's laughter gave away the fact that her plan wasn't as simple as Cassandra obviously believed.

"But . . . ?" Amy asked.

"But once they order dessert, Uncle Yank plans to suggest Harrison choose someone more suited to play the role he wants for Cassandra. Someone more worthy. Someone who will come cheaper. Someone named Lola." Micki snickered.

Amy shook her head, glad she wasn't anywhere near New York City during this lunch. "Go on."

"Harrison, who is infinitely wiser and more cunning than Roper's mother, and who has a stake in the outcome of this lunch, has agreed to agree with Uncle Yank. At which point we expect Cassandra to scream, become offended that he'd give her role away to someone unknown, and then take the role back on principle," Micki said, sounding pleased with herself.

"But as soon as Cassandra comes to her

senses, she'll walk away again." Amy massaged her suddenly aching temple.

"Not so fast," Micki said. "Harrison's assistant is waiting for the phone call that it's a done deal and she'll immediately 'leak' the news to the press that Cassandra Lee is back, making it impossible for the woman to dispute it or back out without looking foolish. Especially when Uncle Yank confirms Harrison's claim that she agreed."

Amy chuckled at the absurdity of it all. "You know, it's so crazy that it just might work. Anything else I need to know about?"

Micki exhaled loudly into the phone. "Well, if the role ties Cassandra up the way we hope, she'll stop booking twelve-piece bands and let her daughter and soon-to-be son-in-law plan their own small wedding."

"Twelve pieces?" Amy yelled loudly until Hannah placed her finger over her lips, reminding her she was in a quiet restaurant.

"Twelve pieces and Barry Manilow, but Cassandra claims he'll do it for free, as a favor for an old flame," Micki said.

Amy cringed. "Eew. Too much information."

"Harrison said she was full of it. And Sabrina isn't answering her phone until her mother sees reason," Micki said.

Amy raised a finger to Hannah, indicating

she'd only be another minute. "Listen, you need to make sure this plan works or Roper will have a coronary," she whispered to Micki.

"I know. But I think I have it under control . . . except for one teensy little thing," the other woman said.

"How little?" Amy asked.

Micki grew alarmingly silent.

Amy stiffened in her seat. "What is it?"

"The stalker is at it again, except now he's turned to threats. He sent a generic baseball in a brown box to Roper's apartment. It was forwarded to the Hot Zone. Untraceable and untrackable, of course. The inscription on the ball read, 'Whack the ball or you'll be whacked instead.' "

Amy's stomach churned. "Did you —"

"Report it to the police? Yes, along with all the other incidents. At least the ones Roper told you about. They want to talk to him, but I managed to stall that for a while. And I let Vaughn know what's going on. He's hired extra security for the lodge just in case. The good news is that since the stalker sent the package to Roper's apartment as usual, we have no reason to believe he knows where Roper is."

Amy exhaled long and hard. "But the papers are quiet?"

292

"Just a mention by Buckley that Roper's lying low, probably hiding out in embarrassment. Roper would be pissed if he knew, but since he doesn't, all's well."

"You weren't kidding when you said everything's wrong."

"As long as you tell me everything is right there, I'll be happy," Micki said.

Amy glanced around at the dark wood decor and her peaceful surroundings. "Everything here is perfect. Roper is relaxed, baseball focused, rehabbing and he isn't worried about home. It's going exactly the way we wanted it to," Amy said.

"Excellent! I have to go, but I'll check in again soon." Micki hung up and Amy turned back to her breakfast companion. "I am so sorry about that."

"Hey, I understand when business calls. Everything okay?" Hannah asked.

Amy nodded. "Nothing my boss can't handle." Which was true. Except for the escalation in the stalker's actions, which Roper wasn't around to deal with, everything was status quo. His family was as needy and crazy as usual, but they had another audience to perform for, at least for a while.

The waiter had cleared the plates while Amy was on the phone.

Hannah leaned forward on her arms. "Then why do you look upset and worried?"

"I do?"

Hannah made a show of studying Amy. "Wrinkled brows, pursed lips, frowning . . . yup, you look worried."

Amy laughed. "I guess I'm just pre-occupied." And concerned about how Roper would feel if he found out about the news from home. He'd want to know everything. But as long as she could shelter him, he could continue to relax, something he desperately needed to do. But she couldn't share his personal troubles with Hannah because he was her client.

So instead she decided to be up-front about her own issues — getting involved with a famous baseball player who came with a load of baggage of his own. She asked Hannah for advice.

"As someone whose life is a media mess, I'm not going to lie and tell you it's easy. I'm also not going to tell you what to do, because I've seen too many celebrity mar-riages break up because public life inter-feres." Hannah signaled for the check.

"You sound older than your years," Amy said.

"Not older, just more jaded." She glanced down. "I believe in going after what you want in life, but I also believe in weighing the odds. What's the point of getting involved with someone if it's doomed from the start? Or if you think it is?"

A shiver raced down Amy's arms. She had no answer, nor did she want to think too much about it right now. "For as long as we're up here, it isn't something I have to worry about."

Hannah inclined her head. "Good point. You might as well enjoy what you've got while you've got it."

Amy smiled. Truer words were never spoken.

She'd enjoy the here and now. Tomorrow would show up soon enough.

There was no *awkward* morning after. For the next few days, Amy and Roper fell into a routine that included sharing the same bed, then going their separate ways after breakfast while he worked out. They'd meet up again for a quickie or just to hang out and talk. She enjoyed their conversations, which ranged from politics to sports and even music. There were never silences that weren't meaningful or comfortable. There were never issues between them that couldn't be resolved with a quick discussion.

Amy could hardly believe this was a job, that she was being paid to watch over Roper. Once they returned home she was certain things wouldn't be so easy, but for now, life was good.

After a swim, Amy returned to her room, showered and changed for the day. Since Roper had an appointment with the physical therapist, she knew he'd be tied up for a while.

She lay down on the bed and memories of last night washed over her in full Technicolor detail. Every stroke, every caress replayed itself in her mind until she was as aroused now as she'd been then. By the time she realized someone had been knocking on her door for a few minutes, her entire body was on fire. She swung her legs over the side of the bed, rose and headed for the door.

On the other side was a lodge employee with fully loaded shopping bags in his hands. "These are for you, Miss Stone."

She narrowed her gaze. "Are you sure? Because I didn't order anything," she said, confused.

The young man nodded. "I'm sure. There's a note here for you. Mind if I put these inside?"

"Of course not. Come in." She pushed

the door open wider and he walked in, unloading his bundles in the entry area of the room.

She tipped him, and once he was gone, she opened the note he'd left with her. *"I promised you a day in the snow. Get dressed and meet me at the lobby entrance at noon. John."*

She tore into the packages and discovered a winter wardrobe filled with items she'd never had a reason to buy for herself before. She examined the goodies one by one: a white down winter jacket with brown piping and matching snow pants, a ski hat with a pompom on top, brown gloves and thermal underwear. She checked the sizes and was shocked to discover Roper had gotten it right. Another bag revealed fur-lined snow boots and a pair of white-rimmed polarized sunglasses, especially designed for winter glare.

Excitement surged through her and she was instantly reminded of her childhood and Christmas mornings past, when she'd open all the wild and extravagant gifts beneath the tree. Thanks to her father's life insurance, her mother had been well-off enough to support them, but her uncle Spencer had always made certain she was spoiled, too. He thought of Amy as the daughter he'd never had. When Amy had found out that he was gay, but that he'd had a son, Riley, whom he'd allowed another man to raise as his own, Amy truly understood the depth of the void she could only partially fill in her uncle's life. He'd given up so much and had only begun to forge a relationship with his son now.

She turned her attention back to the gifts from Roper. She couldn't believe how he'd managed to have all these things picked and sent over so quickly, but she supposed fame and money had its perks.

And he'd chosen to bestow it on her. She marveled at his thoughtfulness and generosity, as gratitude and much more filled her heart.

A couple of hours later, she was dressed and headed for the lobby, ready for her first adventure in the snow.

Roper'd had a great session with the physical therapist and then an appointment with the orthopedist in town. His time at the lodge had been rejuvenating. He was feeling an overall natural high. He still didn't know if he'd be ready in time for spring training, but for the first time, he could live with that because he *knew* he'd be back. He felt good about his life and career.

Amazing what some self-indulgence could do. He felt like himself again, in no small part thanks to Amy. He could think of only one way to show his gratitude, and now he waited for her by the front of the lodge, curious to see how she liked his surprise.

The shock was on him when she finally strode into the lobby, ready for a romp in the snow. Her brown curls contrasted beautifully with the white North Face down jacket he'd ordered, and her face glowed with excitement.

She caught sight of him and smiled, waving as she joined him. "I can't believe you sent me all of this!" She wrapped her arms around his neck and pulled him close, her hug of gratitude so warm and genuine, his heart beat even faster in his chest.

"My pleasure." He held out his hand and she placed hers trustingly in his.

Amy's reaction to her clothing was the same as another woman might react to diamonds or jewels. A gift from the heart, he thought. And he refused to ponder deeper.

The snow fell softly as they made their way outside. One glance at Amy in her winter gear had him on fire. It didn't matter how cold the temperature, nor did it matter that they'd made love last night. Nothing stopped the wanting. Her bright smile and genuine appreciation for the simple things was something he needed. Something he'd been unaware of until she took control.

He trusted her.

She said his family was being taken care of and he believed her. And thanks to that trust, he sensed a shift in his own outlook on the future, in his devotion to his career and his craft. All because he'd taken a time-out from his life. He no longer fought the guilt, no longer felt the desire to find a phone and check on his mother and sister. His own needs had to come first, and for once he was putting his priorities in order.

"Wow, this is way better than looking at things through the window," Amy said, bringing him back to the present.

They'd reached the back of the lodge, the place they'd viewed from the solarium where they'd also . . . He yanked his thoughts away from their first sexual encounter before he tackled her into the snow and had his way with her *here.* She pulled her hand from his and spun in circles, laughing and appreciating the cold winter air and the snow around their ankles. Coming to a stop, she waited while the dizziness wore off, then turned and stared off at the expanse of pure white landscape behind them.

"I can't believe I missed out on this growing up." She shook her head, staring in awe.

"Definitely something everyone should experience," he agreed.

She nodded. Without warning, she took off running — or running as best as she could run while laden down with winter wear.

"Very graceful," he called out wryly.

She paused and stuck her tongue out at him. Then, laughing, she bent down and picked up a handful of snow, packing it into a ball. "The snow is so much softer than I thought it would be," she said.

"And harder to keep together. It depends on the kind of snowfall you get, whether or not you can pack a solid snowball," he explained. "Ben and I used to build forts and have snowball fights all the time on our Colorado vacations. We'd be outdoors for hours on end."

Funny, but he hadn't thought about Ben as his fun-loving little brother in a long, long time. Age had divided them, Roper thought. Age and talent — or lack thereof.

Amy stepped closer. "Hey. What's on your mind?"

He shrugged. "I'm just thinking about

how relationships change." And not for the better.

She placed her hand on his shoulder in understanding. "They could change back if you wanted them to. Or at least you could try to reach out to Ben without any expectation and see what happens. Maybe you need to try an approach you haven't used before. One that doesn't make him feel as if he's second-best."

He met her gaze. Her cheeks were flushed red from the cold, her eyes hidden behind the sunglasses he'd chosen. She looked hot enough to melt the entire field they stood on.

While he was lost in thought, she had trudged through the snow until she was a decent way from him, then she wound up, took aim and threw the snowball, hitting him squarely on the shoulder.

She wiped her hands together, obviously pleased with herself. "Not bad for a rookie."

He bent down for some snow and packed a weapon of his own. "You'd better watch out because I've had a lot of practice at this," he warned her.

"Throwing or making snowballs?" she asked as she stepped backward. And back some more.

He grinned and narrowed his gaze.

"Both." He pitched his ball at the same time she took off at an awkward run, so he ended up hitting her squarely in the back.

He took off after her, catching up in no time. He tackled her to the ground, bringing both of them onto the soft but thick snow. He rolled her onto her back to discover she was laughing. Having fun. Doing exactly what he'd wanted for her when he'd purchased all this winter apparel.

She gazed up at him, smiling.

His heart swelled even bigger. He cleared his throat. "Hey. Do you want to make your snow angel before you get too cold to stay out here much longer? After all, your blood is much thinner than mine, what with you being from down South and all."

"You say that like it's a bad thing. You northerners and your pasty skin, you make a pretty pathetic sight if you ask me."

He shook his head and laughed. He liked teasing her because she took it so well. "Pasty skin, huh? You say *that* like I'm unattractive and don't turn you on. Don't forget I have seen, felt and tasted some pretty distinct evidence to the contrary." With each word he spoke, he leaned closer, until his lips pressed down hard on hers.

Warmth surged through him, licking at him like flames on logs in a fireplace. She opened her mouth, letting him slip his tongue inside to delve deep and swirl around and around, devouring her because he couldn't get enough. Making him wonder if he ever would.

By the time they broke apart, panting and out of breath, he was ready to curse the confining clothing.

But she wasn't finished playing in the snow. She gave him a playful shove so he fell onto his back, carving out more room for herself. She lay down on her back and began to swipe her arms and legs in broad strokes, creating the snow angel she'd talked about earlier.

He watched her, realizing she was his angel. And despite how much time they'd spent together here, he wasn't ready to let her go just yet.

An hour later, Amy and Roper had showered — together — and redressed, heading down to the coffee shop for something hot to drink. Amy needed to pick up a few personal items in the shop, while Roper went ahead to get a table and put in their order.

Once seated, Roper ordered himself coffee and Amy a hot chocolate, and settled in to wait for her to return. He barely had time to take in the rustic interior when Hannah stopped by.

"Mind if I join you?" she asked, and in her usually friendly fashion, didn't wait for an answer before sliding into the booth beside him.

The waitress placed their drinks down.

"Do you want something?" Roper asked Hannah.

She shook her head. "No, thanks. I just was hoping to give you a message for Amy."

"If you wait five minutes you can tell her yourself. She'll be back anytime now."

The other woman shook her head. "I need to make myself scarce." She glanced around as if looking for someone. Nervously looking for someone. "Just tell Amy that Big Mama's here and it isn't pretty. She'll understand," Hannah whispered right into Roper's ear. "Tell her to use my personal cell to reach me. I need to talk."

Roper nodded. "Who's Big Mama?" he asked, obviously too loud for Hannah's liking, because she smacked her hand right over his mouth.

"Shh. Ask Amy. She'll explain."

Women. He would have rolled his eyes but he didn't want to insult Hannah. "Whatever you say," he told Hannah.

She smiled. "You're as great as Amy thinks you are."

Amy thought he was great? Now, that was something Roper could live with, he thought wryly.

"Thanks, Roper." Hannah leaned in and placed a grateful kiss on his cheek.

At the same time a small cell-phone camera captured the moment.

Everything that came next happened in a fast-moving blur. A security guard tried to grab the phone, but the woman holding it, an Amazon by anyone's definition, ducked and ran toward the door.

Hannah yelled and took off after the woman, shrieking for her to come back. By the time security had stopped the female photographer and her phone, Roper had a hunch the photo had already been sent to the highest bidder or whoever was in place ready to receive and run with it.

He didn't plan on sticking around to find out. He had to do damage control. He groaned and swiped his hands over his eyes. Drawing a deep breath, he reached the door, coming face-to-face with Amy, who appeared stunned by the commotion around them.

"What in the world is going on?" she asked.

He explained the situation as quickly as he could, hoping she'd take it in the spirit in which he relayed the tale. He wasn't worried about himself. He was worried about Amy and her reaction to photographers. To one catching him with Hannah in what the tabloids would call a "canoodle." To their idyllic time here being over.

"Typical photographer bullshit," he said. "Hannah and the security guard went after the woman. Hannah seemed way more upset than I was." He was so used to the unwanted photographs and the way reporters twisted reality, he could ignore it with the best of them.

And the lighter he made the situation, the lighter Amy would hopefully react. Because as he'd come to realize earlier today, he wasn't ready to give her up yet. Or for his lifestyle to intrude and yank her away before he'd had a chance to cement the bond building between them.

Amy bit down on her lower lip, obviously upset. "Do you think Hannah was worried that Mike might think the two of you are more than friends? Is that why she was so upset?" Amy asked.

She was worried about Hannah and not them? Typical Amy, caring for others almost to a fault. He assumed the realities of their situation hadn't hit her yet.

"I'm not sure what had Hannah so crazy,

considering she's as used to the press as I am. But she did have a message for you right before the photographer took that picture."

Amy raised her eyebrows. "What did she say?"

"She told me to tell you that Big Mama's here and it isn't pretty. Or something like that. She wants you to call her on her private cell," Roper said.

And then he remembered something else. "When Hannah ran screaming after the woman who took the picture, she called her Mama." He narrowed his gaze. "That big woman photographer was her *mother?*"

"Sounds like it. They do call her Big Mama. I guess now we know why. Was Hannah okay?" Amy asked.

"Last time I saw her she was running after her mother, so I'm really not sure."

"Do you think anyone retrieved the camera before the picture was sent?" As she spoke, Amy was pulling out her BlackBerry from her purse.

Funny how, now, she was the one in contact mode. Or maybe it wasn't so hysterical after all, Roper thought. "You do realize it doesn't matter whether or not the photo was retrieved before it was sent," he said.

Amy's eyes, which he'd grown used to seeing full of laughter and delight, now dimmed. "I know. Big Mama knows where her daughter is and that she's been with you. It won't be long before the world knows it, too."

Her voice dropped along with the light mood he'd been savoring for days. They were both keenly aware of the fact that their idyllic time together was at an end.

Chapter Thirteen

Cassandra paced the floor of her hotel room in bare feet. The rooms had been renovated and hardwood floors replaced what had once been plush carpet. She appreciated the chic modern look, but the last thing she needed or wanted was for her next-door neighbor to hear her and know she was back in her room. She still didn't know who Harrison had bribed to place him in the suite next to hers, but if she ever found out, she'd make sure that person was fired.

She marched to the window and back, her silk loungewear sweeping the floors. At this rate she could save the hotel money on vacuuming and dusting. A glance at the iHome clock radio/stereo on the shelf told her that it was time for Buckley's show.

Since her son's sudden departure, she'd taken to listening to Buckley the Bastard, hoping he'd hear about Roper's whereabouts before she did. He had spies everywhere. But since Roper and Amy had been gone, all Buckley had done was call John a coward for leaving town. The man was all about name-calling. Yet he was persistent, and somehow, someway, he'd find out where her son had gone.

And she'd be listening when he revealed all. She flipped on the cable station that broadcast his radio show simultaneously.

The man droned on about hockey and she sighed.

A knock sounded at her door. She assumed it was Harrison and she sat quietly, hoping he'd go away. He knocked again.

"I died and went to heaven," she called out to the person on the other side of the door. Her stomach flipped like a schoolgirl's. Like the schoolgirl she'd once been the last time they were together, when she'd been head over heels in love with him.

She'd been in love since, but she'd never had the depth of feeling she'd had — *still* had — for Harrison. But those feelings scared her because he was as strong a personality as she was. And she'd been on her own for so long, she feared his ability to twist her to his whim would cause her to lose herself. And even if his whim suited hers, she didn't want him to know he was in control. In essence, her feelings for him and the influence he wielded over her, scared her.

"You'd be in heaven if you'd just let me in," he yelled back, his voice deep through the closed door. "We have business to discuss. I have some head shots of actors and actresses I want to screen-test for the show."

Business or not, she didn't want to be alone with him. "I'm sleeping," she called back.

"You signed the contract, Cassie. You're in this project. Working with me. So open the door." He banged harder.

She cringed and hoped the guests in the neighboring rooms didn't call and report them.

Yes, she'd signed the contract. She'd been tricked. She just wasn't sure who'd done it. One minute she'd been having lunch with Yank Morgan and Harrison, who'd insisted on coming along. She'd been certain she could charm John's whereabouts out of Yank. The next minute the subject changed from her son to the TV series and Cassandra's resistance to the project. Yank had declared he had the perfect replacement for Cassandra. An unknown. A woman who'd never acted a day in her life. He'd suggested Lola, his wife, a lovely although plain

312

woman, who couldn't hold a candle to Cassandra, not in her heyday, and not now.

She'd looked to Harrison, expecting him to laugh. Instead he'd nodded thoughtfully and he'd *agreed.* Cassandra had lost it then. Even though she'd played into Harrison's hands, she'd stood up in the middle of the restaurant, in front of the maître d' and everyone, and announced there was nobody better to play the role than she.

Harrison had whipped out a contract and she'd *signed.* She'd signed without her agent, without her attorney, on principle and acting in anger. Next thing she knew, Harrison had called his assistant and the news had hit the press.

They'd conned her and she'd allowed herself to be conned.

Suddenly she heard Buckley's voice loud and clear again. It had turned quiet and she realized Harrison had stopped banging on the door.

"Whew." She hadn't thought he'd give in and walk away so easily.

And though it was what she'd wanted, she found herself disappointed in him, anyway. She lowered herself to the couch and five minutes later, the key card sounded in her door and housekeeping let him inside.

"Your room," the maid with a heavy accent said, smiling shyly up at him before she walked away.

The door slammed shut behind her, leaving Harrison inside Cassandra's room.

She jumped up from the couch. "Well, of all the nerve!" she said, striving for her most indignant tone.

He walked forward, toward where she stood by the couch. His masculine, sensual cologne wrapped around her, touching her inside and out.

"Cassie, Cassie. When are you going to stop fighting the inevitable?" he asked.

He was as handsome now as he'd been back then, while she'd had to endure Botox and Restylane and even a face-lift. She resented it. "I believe I stopped fighting the moment you tricked me into signing that contract." She fluttered her eyelashes and spoke too sweetly.

He laughed. "If you think you were tricked, sue me." He grinned but didn't say one gloating word.

Damn him. At least then she could have snapped right back.

He placed folders on the table by the couch. At least he hadn't lied about wanting to do business.

"Besides, I'm not talking about you giving in on the role. I'm talking about giving in on us. We're inevitable."

Her heart fluttered inside her chest. Perhaps he'd only used business as an excuse to make his way into her room. She feared her heart would be next. "No, we're not."

He shook his head in that determined way he had, his jaw clenched. "I've waited long enough for you and I'm not about to walk away now." He reached a strong, tanned hand toward her face.

She turned away before she could give in. She was afraid. Afraid of doing as he suggested and ending up as the wife of the most powerful director in Hollywood. He'd turned from movies to television and hadn't looked back. He wanted her to do the same. Then where would she be?

At his beck and call.

At his mercy.

She'd have no protective barriers left because he understood her better than any man ever had, and he got her to do things she knew weren't right for her. Or maybe they were exactly what she needed, but she feared losing control of her life — which she'd lived on her own terms for so long. She just didn't know anymore.

"Why don't we look at the head shots?" he suggested, backing off personal subjects.

Grateful, Cassandra turned back around and they settled beside each other on the couch. He opened the folder and revealed the next crop of young, beautiful perfection. They sought fame and fortune in Hollywood. She'd been like them once, wide-eyed and innocent, ready to make it big.

She was too old to consider them her competition. Rationally she understood that, but she couldn't help but be a touch envious that the hardships of life hadn't touched their youthful faces yet.

"I was thinking . . ." Harrison paused to flip through the photographs.

"I've had so many e-mails and phone calls asking me when I was going to touch on my favorite least-favorite subject, John Roper." Buckley's voice carried through the television, John's name capturing Cassandra's attention.

"One minute," she said to Harrison, and grabbed the remote control to raise the volume.

Buckley adjusted the microphone in front of his face. "It's been frustrating for me to have no gossip to report on Roper since he unceremoniously disappeared. Or should I say ran away?" the disgruntled man asked.

"His harassment helped drive John underground," Cassandra said bitterly. At least that was what Yank and Micki told her. That John needed time for himself or else there would be no next season for him. He needed, they'd said, a break from the media, the fans and, yes, even his family. That remark had hurt.

Maybe because she could understand why he'd need to get away. Which didn't mean she wasn't going to scold him the next time she got her hands on him for a hug. He'd abandoned her to Harrison's clutches.

"Well, I finally have a big reveal," Buckley said proudly. "Right after this message from our sponsors."

"Are you okay?" Harrison asked, wrapping an arm around her shoulder. He understood how she felt about John abandoning her.

She wished he didn't. She wished he wouldn't be so kind or make leaning on him so easy.

Cassandra nodded and bit the inside of her cheek.

After a short break, during which neither Harrison nor Cassandra spoke, Buckley returned. "Many have been looking for our friend, John Roper, the Renegades' highest-paid coward, and *People Magazine* finally got the inside scoop."

Cassandra leaned in closer, her anticipation rising. Just where was her son?

"Inside this week's issue is a cell-phone photo taken from the Web site of pop diva Hannah Gregory in the restaurant of the exclusive lodge in Greenlawn, New York, owned by Brandon Vaughn."

A grainy but clear enough to be recognizable shot of John and the singer with her lips against his cheek showed on the television screen. Buckley continued. "John Roper isn't away rehabilitating his shoulder and getting ready for the season. He's making time with a hot star on the Renegades' dime. Wonder what happened to Amy Stone. Our boy Roper really gets around." Buckley cleared his throat. "The phone lines have just lit up like a Christmas tree," he said, laughing. "Hey, don't shoot the messenger. I just report the truth, folks. I'll take calls next. The Buck Stops Here!"

Cassandra hit the off button on the remote. "Damn the man for being so rude to John," she said as she rose to her feet. "But thank God he was persistent and found him."

"Where are you going?" Harrison asked, jumping up to step around her and block her way.

Cassandra rolled her eyes. Men could be

so dense. "I am going to see my son!" She darted around him. Now that she knew where John was, she was going to find him.

Ever since Ben and Sabrina's father had left — and good riddance — John had stepped up as man of the house. She'd come to rely on him. He was her rock. And now, when she was bound to Harrison and close to being seduced by him again, she needed her son's level head to steady her. It was what she was used to in times of crisis. And this was her own personal crisis.

Still, she wasn't surprised when Harrison hooked his arm through hers and said, "I'm going with you. I'll call my driver and he'll meet us downstairs in twenty minutes." He pulled out his cell phone. "Does that give you enough time to pack?"

She dug her heels into the floor. "Why? Why are you coming with me?" She needed to hear his reasons.

He shook his head. "I'm sorry you need to ask. Because I love you, silly woman. And you need to see your son. Where else would I be?"

Her throat filled. Fear warred with an emotion she didn't want to name. An emotion, she feared, that was close to love.

"Now, I asked if you have enough time to pack." He didn't push her to reciprocate his words, she realized.

"Yes, yes, I do," she said, grateful for him. She knew that with her behavior, she didn't deserve him. She needed to get her head on straight or she'd drive him crazy.

She grinned.

"Good," he said. "I'll go throw a few things together, too. Don't even think about leaving without me."

"I won't," she promised, meaning it.

He strode to the door.

"Harrison?" she asked, stopping him.

"Yes?" he asked, his voice gruff.

"Thank you." From the bottom of her heart, Cassandra thought.

Roper felt as if a soap opera was playing around him and he might as well watch the episode until his own reality intruded. Which he figured shouldn't be too long.

Hannah's mother had taken a room at the lodge, even though Hannah refused to deal with Big Mama until she accepted her daughter's relationship with Mike. The drummer, meanwhile, refused to speak to Hannah because she'd gone behind his back and informed her mother of their relationship before he was ready to go public.

He feared for his career, and if Roper's hunch was right, he also feared for the relationship. Roper felt sorry for all parties involved except for Big Mama, who, true to her name, was larger than life and intrusive to a fault, like some other mothers he knew too well.

Amy had already informed him that Big Mama's cell-phone photograph had appeared in *People Magazine's* Web site the day after it had been taken. Big Mama no doubt chose the magazine on purpose, knowing she wouldn't have to wait a week to get her daughter's face splashed in the tabloids. As if Hannah's fans would forget about her in one short month. As if Roper's hate club would forget him, either. No such luck. The day after *People Magazine's* exclusive photo was aired, Roper's nemesis Buckley picked up on the news. Between *People* and Buckley, he figured Cassandra would arrive anytime and destroy his newfound serenity.

Once again, he was the center of attention. In Hannah's circles the gossip revolved around Hannah Gregory's top-secret new lover, baseball star John Roper. In Roper's circles, the dirt speculated that Roper's priorities were so far out of whack, he cared more about getting laid by a hot young musician than about recuperating.

Put together, Roper had been made to

look like a lazy, inconsiderate, cheating pig who didn't give a rat's ass about his new girlfriend, Amy Stone, or his lucrative career. Nothing, of course, could be further from the truth.

He nursed a beer in the lobby bar, thinking about what on earth he could do to help diffuse the current situation, but nothing came to mind. Amy, meanwhile, was busy on the phone arranging an exclusive with *Sports Illustrated* to counter the bad press. Roper didn't give a damn who the media paired him with romantically as long as Amy didn't believe the hype.

She didn't.

But from the moment the picture had shown up in *People,* only to be copied on the Internet and the rest of the free world, Amy had withdrawn. She might not believe he was having an affair with Hannah, but Amy had stopped sleeping with him, anyway. And he knew why.

The world had intruded on their private time, making them fodder for public dissection. And she wasn't having any of it. It didn't matter how strong their bond was or how well they understood each other. She was going to let outside forces drive a wedge between them.

Unless he stopped her somehow.

He raised his glass to his lips at the same time his gaze settled on the front entrance, taking in the two people making their way inside.

His mother and Harrison Smith.

Both in full-length fur coats, his mother wearing a matching fur hat on her head, Harrison in a wide-brimmed cowboy hat. Both dressed in a manner guaranteed to attract attention. Lots of it.

Sure enough, the normally low-key staff grouped around the couple, bowing and scraping as if the king and queen of England themselves had arrived. Roper didn't know if the staff knew who the famous couple was. Harrison and Cassandra probably just looked important enough to warrant extra attention.

Roper finished his drink in one long sip, placed the glass on the bar and rose to greet his mother.

Amy arrived in the lobby at the same time Cassandra Lee and Harrison Smith made their entrance. Her success at securing an appointment with *Sports Illustrated* to interview Roper suddenly didn't feel like such a coup. Instead all she could do was fear that he'd forget the lessons learned at the lodge about putting himself first and revert to the

dutiful son who catered to his mother's
every whim.

"Maybe I don't give him enough credit,"
she muttered.

"Give who enough credit?" Roper joined
her at the bar entrance.

She hadn't meant to speak aloud. "No
one," she murmured. "Have they seen you
yet?" she asked, tilting her head toward his
mother and the director.

He shook his head. "But it's only a matter
of time."

"John!"

His mother noticed him. "That was
quick," he muttered.

Amy drew in a deep breath and together
they headed toward Cassandra, who was
waving madly.

Harrison stepped away, having a conversation with the luggage valet.

"Darling!" Cassandra called.

Amy winced at the long-haired fur she
wore, which was really noticeable in a day
and age it wasn't considered politically correct.

"It's so good to see you!" Cassandra came
at him with open arms, enveloping him in
chinchilla.

"Isn't this a surprise," Roper said drolly,

once he'd extricated himself and stepped back.

He tried to sound upset with her, but Amy couldn't help but notice the warmth and affection in his tone despite his mother's unwanted intrusion.

"You and I have so much to catch up on. I won't even scold you for dropping off the face of the earth without so much as a word to your own mother." Cassandra's pout was actress perfect.

"I think you just did," Roper said with a grin.

Ignoring the subtle rebuke, Cassandra turned to her companion. "Harrison," she called. He stepped back toward her. "Be a dear and see to our rooms. Plural, remember? That means two. Preferably on different floors or opposite ends of the hall if I have no other choice." Without waiting for an answer, she hooked her arm through her son's. "I want to hear all about your time here," she said to Roper.

Not a word to Amy, not even a greeting. Amy wasn't surprised since she was the one who had helped orchestrate the separation between the actress and her beloved son.

"Hello, Cassandra, it's nice to see you again," Amy said, unwilling to meet rudeness with rudeness.

Cassandra lifted her chin a notch. "Hello," she said stiffly.

Amy sensed the hurt behind the cool facade, but she couldn't apologize. Not without losing her edge in this situation.

"Come, darling, show me where you've been hiding out." Cassandra pivoted and tugged on Roper's arm, urging him to walk away with her.

Amy glanced at her watch before meeting Roper's gaze. "You have an appointment with the physical therapist in ten minutes," she reminded him.

Cassandra let out a frustrated, exaggerated sigh. "You've probably been seeing your therapist daily while I haven't had five minutes with you in the past two weeks. I didn't even know where to find you. Surely you can skip just one appointment so we can catch up. You can't imagine what Harrison and that horrible Yank Morgan put me through."

Amy bit the inside of her cheek to keep from telling the prima donna that she didn't deserve what Yank and Harrison had done. They'd pushed her into taking a role that would put her back in the public eye, make her a ton of money and give her back her sense of self.

No, Amy thought, watching her manipulate her son, she didn't deserve such good fortune. It was time for her to grow up. But Amy didn't expect Cassandra Lee to understand just yet. She did, however, expect Roper to make his mother see the light. Surely he'd experienced enough freedom of thought, mind and body while here to know he needed it to survive. Surely he could see his mother needed to be pushed away from him in order to make her own way in life once more.

He had to set parameters with his family and this was the ultimate test.

"John?" his mother asked.

Yes, John, what will it be? Amy wondered, but she remained silent. She folded her arms across her chest and waited for him to decide — physical therapy and his career or his mother and her whims.

Roper had never felt so torn in his entire life. There hadn't been a day when he'd ignored his mother's needs. She'd been the rock in his life after she split with his father and again when Ben and Sabrina's dad took off for good.

To his surprise now, he resented her intrusion into the progress he'd been making in his rehabilitation, his thought processes and with Amy. But as she pleaded with him now, desperation and fear in her eyes and her voice, he didn't know how to shut her out.

He'd have to explain it to her, of course, and maybe start slowly with real rules she had to follow. But he couldn't turn her away cold turkey.

Both women waited. He wanted to please them both. *Because he loved them both.*

He loved them both.

Which meant he loved Amy.

Holy shit.

His palms began to sweat and his body overheated at the sudden, but not so unexpected realization.

He needed time to process the revelation as much as he needed time to ease his mother into the way things would be between them from now on.

"I'm going to skip this one appointment and talk to my mother," he said to Amy. He met Amy's gaze, silently imploring her to understand the choice he'd made.

A flash of pure disappointment crossed her face. "I have some things to do in my room." She turned and walked away.

His stomach plummeted, but he'd just have to explain later tonight when they were alone.

When she always seemed to understand what he wanted and needed.

And he needed her.

■ ■ ■ ■

"I am so done," Amy said as she pulled her suitcase out of the closet and tossed it onto the mattress.

Hannah flipped the top closed. "No, you are not. You can't walk away from Roper."

Pausing by the bed, Amy opened the suitcase again. "Watch me." She headed to the drawers and began pulling her clothes out, packing her items in the large bag. "I called the Hot Zone and Micki agreed. If Roper can't stick to his schedule within five minutes of his mother's return, then he can damn well fix his career himself."

Drawers emptied, Amy turned to the closet and laid her pants, jeans and sweaters neatly inside the suitcase, then wedged her shoes in the sides.

Hannah seated herself on the bed and curled her legs beneath her, watching Amy's manic packing. "I'm not talking about his career or your role as his publicist. I'm talking about you, Amy, the woman, walking away from John Roper, the man."

"Have *you* made any progress getting Mike to forgive you for calling your mother?" Amy asked, moving toward the bathroom for her toiletries.

"No, but he's a man and he's stubborn. But you don't see me leaving him because I don't like the decisions he's made," Hannah said, loud enough for Amy to hear as she pulled her shampoo and conditioner out of the shower.

"Here's the thing," Amy said, rejoining Hannah and continuing to pack. "I got involved with Roper while we were here at the lodge so that I could stop fighting the attraction while we were living in such close proximity. It made sense." She placed the sealed bags filled with her things into her suitcase and zipped it closed.

"Go on," Hannah said, her skepticism obvious.

Amy ignored her tone. "But now that things have blown up with the press, it's time to go home. I can't help a man who doesn't want to be helped. So I'm leaving."

"Craving satisfied, man out of your system?" Hannah asked wryly.

Amy drew a deep breath. "Exactly."

"Liar."

Maybe, Amy thought, but she wasn't about to admit it aloud. She was disappointed in Roper. Disappointed in how he handled his first crisis. And she was disappointed in herself for falling hard for a man who was the opposite of everything she wanted and needed in her life.

"I'm not going to argue with you," Amy said. "I am, however, going to insist you keep in touch. I'm new in town and I don't have many friends, remember? So when you're visiting New York, I expect to see you. And when you're home in L.A., I want you to call, okay?" Amy changed the subject. She wanted to leave one conversation on a good note.

Hannah rose from the bed and gave Amy a hug. "Okay. As long as you know I'm not finished harassing you about Roper."

Amy rolled her eyes. "Fine," she said, knowing she couldn't deter Hannah. If the woman could stare down Big Mama, Hannah had persistence and staying power.

Amy glanced at her watch. She had a car service picking her up and she needed to get going. Before she could think too long or too hard about all the reasons she didn't want to leave Roper. But she had no choice. The only way he could decide what he wanted in his life, what kind of relationship he wanted to have with his family and how he could put his career first, was for Amy to step aside. Leaving him alone to compare life before and after Amy Stone.

He popped a beer in celebration. Roper had

been found. It had been a long, dry spell. Boring. He'd had no one to blame for his troubles. Now that was over. The fun could begin again.

CHAPTER FOURTEEN

Roper had been home for one week and he still couldn't believe Amy had picked up and left him at the lodge.

Could. Not. Believe. It.

Worse, now that he'd shown up at the Hot Zone to get his best friend's support, Micki sat behind her desk, backing up Amy's move both professionally and personally. "So much for turning to my best friend for support," he muttered.

Micki raised her eyebrows at him, not looking at all sorry. "You turn to your best pal for the *truth.*"

He shoved his hands into his pants pockets and stared out the window at the gray sky, which matched his mood. "I had every intention of following Amy's advice after I explained things to my family. She didn't have to take it so personally."

"Well, let's see. Have you followed her advice since you've been home? Have you been as single-minded as you were at the lodge?" Micki asked.

No, he hadn't been. Because as soon as he'd returned, so had old habits. "They need me." But he planned to talk to them. Soon.

"You need you," Micki said, her voice stern. "Have you spoken with Amy since you've been back?"

He turned to face her. "She was with me at the *Sports Illustrated* interview and she set up a few more media hits to counter the Hannah thing. Just so people would know I'm coming back stronger than ever."

Micki nodded, a satisfied look on her face. "I've guided her through some of it, but she's really got a knack for this job."

"If you knew, then why did you ask?"

She grinned. "Because I am trying to get you to see the obvious. Which is that Amy is damn good at her job. She had you completely focused on your career, and the minute your family starts pulling at you, you forget all lessons learned." She leaned forward, elbows on her desk. "Amy took it personally and I can't say I blame her. That's my professional assessment. Get your head on straight again or you might as well kiss your career goodbye. You can't handle the distractions right now."

She was right.

So was Amy.

"You said that was your professional assessment. What's your personal one?" he asked, sure Micki had more to say.

"That you've fallen in love with Amy." Micki smiled with a knowing certainty.

He *had* fallen in love but he'd never admitted his feelings aloud, not even to his best friend. "And?" he asked, wanting to hear what more Micki had to say.

"She's not willing to see you on a personal level now that you're back in the city and it's driving you insane." Micki shook her head and laughed.

"And for some reason you're enjoying watching me suffer?"

"I'm enjoying the fact that you're in love for the first time in your life. That you have to work hard for something for the first time ever. That Amy isn't falling at your feet like every other woman in the universe," Micki said. "But no, I'm not enjoying watching you suffer. I just think you two have more stuff to go through. Like all couples that are meant to be."

He frowned. "You sound like a romantic."

She rose from her desk. "Just telling it like it is. Have you?" She began to collect files from her drawer, which told him she had a meeting and their time was through.

"Have I what?"

"Told Amy how you feel about her? That you're in love with her? Maybe knowing she's *the one* will help her settle things in here." Micki tapped her head. "She can't read your mind, you know."

"No, I haven't told her." He hadn't put her first, either.

He missed Amy like crazy and Micki was right. Amy was driving him insane by not falling at his feet.

"Any reason why not?" Micki asked.

He shrugged. "It's not every day I make a realization like that one. I guess I wasn't ready."

"You ought to get yourself ready," Micki suggested. "Before you lose her for good."

"Thanks for the advice," he said, coming around the desk and pulling her into a big hug, which she easily returned.

"Anytime."

He didn't bother telling Micki he wasn't holding out much hope that if he bared his heart and soul to Amy, they were guaranteed a future.

Amy wouldn't consider returning to the way things were at the lodge. She claimed it was because she was his publicist, but he didn't believe her. She had deeper reasons for avoiding him — and his bed. His life in the public eye was one heavy part of her reasoning, but he sensed there was more and he didn't know what that more was.

He wasn't even certain Amy, herself, knew why she was avoiding any emotional closeness between them. But Micki was right about one thing. Amy needed to know how he felt.

He needed to break through her defenses and hope that he was wrong.

That the three little words women loved to hear would actually make a difference.

He walked from Micki's office directly to Amy's. He was a man on a mission and not the gentleman she'd been dealing with during their time at the lodge. He was determined not only to make his point but to get her to see the error in her thinking. Either she listened or he was shit out of luck. He didn't want to think about that possibility.

He entered without knocking.

Startled, both Amy and Yank, who sat across from her desk, turned to stare.

"Roper!" they both said at the same time.

Suddenly he felt like an ass. But his reasons for barging in hadn't changed so he kept walking toward her. "Hi, Yank," he said to his agent. "Bye, Yank."

As if agreeing with Roper, Yank's fluffy

dog barked.

"Of all the nerve!" Amy strode around her desk and stepped between the two men. "You can't barge in, interrupt a private meeting and expect to get your way. Yank, you aren't going anywhere," Amy said, her cheeks flushed pink with anger.

The older man leaned back in his seat. "You heard the girl. I ain't goin' nowhere," Yank said, his tone not only smug but amused.

Roper wasn't worried. He still held the trump card. "My career may suck at the moment, but I'm still worth money. If you want to be the one who gets me the deals, you'll give me and Amy some time alone." Roper stared his agent down because otherwise Yank, who loved drama and gossip as much as any female, would have kept his ass in the chair.

Yank groaned. "Man, you're taking what little fun I still get out of my life," he muttered as he rose from his seat.

"You'll survive," Roper said wryly.

"It's my office. I have the final say." Amy perched her hands on her hips.

Roper took a moment to admire her high-waisted black slacks and fitted buttoned-down shirt, which accentuated the curves he'd learned well, both with his hands and his tongue.

He shifted positions before dealing with the task at hand. "I'm sorry to tell you this, but I'm the client. And the client is always right," Roper said to Amy. Then he turned to Yank. "Tell her I'm right."

He ran a hand through his shaggy hair and groaned. "We'll talk later, girlie," Yank said. He pulled on Noodle's leash and he and the dog strode out of the room.

They were alone. Roper might have won the battle but he didn't kid himself. He hadn't yet won the war.

Amy's heart beat fast in her chest and her head pounded so hard she thought both might explode. "How dare you!" She faced Roper and poked him hard in the chest. "This is my office. Where do you get off walking in here and calling the shots?"

Despite her words, a traitorous part of her was glad to see him. In the time since she'd been home, she'd been fighting her deepest feelings. The rational part of her understood that she and Roper were trouble waiting to happen. But looking at him now, it was difficult to remember why.

"You need to calm down and listen."

She inhaled deeply. "What?" she asked, her voice deliberately cold.

He shook his head and laughed. "You

don't make things easy."

She opted for silence.

"We grew close at the lodge," he said in his most seductive voice.

She swallowed hard.

He stepped nearer. She stepped back. He stepped closer. She stepped back. The dance continued until her back hit the radiator by the window and he had her cornered.

Just as he had at the solarium. Memories and seductive heat swept through her.

"Very close," he said as he took his final step, his thighs coming into direct contact with hers. "Remember?" He stroked her cheek with his hand.

"It's over," she said in a shaky tone. Damn, she hated the effect he had on her. The longing and wanting threatened to make her forget her reasons for not being with him.

"Actually, it's just beginning." His eyes bore into hers and his fingertips stroked her face, her cheek, her throat. "I love you, Amy."

She couldn't have heard him correctly, though everything inside her turned to liquid, molten heat and a sudden yearning for so much more settled inside her chest. "You —"

He inclined his head. "I love you and I

believe you love me, too."

Oh, my God. Oh, my God. How long had she dreamed of the day when the man she loved would tell her he felt the same?

And she did love Roper. She knew it in a soul-deep way and had for a while, though denying and pushing it away from her consciousness had become second nature.

"Tell me, Amy," he said, his lips inches from hers.

She was enveloped by the sensual cologne he wore that made her weak. She wanted to let herself be swept away by the dream. But she couldn't.

Because it was nothing more than a dream.

"I can't."

"No, you won't. You're scared. I understand that. I've never said those three words to any woman before in my life. But we can make it work." His tone was low and imploring.

She drew a deep breath, steadying herself. Reminding herself of the reasons she'd left the lodge and had steered clear of him since. "We can't. I gave you all the tools to fix your life. I took you away, I showed you what you needed. But the first time you were faced with a choice, you chose to cave into your family's needs."

"Let me explain."

"In a minute. I need to finish first. Until you can make that separation between yourself and your family in a way that leaves you healthy emotionally, you aren't remotely ready for the kind of relationship that love entails." Her heart and her voice cracked as she spoke.

"Are you saying you love me, too?"

When she didn't reply, the knowing smile that had teased the corners of his mouth disappeared. "I *will* handle my family. You just can't expect me to shut them down with no explanation after a lifetime of doing just the opposite."

He made sense. He did. But it wasn't enough. She merely shook her head.

"There's more bothering you than just my family," he stated with certainty.

She trembled, unwilling to admit to anything more. She couldn't put it into words herself. "The family issue's enough, considering it's not going to change."

"It will. And when it does, are you going to admit you love me? Or are you going to use the press as another excuse to stay away?" Once again, he spoke as if he knew the answer.

She wondered why he even bothered asking the question. "The press is another part of the problem," she admitted.

He narrowed his gaze. "But there's more, isn't there?"

Before she could answer, his cell phone rang.

Both Amy and Roper froze.

He glanced down at the number. "It's Ben," he said, meeting her gaze. "Ben never calls."

"Unless something's wrong. Go ahead and answer it," she said, resigned, as she raised her hand, waving him away.

She wasn't surprised at the intrusion. She supposed it was just as well. She didn't want to have this painful talk, anyway.

"I'm going to handle this. I'm going to break my family into the way things are going to be from now on. And then I'm coming back to finish this conversation. We aren't done. Not by a long shot," he said, before answering his phone.

Oh, yes, we are, she thought as she watched him engage in the same frustrating discussion with his brother that he always had.

Then he left without another word.

They were over.

It was exactly what she told herself she wanted and needed. Yet she'd never felt so miserable in her entire life.

■ ■ ■ ■

Ben hated sleeping on a friend's couch. He hated feeling like a loser who couldn't hold a job or make a go at any career he started. And he absolutely hated having to ask his brother for money.

"I just know I can make this gym thing work," he muttered. But Roper didn't want to talk about money. He wanted to talk to Ben about taking a demeaning coaching job. One that was beneath him.

But his big brother in the major leagues wouldn't understand that he wouldn't compromise his principles. Everything came easy for Roper. A father whose genes guaranteed talent and the magic touch with both women and baseball. So what if he was having one bad season?

It wasn't the same as having a bad life.

"Are you moping again?" his friend Dave Martin, whose couch he currently occupied, asked.

Ben shrugged. "Feeling sorry for myself, I guess."

"Well, your brother surfaced, so that ought to cheer you up. It means you can talk to him about our gym idea. My friend still hasn't found a buyer, but he is talking with some people, so you need to step up the pressure before we lose out." Dave sat down beside him and kicked his feet up on the table.

"At least you have a decent, well-paying job."

"Being a trainer at Equinnox means I work for someone else. I want to work for myself. Make my own hours, boss someone else around. I've been there more than ten years and I have the experience."

"You just don't have the money. I know." And he was counting on Ben for the cash. Or rather Ben's famous brother. "It just so happens my brother called a family meeting. I'm heading over to my mother's suite for lunch."

"Good. Just make sure you get some time alone with Roper and be your charming, persuasive self," Dave said. "Your brother shouldn't be so stingy with his money. He ought to share the wealth with his family. Besides, it's not as if he's doing anything to earn it lately," Dave said in a round of Roper-bashing Ben had become used to.

It bothered him, though. Ben didn't mind complaining about his brother, but it irked him when others did it. For all Ben's jealousy, Roper had been good to him and they *were* brothers. Which Ben was counting on to convince Roper not to give up on him just yet.

"I'm going to shower," Ben said, rising. "And for the record, it's not my charm I'm worried about. It's my brother's built-in immunity."

"Make it happen," Dave warned him. "Or else."

Or else he'd be out a couch and on the street, Ben thought, finishing his friend's sentence in his mind. There wasn't much else he could do.

As much as Roper wanted a quick fix to his and Amy's problems, he also understood he had obligations to his team, and so he threw himself wholeheartedly into his rehabilitation. Not only did he hope to return as quickly as his body allowed, but he hoped to prove to Amy that he was a man who learned — from his mistakes and from good, solid advice. That he was a man who kept his word.

Through it all, he also dealt with the daily traumas from his family that never seemed to cease. Complaints from his sister that his mother was lining up people and events for the wedding she wanted no part of. Meetings with his mother and Harrison, mediating in order to keep his mother from being in breach of contract before actual work on the television project began. Ben wanting to show him the gym he wanted to invest in, all the while constantly pushing him for money.

Roper tried to tell them things had to change, but they weren't listening. Or maybe, he realized, he wasn't speaking clearly.

Just as Amy wasn't coming after him. It was time he took charge in a decisive way, then acted on it.

So he'd called a family meeting. He wasn't surprised when his mother balked at going out and insisted on hosting the family at her suite. Her new ploy to irritate Harrison was to avoid the public and the reporters questioning her about her new television series. He wanted them to be seen in public, so she adamantly refused to be seen at all.

Cassandra hadn't come to terms with her contract and she was still running from Harrison Smith's presence in her life. Ironically, Roper was beginning to accept and like the man. He appreciated the stability Harrison provided Roper's mother and how he encouraged her independence and her career even if he had to manipulate her into agreement. Harrison could aid Roper's need to free himself from his mother's neediness

— Roper just had to make the break, as guilty as he felt doing it. If Cassandra chose to rely on Harrison more instead of becoming more independent, that was *her* decision.

Roper would just have to assert his priorities in a way his family couldn't misunderstand. Then he had to follow through. He hoped once his family understood, they'd support his efforts, if not now, eventually. In the meantime, he'd get his ducks in a row, so to speak, and then challenge Amy to step up as he had.

That was in a perfect world, Roper thought. He entered his mother's apartment to find his family already assembled. This was *his* world, and here, anything could happen.

"I'm glad everyone could make it," Roper said.

"I was under the impression it was a command performance," his mother said, obviously miffed.

He laughed. "Yes, it is. We're *here* at *your* command," he said. "The food looks delicious. Everyone dig in," he said, figuring they should have full stomachs before they heard what he had to say.

He chose a chicken wrap and a bottle of water and was on his way to sit beside Sabrina and Kevin when Ben grabbed his arm. "Got a minute for your brother?" he asked.

"Sure." After today Roper would control his own minutes, so he didn't mind talking to Ben now. He refrained from asking, *what can I do for you?* knowing he probably wouldn't like the answer.

They made their way to the empty kitchenette area. Ben pulled a can of Coke from the fridge, popped the top and took a long drink. Roper ate his lunch standing, waiting for his brother to talk first.

"How's the rehab?" Ben asked.

Roper wiped his mouth with a paper napkin. "Coming along," he said warily.

It pained him to realize that gone were the days when he could confide in his brother about anything — and vice versa. Sure, Roper knew Ben bounced from idea to idea and rarely held a full-time job, but he didn't understand why. Communication between the brothers had died a slow death about the same time Roper's major league career had started to soar.

"Are you still crashing on Dave's couch?"

Ben nodded. "It's not bad. He's got a fifty-inch flat screen so he can catch the Renegades away games and feel as if he's really there."

"He's a fan," Roper said.

"Season ticket holder."

Roper nodded. The small talk wasn't working for him. "What's going on?" he asked his brother.

Ben shifted from foot to foot. "Here's the thing. I need to talk to you and I don't want you to turn me down without hearing me out."

Here it comes, Roper thought. "Okay, what's your pitch?" he asked, then listened to Ben expound on the perfect gym location in SoHo and how he hoped to bring the money, while Dave would bring the experience, and together they'd set up a fantastic business.

"There's just one problem," Roper said to his brother.

"What's that?"

"You don't have the money." He had no choice but to lay it on the line for Ben in a way he'd never done before. He'd come here today to do just that with each family member, and Ben had given him the opening first.

Ben's eyes opened wide in disbelief. "But you —"

"I don't have it, either, and before you argue, call my accountant if you don't believe me. Incoming money is tied to endorsements and performance. The rest is tied up for the future. My future." He squared his shoulders and faced the brother he'd rarely refused.

This gym proposal was probably the only thing Roper had pushed aside and refused to discuss — proof he'd already been taking a stand even before Amy had entered his life.

"What about me? It's not as if I have the talent to make it the way you did." Ben's voice dropped to a whine and his expression turned to a pout.

"That's what I came here to talk about. Even if I did have the money in liquid cash, I wouldn't be giving it to you. It's time you stood on your own. You may not have what it takes to make it in the majors but you have plenty of other talents. Certainly enough to make a living and support yourself. More than support yourself, really."

Ben rolled his eyes. "Oh, here it comes again. The old 'why don't you take a high school coaching job' speech."

"Why *don't* you take a coaching job?"

"Because I'm better than that. But you wouldn't know what it's like to fall short, now would you?"

Roper had to laugh at that. "I know better than you think. I know exactly what falling short means. I know what it's like to disappoint my family and my teammates. I know what it's like to have fans boo me from the stands and throw things at me onto the field. I deal with criticism from everyday people on the street and from the media. I can't name one source I don't get shit from, so don't tell me I don't know what it's like to lose. The difference between us is that I'm not afraid to step up to the plate. Whatever plate that may be. If I had to walk away today, I'd be damn happy to have a coaching job, Ben. No joking here." He blew out a stream of air, shocked at how direct and hard he'd been with his brother.

He glanced at Ben, who appeared stunned, too.

"I'm sure that's easier to say with money in the bank," Ben muttered.

"I put that money in the bank." He jabbed himself in the chest. "I earned it. When your father took off and mine was nowhere to be found, all I could think about was stepping up and making sure the family was taken care of. I mowed lawns while Mom worked. I did what I had to and I never asked a damn thing in return. But I'm asking now. No, I'm telling you now. Grow the fuck up. Get a job and hold your head up high for once," Roper said, his heart accelerating in his chest.

Ben looked as if Roper had slapped him.

"What's going on in here?" Cassandra asked, walking inside to join them.

Roper glanced at his younger brother. "Nothing. Give us another minute, okay, Mom?"

Cassandra nodded. "Just stop with the raised voices or I'll be thrown out of here and then —" Her eyes lit up. "Then I can find a place where Harrison will never think to look!" she said, the idea obviously just forming.

Roper shook his head and groaned. "Remember your contract, Mom. We'll talk in five minutes. Don't do anything until then," he warned her.

She laughed and walked out, probably already planning.

Roper quickly turned back to his brother. "Ben —"

"Not now. You've said enough." Arms folded over his chest, he looked like the hurt little boy Roper remembered. It took everything Roper had to steel himself against the manipulation.

"Listen, Ben, my point is this. You have more inside you than you give yourself credit for. You could do a world of good coaching kids. You could tap into their psyches — those that already believe in themselves and those that don't but should. You can steer them in the right direction from the start." He placed a hand on his brother's shoulder.

Ben shook it off.

Roper swallowed back the hurt, knowing he had to let things settle and hope someday his brother would come around. "Let's go join Mom and Sabrina," Roper said.

"Why bother? I'm finished here." Roper waited in the kitchen while his brother stormed out of the room, said his goodbyes and left, slamming the door behind him.

One down, two more to go, Roper thought.

Chapter Fifteen

Roper glanced around, studying the female members of his family who gazed at him with curious eyes. Ben's abrupt departure had left them stunned, Roper was sure.

"Obviously Ben's upset about something. What's going on?" Sabrina asked. She sat beside Kevin, holding his hand. At least she seemed genuinely happy.

And that, Roper thought, was what this part of his day was all about. He needed to use his sister's happiness as the springboard to give him the courage to lay down the law with his mother — and undoubtedly hurt her in the process.

Before he could speak, a noise sounded from outside the door and suddenly Harrison entered, key card in hand. Roper raised an eyebrow but didn't say a word. He already knew there was more to this relationship than his mother wanted to admit to her children *or* to herself.

"You shouldn't just barge in as if you own the place," Cassandra chided him.

He raised an eyebrow. "Considering I gave up my own room, you can't expect me to knock first. Hello, everyone," Harrison said.

Roper shook the other man's hand.

Sabrina managed a wave. From her pale face, she hadn't known about their mother's living arrangements, either. It seemed as if Cassandra was keeping up the pretense of not wanting to be with Harrison for no one's benefit that Roper could figure, except maybe her own.

Cassandra scowled at him. "John was just about to say why he called us all together. It's a family meeting so you might want to —"

"Stay," Roper added before his mother could send the other man away. "And do not argue with me, Mom."

Harrison grinned. "Thank you," he said to Roper.

"No problem."

Cassandra needed the older man more than she wanted to admit and Roper was glad she had him, especially since he, himself, intended to take back his own life. He was grateful and relieved he wouldn't be leaving his mother alone to her own devices.

Cassandra folded her arms across her

chest. "I wasn't going to argue. If Harrison wants to pretend he's part of this family, who am I to stop him?" She sniffed in her haughty way.

Harrison laughed and slung an arm around her shoulder. "Go on," he said to Roper.

"Please," Sabrina said.

Roper drew a deep breath. "Okay. Here goes. For as long as I can remember, I've been here when you all needed me. Twenty-four/seven, at your beck and call."

"Well, I'm not sure I'd phrase it so callously," his mother said, only to be silenced by Harrison squeezing her shoulder in warning.

"You've been a wonderful son," she said, her voice sincere.

"Thank you." He wasn't fishing for compliments, just stating reality. "The thing is, that by doing everything you all wanted when you all wanted it, I've neglected my own life."

"I can see that," Sabrina said softly. "I have for a while. It's just that old habits are hard to break."

He smiled at his little sister. "Tell me about it."

"So what are you trying to say?" Sabrina asked.

"That it's time for you all to live your own lives."

"As if we haven't?" Cassandra asked.

The sad thing was that Roper knew she believed her words, which made what he had to say all the more difficult. "No, you haven't. If I was in a meeting and one of you called, I dropped everything. If I was on a date and you needed me, I cut it short. Don't get me wrong, I did it because I wanted to —"

"And you don't anymore?" his mother asked, insulted.

He wanted to say no that, of course he wanted to, he just couldn't do it anymore. But that would be a lie and he'd promised himself and Amy — even if she wasn't aware of the promise — that he'd be completely honest. For everyone's sake, including his mother.

"No, Mom, I don't want to. I want to concentrate on my career. The time I spent at the lodge showed me the difference less stress could make on both my body and my mind."

"This is all that woman's fault."

"That's not fair, Mom," Sabrina objected. "And it's not true. Besides, I thought you liked Amy. You said she's bright enough to hold her own with John, and she didn't bore you like the other bimbos he's dated." Sabrina shot him an *I'm sorry* look. "No insult intended," she said.

"None taken. And I'm glad you like Amy. Because if I have my way, she's going to be around for a long, long time."

Sabrina let out a whoop and ran to Roper, giving him a hug. "I hope you find the happiness we have," she said, nodding toward Kevin.

His mother remained silent. Sulking.

And Roper wasn't even finished yet.

"Thanks," he said to his sister. "We'll see. There's a lot to work out between us." An understatement if he ever heard one. "Still, I want to be clear on what this means to all of you."

"Do tell," Cassandra said, curled up in the corner of the couch, sulking like a petulant child.

He realized now what a complete disservice he'd done his mother by being at her beck and call. He'd never allowed her the chance to stand on her own. He hoped she did so now and didn't just transfer her needs from Roper to Harrison.

"I love you, Mom, and I will always be here for you if you need me. I want to see you. I want to have lunch or dinner with you and I want you to call me when you want to talk."

"But?" she asked.

"But you can no longer expect me to drop everything I'm doing to fix things for you. You're a grown woman with a new career and you're going to love it."

Harrison applauded.

Roper rolled his eyes. "You're also able to support yourself now, and I'm hoping you'll love the freedom it gives you. Don't close your eyes to new opportunities. Accept and embrace who you are and what you can do today, not twenty years ago," he said, hoping she heard the love and respect in his tone. "America is going to adore you on this series. It's going to open up all sorts of new doors for you. So don't be stubborn like you were with Harrison. I'm betting you're going to love what happens to you next and I want to be there to share it."

"On your terms."

Okay, so she didn't *get it* yet. He had faith that she would.

"On *our* terms, over time," he said.

"I need to lie down."

Harrison shook his head, but Roper met the other man's gaze and silently told him he'd expected this reaction. There would be more discussion, and hopefully, understanding, in the future.

Harrison escorted Cassandra out of the room.

Roper turned to his sister and her fiancé. "As for you, Sabrina, you're marrying a good man."

Kevin cleared his throat. "Thank you," he said, clearly embarrassed.

Roper inclined his head. "Sabrina, you have the world ahead of you. If you continue to work as a paralegal, good for you. If you decide not to work, that's between you and your husband. Whatever you two decide, I stand behind you. I'll be there for you, but I won't undermine Kevin by sneaking money to you or providing things he can't. Unless he agrees," Roper said, grinning because Kevin was nodding at everything he said.

Sabrina seemed surprised but okay with his words. Relieved, even.

"One last thing. About the wedding." This was the best part of his day, Roper thought, reaching into his pocket.

And damned if he didn't deserve some fun after the nightmare he'd been through.

"Your wedding should be everything *you* both want. I want to give you the wedding of your dreams." And he already knew that Sabrina's dreams weren't his mother's. "So here," he said, walking over and handing them the check. "Plan your wedding the

361

way you want. Or don't plan the wedding and use this toward your future. The choice is yours."

Sabrina glanced down at the paper in her hand and her eyes widened. She squealed and threw her arms around Roper's neck. "You are the best, John. The very best."

"Do it your way, baby sister," he whispered in her ear. "And be happy."

Kevin shook Roper's hand. "I can't thank you enough."

Roper shrugged. "If Mom had the money, she'd do it herself and you'd be ducking dove shit. So this is my pleasure," he said, laughing.

Kevin smiled. "She's going to have a fit when she realizes you've effectively taken away her power."

"I'm hoping that by giving it to Sabrina, she'll include Mom on the right things, shut her down when she doesn't belong, and eventually we'll all be one big happy dysfunctional family," Roper said.

"We can hope," Kevin said.

"Will that family include Amy?" Sabrina asked.

Roper groaned. "I honestly don't know."

But he couldn't wait to find out.

Amy kept busy. At work she'd been given

new clients and she'd also shadowed both Annabelle and Sophie through various events and meetings, learning by example. Her uncle Spencer was pleased with her progress at the Hot Zone and he took her to dinner to tell her so. She joined a gym and went there at night so she didn't have to spend so much time in an empty apartment. There she met other single women in a yoga class, one of whom she'd become friendly with. All and all, her life was exactly what she'd wanted when she'd planned to come to New York.

Unfortunately the life she'd imagined hadn't included John Roper. Having been with him, she was afraid she'd never be the same without him. And working at the Hot Zone, where she read the papers and blogs to keep up with damage control, guaranteed she was reminded of him daily. Buckley hadn't let up on him, but the rest of the papers had, due in the most part to the fact that he'd been at the gym every day.

But Amy was reminded of him nightly when she lay in her bed, tossing and turning. How could she not when their last encounter had included his declaration of love.

One she hadn't been able to verbally reciprocate even though she knew without a doubt, she felt it deep in her heart. How could she not love a man who was so kind and generous, thoughtful and caring? Not just to his family but to her, as well. He'd made her wish for a day in the snow come true in a way that went beyond special. He could have just taken her outside. Instead he'd planned a fantasy afternoon.

But that was the problem. No matter what they both felt in here, she thought, her hand rising to her chest, it had been a moment out of time. Real life meant obligations he couldn't extricate himself from and cameras that followed him everywhere he went.

That was a life of his choosing. Not hers.

Frustrated with her train of thought, she tossed her pen down onto her desk. Obviously she couldn't concentrate on work. A glance at her watch told her it was late in the afternoon. She'd had it for today. With nothing pressing keeping her at the office, she decided to head home.

She began packing her bag, taking select things to review with her when she heard a knock at her door. "Come in," she called, hoping nobody had an assignment that would keep her in the office later. She was more exhausted than she'd realized.

She glanced up at the same time her visitor strode inside. "Roper," she said, surprised to see him. Her stomach flipped, nerves fluttering inside her.

"Hey, there," he said casually. As if nothing important had happened the last time they'd met.

I love you. She considered that important.

He looked healthy and well. She knew from Micki and Yank that, despite his family obligations, he *had* been focusing on his recovery. Though he'd miss the beginning of spring training, the doctors were hopeful for a full recovery. But also according to Yank and Micki, his family still pulled his strings.

And he still let them.

"Let me guess. You just happened to be in the neighborhood. Visiting Yank or Micki?" She gripped the handle of her tote bag hard, yet strove for normalcy in her voice. Like in the deodorant commercial, she wouldn't let him see her sweat.

"Nope." He shut the door behind him. "I'm here to see you."

"Oh." Her mouth grew dry. "I was just leaving for the day."

"Then I can walk you out."

She shrugged. "That's fine."

He helped her on with her coat and they started for the door. "You look good," he said.

Such a simple compliment and yet she grew warm all over. "Same for you. I hear your therapy is going well," she said.

"I'm trying. The shoulder's getting stronger. It helps that I've lowered my expectations of trying to be back in time for spring training. I find I'm more focused."

They rode down the elevator and walked onto the street. "I was going to take a cab, but it's a little warmer today so I think I'll walk a bit," she said.

"Sounds good. I'll join you."

They walked in silence, but the comfortable feeling they'd found at the lodge was gone. "How's your family?" she finally asked when she couldn't stand the stiff silence between them any longer.

"Good, actually." He perked up at the question. "I'm glad you asked. It ties into the reason I wanted to talk to you. My mother has her hands full with Harrison and —"

The sudden singing noise from her cell phone interrupted him. She dug into her jacket pocket and pulled out her phone. "Sorry," she said, glancing down and seeing a 718 phone number she didn't recognize.

"Hello?"

"Amy, it's Uncle Spencer," his warm voice said.

"Hi, Uncle Spencer," she said, more for Roper's benefit so he'd know who was on the phone. "What's up?" she asked.

Roper shoved his hands into his jacket pockets and waited patiently.

Her uncle went on to explain the reason for his call and a familiar panic settled deep in her bones. "Mom is *where?*" Amy yelled.

A young couple passing by her on the street turned and stared.

Roper immediately huddled near her side, placing a hand on her shoulder. She appreciated the support.

God, this couldn't be happening. Not when she'd just carved out a perfectly sane, normal life for herself. She shut her eyes for a brief moment before she pulled herself together.

"I'll be right there," she told her uncle, ending the call. Then she turned to Roper. "My mom and my aunt are being held by security at JFK Airport."

She stepped off the sidewalk and into the street, glancing around for a free taxi cab to take her to meet them.

Roper grasped her hand. "I have my car in the lot downstairs. I'll drive you. It'll be cheaper and quicker. Come."

She drew a deep breath and met his gaze. "Thank you," she said, grateful for his unquestioning support.

He steered her back toward the Hot Zone offices and to the elevator leading to the underground parking garage.

"I didn't even know my mother was coming to town. Apparently they wanted to surprise me." And she hadn't seen it coming, Amy thought. "Uncle Spencer has a meeting he can't miss, so it's up to me to get them out."

"And we will," Roper assured her.

Amy was sure they would. As good as her mother and aunt were at getting into trouble, they were equally adept at talking themselves out of it. Or letting Amy do it for them. And to think, she'd been so anxious to start her new life, she'd let her mother remain in Florida unsupervised. She'd underestimated the older woman yet again.

Roper handed his ticket to the attendant and within minutes they were in his car and on their way. Amy finally started breathing again.

"I almost took the Porsche but I knew with all the stop and go traffic, there'd be no point. It was a good thing, too. At least I can fit them in the backseat."

She nodded, grateful. Even in the midst of her panic, she could see how quickly, calmly and efficiently he'd taken charge. What a guy.

"Why are they being held by security?" he asked.

"Uncle Spencer didn't give me a straight answer, which isn't surprising given my mother and aunt. I'm sure we'll find out soon enough."

There was some traffic, but it moved at a decent pace and soon they'd pulled into the airport.

"I'll drop you off, park and meet you in there," he said, easing the car to the curb in front of the terminal.

She bit down on her lip. "You can drop me off and leave. I'm sure you have somewhere more important to be and —"

He placed his hand on hers, his touch doing more to calm her than anything could. "Nothing is more important than helping you through this," he assured her.

Strong and capable. Roper had to be the perfect man.

For the first time, she could understand firsthand how and why his family had come to rely on him for everything. She couldn't allow herself to do the same, especially since she'd faulted him for responding to them on cue.

"Really, I'll be fine. I can take them home

with me in a cab and —"

"I will be inside in five minutes. You'll get to them sooner if you stop arguing and go," he said, giving her a gentle yet firm push.

She inclined her head. Then, knowing she should just turn and head inside, she acted on impulse and placed a thank-you kiss on his cheek.

At least she meant for it to be on his cheek. But the scoundrel anticipated her move and with a quick shift of his head, he caused her lips to land squarely on his.

She didn't pull away. Instead she leaned in closer. Her eyes closed, and for a sweet short time, she was back at the lodge, where real life couldn't intrude. His lips parted, and his tongue swept over her lips, her teeth and then tangled with hers. Warmth eased from the pit of her stomach, shooting outward, overwhelming her senses . . . until a car honked, startling them and breaking the intimacy of the moment.

Flustered, she gathered her bag and darted out of the car.

Roper managed to park and catch up with Amy before she was allowed in to see her relatives. A stiff man in a suit, who turned out to be the federal marshal on the plane, escorted Amy and Roper to the area where

Darla and Rose were being held. The marshal explained that he worked with TSA, a component of the Department of Homeland Security and they were trying to assess whether Darla and Rose were terrorist risks.

More like attention seekers, Roper knew.

First, Amy introduced Roper to her family and they shook his hand, but they were too impatient to tell their story to spend time on pleasantries.

"So we were talking about how what happened with my luggage reminded us of the movie *Meet the Parents*," Amy's mother, Rose, said.

"And I said it wasn't *Meet the Parents*, it was the second one, *Meet the Fockers*," Darla said.

"It was *Meet the Parents* and the stewardess —"

"They're called flight attendants now," Darla interrupted her sister.

Rose rolled her eyes. "The *flight attendant* had taken my carry-on and gave it to the handlers to put it in the cargo area. I forgot, and when the plane landed in New York, I opened the top compartment to take out my luggage and Darla reminded me that my bag wasn't there. So I said, I thought it was stupid. I could so have fit it on top."

"But the flight attendant wouldn't even

let her try," Darla said. "So we were reminded of *Meet the Fockers.*"

"*Meet the Parents,*" Rose interrupted. "And I said, in a complete and perfect impersonation of Ben Stiller, *It's not like there's a bomb in it.*"

Darla and Rose both spoke with animation, hands waving in the air. "Then some woman obviously misunderstood us and yelled, 'that old lady said she has a *bomb.*' Do I look old to you?" Rose asked Amy.

"No, Mom," Amy said through gritted teeth. "Go on with the story."

Roper held back his laughter because he could see how obviously stressed Amy was. But the women, with their bright red lipstick, overdyed hair and deep circles of rouge on their cheeks, looked more like Kewpie dolls than terrorists. And Roper thought the way they each argued their point was hilarious.

"Of course we don't look old to you," Rose said, ignoring Amy's request. "You see us all the time." Rose then took Roper off guard by walking up to him. "You're a young, handsome man. Do I look old to you?" She nudged him with her elbow and batted her thick eyelashes.

"No, ma'am," he said, holding back a chuckle. "You're beautiful."

Amy shot him a warning look that clearly said *don't humor them.* He couldn't help it, they were so cute.

"Why, thank you," Rose said. "You see, Darla?"

"What about me? Do I look old?" Darla asked him, pushing her sister out of the way.

Roper grinned. "You're absolutely breathtaking, too," he told her.

Pleased, both women relaxed and smiled. "So anyway," Rose continued, "someone yells, 'The old lady has a bomb!' And all hell broke loose. That man who brought you in here had been sitting in front of us and he turned around and practically dove over the seat. The rest of the passengers went into utter panic."

"There was nearly a stampede thanks to that crazy woman," Darla said, nodding.

Amy raised an eyebrow. "You think *she* was the crazy woman?" she asked.

Both relatives ignored her. "Next thing you know, they evacuate the plane and corral everyone into one area, except for us. They brought us in here. Apparently they had to check all the carry-on bags underneath the plane to make sure they didn't miss something in security the first time around. They thought we were planning to blow up the airport!"

"They can't be too careful these days," Roper said seriously.

Rose and Darla nodded. "We understand. If only that woman hadn't made a scene, nobody would have been detained."

"And you don't think you had anything to do with that little scene?" Amy perched her hands on her hips and confronted her family.

Roper thought they blushed, though it was hard to tell beneath the heavy rouge.

"It was a misunderstanding," Darla said. "Not that your uncle Spencer thought so. He was furious, but he promised us you'd be here to handle things."

"Of course she's here. My beautiful, smart girl always rescues us," Rose said, pulling Amy into a hug. "I've missed you."

Amy hugged her mother back. "I missed you, too." She turned to her aunt. "You, too," she said, wrapping her arms around the other woman, as well.

For all her frustration, Amy obviously genuinely adored the women in her family.

Roper watched the byplay with interest. This was the only real firsthand glimpse he'd gotten into Amy's family and background, and a few things jumped out at him immediately. Her home situation wasn't much different from his. Her mother and aunt created situations and she rescued them on command.

It didn't take a psychologist to figure out that Amy dove into handling his family so methodically not because she was used to handling her own, but because she couldn't *control* them. In managing Roper's family issues, she'd been able to take charge in a way she hadn't been able to with her own family. She saw herself in Roper, and when Roper fell back into old habits, she'd backed away.

He'd gotten some insight into Amy's emotions. But he hadn't gotten enough. With her mother here, he hoped to gain even more.

"Mom, you really should have told me you were coming for a visit," Amy said.

"And ruin the surprise? What fun would that be?"

"None at all," Amy muttered. "So how do we get you two out of here?"

Rose seated herself in a metal chair. "The grumpy air marshal said he'd be back. He had to confer with his colleagues."

"Do you think they'll do a background check like they do on the TV show *COPS*?" Aunt Darla asked, walking to the small window and glancing out.

"Oh, Lord." Amy chose the nearest chair

and lowered herself into it.

Roper gave Amy's shoulder a squeeze. "Why don't I go outside and see what I can find out."

Amy glanced up. "I'd appreciate it."

"Not so fast," Rose said. "Amy introduced you and we know you're a professional ballplayer, but she didn't say what your relationship is. What are your intentions? Because when you come to help rescue a woman's relatives from the hoosegow, then you must have some personal interest, yes?"

"Remember, my sister is like a professional lie detector," Darla said. "If you're not telling the truth, she'll sniff it out."

"Oh, for God's sake, leave him alone," Amy said. "Roper, please go find out when I can take them home," she said, pleading with him.

Because her mother and aunt were wackier than his family, he took pity on her and agreed. "Okay. When I get back, we can discuss your questions," he promised the women.

They reluctantly agreed.

So Roper headed out of the room to get Amy's mother and aunt sprung. Afterward, he thought, the real fun could begin.

CHAPTER SIXTEEN

Her family was free. Amy sensed Roper had signed a few autographs and promised tickets to Renegades games in order to hasten the release process. He hadn't said, but the people who'd eventually released her mother and aunt had been huge fans, shaking Roper's hand and thanking him. He refused to say for what.

TSA and Homeland Security actually did perform a background check on the women and discovered their penchant for getting into ridiculous trouble back in Florida. It was soon obvious terrorism wasn't an issue. Insanity was, though, Amy thought wryly. But since the incident had been more of a misunderstanding than any kind of practical joke, the women were released into the general population of New York — complete with a behavioral warning for the future.

Amy was exhausted.

"So what are we doing tonight?" Aunt

Darla asked, from her seat in the back of Roper's car.

Amy closed her eyes and groaned. But at least they hadn't started asking Roper questions about his intentions again.

"I need to make some calls and find you two a hotel. I'm afraid my apartment is too small," Amy explained. "By the time I get you settled, it'll be too late to do anything tonight." Amy turned around in time to see her mother wink at her aunt. "*What* was that wink for?" Amy asked.

"You can go home and sleep. Darla and I want to hit one of the clubs," her mother said.

"Oh, no."

"Ladies, I think I have a solution," Roper said. "Do you want to hear it?" he asked Amy.

She leaned her head back and nodded. "Yes, please." She owed him more than she could say for just being here.

"Instead of a hotel, why don't your mother and aunt share my guest room? It has two double beds and they'll have their own bathroom. And I'll be there to keep them company."

Meaning he'd make sure they didn't get into trouble by sneaking out at night.

The rest of the thought went unsaid, but

378

it was glaringly obvious. "I couldn't impose like that," Amy said. No matter how good a solution he provided. Nobody should be subjected to dealing with her family twenty-four/seven.

"We'd love to!" Rose and Darla said at the same time, ignoring Amy as usual. "That's just so kind of you. We won't be any trouble."

"Are your fingers crossed behind your back?" Roper asked, laughing.

"You have a season to get ready for, remember? You can't afford any distractions," Amy said, her heart beating out a panicked rhythm.

Not only did Roper need to focus on his career, Amy didn't want her family getting close to the man she was trying to avoid.

"My family is a distraction for me. Your family is not," he assured her.

"You see? We're not a distraction."

Amy didn't turn around to see which one of her relatives spoke. They sounded alike and she didn't much care.

He leaned closer, never taking his eyes from the road. "It's different when nobody's pulling your emotional strings," he said softly, so only she could hear. "I can handle them and still keep all my appointments." Roper reached out and placed his hand on her thigh.

She knew he meant to reassure her but he aroused her instead. Talk about pushing emotional buttons, this man had hers down pat.

"It's still an imposition."

"Not when I offer freely. Besides, they want to stay with me."

"We do," the two chimed in from the backseat.

Amy groaned. "It looks as if I'm outnumbered."

"Wait until I call home and tell everyone we're staying with the famous John Roper. You know many of our residents are originally from New York. They still follow the Renegades and you're big news," Darla said.

"I didn't think you knew who I was when Amy introduced me," Roper said, glancing at them from the rearview mirror.

Rose laughed. "Well, we didn't want to embarrass you. We do have some sense of decorum. We know how to behave around a celebrity. Besides, who knows if the room was bugged."

"Oh, give me a break," Amy said. They'd obviously been watching too much television without her there to set up activities.

"We're almost at my apartment," Roper said.

"Good! Thank you so much for your generosity," Rose said. "We won't tell a single soul about your engagement to my daughter until you're ready to announce it publicly."

"What engagement?" Amy practically shrieked.

"The one Roper promised the guard would be happening soon, of course," her mother said, confident she had the whole situation figured out.

"Roper?" Amy asked, her head pounding hard.

He shook his head and grinned. "I promised to speak at his son's graduation."

Amy swirled around in her seat. "Did you hear that, Mom?" she asked, wanting to put an end to their inaccurate assumptions once and for all.

But both women suddenly had iPod earphones on and neither one was paying any attention.

"Maybe it's time to get a job," Ben said, flipping through the Help Wanted section of the paper.

"You're giving up?" Dave, just home from work, pulled out a Vitamin Water and guzzled from the bottle. "What happened with your brother?"

381

Ben had avoided seeing his friend for the past few days, embarrassed to admit he'd failed to get the necessary cash from his sibling. "He cut us all off," Ben admitted. "Mom, Sabrina and me. Told us it's time to stand on our own, if you can believe that." Ben could practically feel his anger and blood pressure rise at the memory. "What does he know about how rough I've got it? The guy's got the golden touch. Even with an injury, life's easy for him," Ben said.

"Damn." Dave shook his head. "I didn't want to believe he'd be so full of himself. I mean, he's a hero, even with last season's mess. But he's so damn selfish."

"You're telling me! He tried to convince me coaching is the way to go," Ben muttered. "He needs to be taken down a few pegs. Maybe then he'll stick his hand into his pocket and give something to the family that stuck by him."

Dave placed his empty bottle on the counter. "Don't you worry, I'm planning just that," his friend said.

Ben glanced up. "Planning what?"

"Remember all the times you wished someone would teach your brother a lesson?" Dave asked.

Ben didn't like Dave's tone. "Yes," Ben said warily.

"I've been doing it. It's been so easy, considering I know where he lives. A few disgruntled fan letters, a bobblehead doll with a knife in the shoulder, all meant to remind him that he's been one constant disappointment. What a waste of money on season tickets," he muttered in disgust. "I'm ordering a vegetarian pizza for dinner. Want some?"

"Make mine half plain," Ben said. "Wait a minute. You've been harassing my brother?"

Ignoring him, Dave picked up the phone and placed the food order before turning back to him. "I wouldn't call it harassing. It's more like teaching him a much-needed lesson. All that money, he should work a little harder instead of doing so much wining, dining and romancing. Pay a little respect to the fans, you know."

Ben's stomach rolled. It was one thing for him to complain about his brother, it was another to hear his friend ragging on Roper when he was down. Despite his own anger, Ben knew Roper was pissed at himself for this past year's performance. It wasn't like he'd screwed up on purpose.

"Back off," Ben warned his friend.

Dave stepped back and stared at Ben in disbelief. "You're sticking up for him now?"

"I'm just saying he works hard. When he

wasn't playing well, it wasn't his fault. Just like it isn't my fault that my minor league career didn't work out," Ben said, hearing his words as if someone else were speaking them.

Understanding them, maybe, for the first time.

If it wasn't Roper's fault that he'd had a bad season, could it really be Roper's fault that Ben's life didn't turn out the way he'd hoped and dreamed?

Holy shit. Talk about an *aha moment.*

"This is frigging unbelievable," Dave said, pacing the kitchen. "What happened to the man who wanted his brother to suffer the way he was?"

Ben jumped up from his seat. "Those were words, man. A fantasy. We all have those. I'm not happy with my brother at the moment. But he's my brother." Hell, Ben had just come to realize he wasn't happy with himself, either.

After all, he'd leaked news of his brother's whereabouts to the press. His mother would casually mention what Roper had been up to and Ben would put an anonymous call through to Buckley, Roper's number-one nemesis. He'd tell the guy where Roper had been and with whom, usually making things seem more frivolous than they were.

Ben had gotten perverse pleasure in seeing Roper on the receiving end of bad press for once, but Ben's actions had been harmless fun, or so he'd thought at the time. Looking at Dave's twisted view, Ben was coming to see that even his phone calls had done damage to the brother he was jealous of — the brother he loved.

Dave went on to describe some of the better packages he'd sent Roper, including the dog shit he'd paid a dog walker to hand over, and Ben thought he'd be sick.

Roper was his brother, Ben thought, repeating his own words.

The same brother who had stepped up to the plate when Ben's father took off. Who'd introduced him to coaches in the minors and who'd funded more failed businesses than Ben cared to remember. Jeez, he'd been living with his head up his ass, Ben thought.

"So do me a favor and leave Roper alone."

Dave shrugged. "Can't do that. It's too late."

Ben's skin chilled. "What do you mean?"

"The way you've been ducking me the past two days, waking up before I leave, coming home after I'm asleep, I had a feeling you struck out with big brother. So I put the ultimate revenge in motion."

Ben grabbed his friend by his shirt. "What the hell do you have planned?" he asked.

Dave laughed, but there was nothing remotely funny about the situation. "Nothing I'm going to tell you about, that's for sure. And Ben?"

"What?" he asked, releasing Dave's shirt.

"Find yourself a new couch. Mine's off-limits."

Amy sat in Roper's kitchen, her stomach cramping as he read, first from the *Daily News* and then the *New York Post*. He hadn't said much since she'd arrived except to warn her that her mother's adventure at the airport had made the news, thanks to an overzealous fan who'd spotted them. The guy had called the Gossip Zone, another online site. And when one rag got hold of the news, the rest followed.

Roper watched Amy warily, as if waiting for her to explode at any moment. And he was right to worry.

Amy's fuse was lit, her nerves strung tight. But she had to see the damage for herself. "Give me that."

She snatched the newspaper from Roper's hand and glanced at the article, reading aloud. " 'As opening day of baseball season approaches, Renegades star John Roper is busy. Just not in the way his fans would expect.' "

As she spoke, he rose and poured his coffee into the sink, rinsing the mug and saying nothing.

She continued. " 'Yesterday, the center fielder bailed his girlfriend's mother and aunt out of trouble at JFK International Airport.' " Nausea rose and remained in her throat. "Why can't my family just act like normal human beings?" Amy asked in frustration.

"Because they are who they are. Besides, that's why you love them," Roper said. His kind tone only made things worse. How was she going to fight her feelings for him?

The newspaper articles instantly reminded her of the last time her mother's antics had made the front page. How she'd lost the job she'd been so proud of, not to mention any potential career in the same field thanks to Rose's behavior. Amy knew a psychiatrist would have a field day with her inability to put the past where it belonged. But it *was* her past and she was reacting the only way she knew how.

"Give me the papers," he said. "They aren't good for anything except recycling," he said, the voice of reason. His reaction seemed strange, coming from a man used to reading about himself regularly in a none-too-flattering light.

But Amy wasn't a celebrity. She hadn't signed on for a life in front of the cameras. In fact, she'd deliberately chosen a career behind the scenes. Yet when she was with Roper, she couldn't remain there.

"I need to read the rest." She folded the newspaper in half and cleared her throat. " 'Amy Stone, niece of sports agent Spencer Atkins, and newly minted publicist at the Hot Zone, has her hands full with relatives who were detained for possible terrorist activity on board an aircraft. . . .' "

"Give me that," he muttered, grabbing the paper and tossing it into the recycling bin in disgust.

But not before she caught a glimpse of the photograph beneath the article. "There's no mistaking us," Amy said. She shook her head and groaned.

"I actually think it's a good picture," Roper said. He settled back into his chair as if nothing had occurred.

As if two elderly women with a penchant for trouble weren't in his guest room getting ready to *hit the streets of New York City* right this minute. There were probably even people with cameras waiting outside the apartment. Ones that had probably watched her come inside. Not that she'd seen any-one, but obviously, that didn't mean a thing.

"I never saw anyone with a camera at the airport." Amy said. Yet there was the picture, taken as they exited the terminal building yesterday.

Her hands grew damp at the thought of dealing with more pictures, innuendos and rumors.

"They could have had a zoom lens or a cell-phone camera. At least we know who called it in. Half the time I'm left guessing about how they found me." He eyed her with obvious concern.

She didn't respond. She was too busy wor-rying about avoiding more photo ops in the future.

"Everyone's looking for a way to make a buck these days," Roper finally said.

"Off of my newfound celebrity status." Since New Year's Eve, she'd somehow become a person of interest, thanks to her connection to John Roper.

She couldn't blame him for her mother's innate ability to attract trouble. Amy had been this route before. But she couldn't risk the potent combination of Roper and her mother placing her squarely in the limelight again. True, her uncle Spencer had as deep a connection to her mother and aunt as

Amy herself, so she wouldn't be fired. But the idea of being the object of public ridicule after spending so many years avoiding it gave Amy more than a headache. It made her want to throw up.

She realized that Roper was staring at her, trying to figure out what was going on in her mind. "It's just insane the way the media focuses on me as your girlfriend," she said, needing to explain her reaction to him in some way he could understand.

"That's not what bothers you," Roper said.

She leaned forward in her seat. "And what does?" she asked, since he obviously thought he knew her so well.

"I'm not sure yet. But I'll let you know when I figure it out," he said.

"Maybe it's that you insist on giving everyone the idea that we're a couple when you know we aren't."

He grinned, that sexy, in-control smile that drove her to distraction. "I know no such thing."

And because of his stubbornness, her mother, her aunt and even the media refused to believe that she and John were just friends. Perhaps because he made it so hard for Amy to believe it herself.

He was doing his best to charm her into

his life and keep her there. Last night he'd taken them to dinner at his friend's restaurant in Little Italy. The one where he'd brought Amy on their first date. She had a hunch he'd chosen the place on purpose, as much for the memories as the good food. He called it *their place,* which caused a stir with her relatives. Afterward they walked around and he treated them to gelato and cannoli.

Then he insisted on dropping Amy off at her apartment first, so her mother and aunt could see where she lived. Amy had allowed him to take charge because he'd had ideas to keep her mother and aunt busy for the night, tiring them out. As much as she wanted to argue with his commandeering attitude, he took the pressure off of her and she appreciated it.

He was a gentleman. A kind, sexy gentleman. And to use her mother's old-fashioned word, he was *wooing* Amy with thoughtfulness, not money. She couldn't let herself succumb, but it wasn't easy.

Last night he'd slipped his hand into hers as they walked, so she couldn't pull back without making a scene. He'd casually placed his palm on her back when they entered the restaurant and once again she'd been powerless to separate them. After a while, the gestures felt too good and she didn't want him to stop. She lay in bed last night, aroused from his touch, yearning for him to ease the ache in her heart and the one that throbbed insistently inside her body. She missed him.

Just as he obviously intended.

But that was before she'd seen the morning paper. Before the past and present collided. John Roper and her eccentric, publicity-magnet mother were a combination Amy could not handle.

"So what are we doing today?" Roper asked.

She rose from her chair. "*We* aren't doing anything. I took the day off to entertain the troops. You are going to the gym or the physical therapist or whatever else is on your schedule." If he wasn't with them, he couldn't get them on tomorrow's front page.

She could keep her mother and aunt under control for a day or two, make them happy and then send them back to Florida without argument.

"I haven't skipped a day of therapy in weeks and you know it. I have a four-o'clock appointment today and I'll be there. Meanwhile, if you have nothing specific on the agenda, I thought maybe we could all do the Statue of Liberty. Then you can take them back here to rest up for dinner while I keep my appointment."

The telephone rang before she could argue, and Roper picked it up on the first ring. "Hello?" he said, then listened.

"Hi, Mom. I can't talk right now. I have company," he said.

Amy watched with interest. He'd taken phone calls from his mother and sister last night, as well, and there was a distinct difference in how he dealt with them now, compared to the panicked acquiescence he'd used when they'd first met.

"Yes, Amy's family is still here. If you'd like you can join us for dinner tonight."

Amy winced. "No!" She waved her hands in front of her face. Between her family and the famous Cassandra Lee, there'd be more than enough drama to create ten scenes. Amy couldn't deal with it and her anxiety built higher at the mere thought.

"I'll talk to you later, Mom," Roper said. There was no hint of frustration in his voice.

If anything, things with his mother seemed almost . . . normal. Such a stark contrast to the episodes Amy had witnessed in the past. It was enough to distract her from canceling tonight's dinner or arguing about today's plans. At least for now.

Roper hung up and met Amy's gaze.

"You haven't dropped everything and run to your mother, not last night and not this morning," she said, realizing exactly why things seemed so off balance to her now. "And Sabrina? Her phone call was calm. She wasn't in hysterics complaining about your mother. And Ben —"

"Isn't speaking to me at the moment, which makes things easier," Roper admitted. "But yes, something *is* different. I came to your office to talk to you about it. But then you got the phone call to rush to the airport and, well, I forgot."

Amy nodded. Subtly and not so subtly, Roper was now his own person. Not an athlete and a son pulled in a million different directions. If his family called, he spoke to them and quickly got off the phone. He met all his obligations and appointments, including those promises he'd made to Amy's mother and aunt, without running off on one emergency after another.

He was focused.

He was present in the moment.

And his career obligations — working out and meeting with the physical therapist — came first.

Wow.

"How? What happened with your family?" she asked.

"In a nutshell, I laid it on the line for them. I told them —"

Suddenly her mother's and aunt's voices sounded from the other room, growing louder as they made their way to the kitchen.

Roper shot Amy an amused glance, but she wanted to hear the rest of his story. Unfortunately her family descended on them, two small women who sounded and acted like a herd.

"We decided what we wanted to do today," Darla said. "We want to go to the Central Park Zoo."

"And then I have something special planned for tonight," Amy's mother said, her eyes sparkling.

"We're having dinner with my mother tonight," Roper said.

"Great! I can't wait to meet Cassandra Lee! And afterward she can join us. I read in the paper that the Chippendales show is in town. Can you use your pull to get us tickets?" Rose asked Roper, snuggling up to his side and batting her eyelashes.

"No, no and no!" It was time for them to go home, Amy thought.

Much as she loved them, they were already driving her crazy. And though she'd loved her job in Florida, she had to admit she'd found a peace in her short time in New York she hadn't realized existed. Her family had shattered it the moment they arrived.

And on the pragmatic side, she wasn't getting any work done. Though her uncle had given her time off, she was too new to have earned it. She needed and wanted to get back to the office. But how could she send her relatives packing after not even twenty-four hours? They'd be devastated. And hurt.

"I'll see what I can do," Roper said, chuckling. "But it's last-minute. I'm pretty sure it's too late for me to get tickets. I'm sorry."

Amy breathed a sigh of relief. Obviously he knew better than to let her mother and aunt Darla loose at a strip show in Manhattan. Short of putting them in handcuffs and chains, Amy barely knew how to contain them herself.

Whether they stayed three days or three weeks, they'd have more than enough time to wreak havoc without a trip to Chippendales on their agenda.

Dave put the finishing touches on his project. He'd been working on it for a while, in between shifts at the gym. It looked professional, if he did say so himself. Enough to cause trouble for John Roper.

Trouble the likes of which he'd never seen before.

Ben had bailed out on him and he wouldn't be getting the money for his gym. Someone had to pay. It might as well be the high-and-mighty John Roper, Dave thought.

Laughing, he clicked Upload on his computer.

Let the fun begin.

CHAPTER SEVENTEEN

At dinner, Roper braced himself for a clash of two women who could not be more different, but his mother and Amy's hit it off. Darla and Rose gushed over Cassandra and she ate up the attention. If his mother found Amy's family odd or eccentric, she didn't show it, for which Roper was grateful. And Harrison, ever the gentleman and ever present at Cassandra's side, kept her grounded.

The same couldn't be said for Amy's female relatives. Aunt Darla was obviously smitten with their waiter, a young man, new to his job, who didn't know what to make of the attention.

He'd taken their orders, with Rose and Darla interrupting him periodically to ask questions. Unfortunately they weren't about the daily specials.

"I have a question," Darla said for the third time. The first two times she'd interrupted the man with personal questions.

"Yes?" he asked, forcing a smile.

"It had better be about the meat," Amy said through gritted teeth.

"Oh, it is," her aunt assured her. She glanced up at the waiter. "What's your address, Hot Boy?" she asked.

Roper chuckled despite himself.

"Aunt Darla!" Amy scolded her aunt.

"I'm going to turn in the order," he said, flustered and walking away.

"Ooh, check out that rear end."

Amy slapped her hand over her forehead. "Would you cut it out?" she scolded under her breath.

"Don't be a spoilsport," her mother said. "It isn't anything personal. This is the one thing we don't miss back home — you killing our fun."

Beside him, Amy gritted her teeth. "I'd think you also miss me bailing you two out at midnight. Aunt Darla told me that my replacement makes you wait until morning."

"This is better than any movie," Cassandra said, laughing.

The waiter returned with their drinks, serving the ladies first, which was his first mistake.

Darla reached out, and before Roper realized what she intended — and definitely before Amy did — Darla pinched the waiter's behind.

The man jumped back, dropping his tray of drinks. "Sorry," he said. Red-faced, he headed back to the kitchen to get something to clean up the mess.

"That's it," Amy said, yelling at her aunt. "You need to apologize to the man."

Roper stood and placed a calming hand on her shoulder.

At the same moment, a man in a jacket and tie approached the table. "I'm sorry to disturb you, but we've had some complaints about your table being too loud," the gentleman said.

Amy's face turned red. "I apologize. We won't cause any more trouble," she promised.

"Thank you. I'll be sending a new waitress to handle your order," he said pointedly. Then he walked away quickly, leaving them all alone.

No explanations were necessary. Darla had run the other man off.

"I hope you're all happy." Amy glared at her family members.

"I didn't mean any harm," Darla said, sounding sincere and embarrassed at the same time.

Roper actually felt sorry for her.

He felt worse for Amy.

She lowered herself into her seat and the rest of the meal passed without a word from her. Her mother and aunt behaved — at least well enough not to get them kicked out of the restaurant.

His mother picked up on the tension and told stories about Hollywood, distracting Amy's family enough to pass the time.

"I heard your daughter is getting married," Rose said to Cassandra at the very end of the meal.

His mother nodded. "She's marrying a wonderful man and they're having a *small, intimate ceremony*," she said, grudging acceptance in her tone.

Since the day Roper had laid down the law, his mother had backed off his sister and stopped meddling in the wedding plans. Of course, the fact that Sabrina had a check in her hand meant there was nothing Cassandra could do but accept her daughter's wishes.

Just as Roper had intended.

And perhaps sensing she was at a crossroads with her son, Cassandra had changed her behavior where he was concerned, as well. Roper was sure Harrison played a strong role in his mother's turnaround and he appreciated the man more than he could say. Harrison obviously made his mother happy, in her own dysfunctional way, and that pleased Roper, too.

Roper gestured to the waitress, who picked up the credit-card slip, fully signed. They could leave whenever they were ready. And he sensed Amy had been ready a long time ago.

"Weddings are wonderful," Rose said with a sigh.

Roper nodded. "I'm going to give my sister away and we're looking forward to Kevin becoming part of the family," he said.

"Speaking of weddings," Rose said, leaning across the table and staring Roper in the eye.

"Oh, no," Amy said. "We're leaving before you can go there." She correctly guessed her mother would begin to pump Roper about his intentions regarding her daughter.

Roper knew his own intentions. Unfortunately Amy didn't share them. Instead she wanted to run from him, far and fast.

After tonight's dinner, he was starting to understand why. Now that she couldn't blame Roper's family or his choices for coming between them, she had it in for the press. But there was so much more to her feelings. When she'd first come to New York, she'd been uptight, diligently planning his life as if her career hinged on his getting it right. At the time he'd chalked it up to the fact that he was her first assignment. But their trip to the lodge proved him wrong.

Only when she'd gotten away from the pressure of her job and her family, when she'd stopped worrying about what people were going to think of her, had she been relaxed and happy. She'd enjoyed life.

There was no enjoyment in Amy now.

Her family pulled her strings the same way his family had with him.

Amy stood and he followed. Everyone at the table did the same. They left the restaurant, at which point Cassandra and Rose exchanged phone numbers. Everyone survived the embarrassment of the evening no worse for wear. Everyone except Amy.

She was barely speaking to anyone. He wished he could help her through what was going on with her family. Unfortunately, he'd learned from firsthand experience that the only person who could fix Amy's situation was Amy. After all, she'd tried desperately to change his and nothing worked until he'd stood up for his own personal space.

She needed to do the same.

Amy couldn't believe her luck. Yank had arranged for an entire day's worth of activities for her family. Curly, one of his and her uncle Spencer's poker buddies, was taking some relatives into town to see the sights and they asked Amy's mother and aunt to join them. Amy showered, dressed and headed for work, determined to forget the events of last evening.

She cringed, her stomach cramping at the memory. She wondered what her father would think of last night's episode. Pushing those thoughts aside, she collected her note-pad and pen and headed for the conference room for the weekly meeting. The room filled up quickly, everyone present and accounted for.

As usual, Yank called the Hot Zone meeting to order. Amy, having already learned the drill, remained standing, hands and coffee off the table until he slammed down the gavel. Then she seated herself and prepared for the list of new assignments.

Yank's first words weren't about business per se. "We're gonna have a firm party at one of the upstate country clubs," he announced without preamble. "It'll be before the start of baseball season and after the NFL draft, so nobody can make excuses. Micki's got media lined up and we're gonna make a splash just because we can," he said proudly. "Everyone needs to be there."

"This is going to be an annual event," Annabelle said. "We have corporate sponsors who want to meet our clients. It's a win-win for everyone. Date to follow soon."

"Amy and Spencer, be sure your family's back home before then. Otherwise we might have a bomb scare," Yank said, laughing.

Amy cringed.

Until her uncle added, "Similar to the fire drill you arranged New Year's Eve?"

Then Amy laughed.

"He's blamin' a blind man for trippin' over his dog! Can you believe that?" Yank asked, rising from his chair.

"I'm blaming you for being a klutz. Being blind's got nothing to do with it," Spencer said.

"Here they go again," Micki whispered to Amy, leaning close. She grabbed the gavel from her unsuspecting uncle's hands and rapped it on the rubber mat. "Move it along," she ordered.

The men sat down, obeying her without question. Another half hour passed with routine business until Frannie burst into the room without knocking. "I'm sorry to interrupt," she said, huffing and out of breath. "But I have news that can't wait."

Amy's stomach churned. She had a distinct feeling of déjà vu, taking her back to her first meeting in this room.

"Let's hear it," Yank said.

"Well, I need to see Amy privately," Frannie said, suddenly realizing all eyes were on her.

Now Amy's stomach churned again, but for good reason. Frannie wasn't the type to get so worked up. This must really be something. Amy rose from her seat, but Micki placed a hand on her shoulder. "We're family here. Nobody is in this room except Uncle Yank, Spencer, myself, my sisters and Amy. We want to help."

Amy sat down again.

Frannie nodded. She leaned forward until she was between Amy and Micki. "There's something on the Internet Amy needs to see. Nobody else should see it," Frannie said.

That was the moment Amy realized her uncle's secretary had a laptop beneath her arm. She placed it on the table, opened it and Amy immediately recognized the banner for Buckley's blog on the top of the screen.

Everyone in the room was silent, obviously recognizing something huge was going on. Amy had never been so sick in her life.

"Ready?" Frannie asked.

"As I'll ever be," Amy muttered.

She scrolled down slowly until the headline caught Amy's eye. *Roper Bares All.* Panic rose in her throat as she tried to concentrate on the words. The effort to understand what she was seeing was futile until she saw *her* own name posted along with Roper's.

A prominent link promised to lead to "an eyeful."

She clicked.

She looked.

And she immediately wished she hadn't.

Her hands began to sweat because somehow, there were photographs of Amy and Roper — *naked* on the Internet.

Having sex.

She ordered herself to breathe. In. Out. In. Out.

Think.

She peeled open her eyelids and looked again. Thanks to the unbelievable angle of the bodies on screen, Amy tipped her head to the side to get a better glimpse.

"When did you get a tattoo?" her uncle Spencer asked from behind them.

"I didn't!" she said tightly, jumping up from her seat, nearly knocking everyone behind her over in her effort to escape the sudden stifling feeling surrounding her.

"Take it easy," Micki said, grabbing her wrist. "They're obviously doctored, so breathe. We'll figure something out."

Everyone around her spoke, but she couldn't hear anything beyond the ringing in her ears. It didn't matter that the body on the screen wasn't really hers. It was her face. And nobody who viewed this photograph would know or care that it wasn't really Amy and Roper doing the deed.

She knew her business. Perception was everything. Thanks to her relationship with Roper, she'd been violated in the most extreme and demeaning way and there was nothing she could do about it.

Tears filled her eyes, along with impotent frustration. She'd felt like this once before. Memories of her mother being photographed as Lady Godiva came back to her vividly. Guilt by association had damned her in the eyes of her employers and made her a laughingstock in the community. She'd let herself down, but worse, she felt her father's disappointment keenly. Amy had coped by withdrawing deeper into her mother's world, doing her best to help them control their behavior. Without others to judge her, she'd been able to live with the insanity.

But here in New York, she couldn't hide

the same way. She hadn't signed up for the privilege of being in the public eye. Nor did she want it.

The price was too high.

She jerked away from Micki, her uncle and everyone else calling her name and headed to find the one person she could vent on. The person who'd caused this mess, intentionally or not.

To her surprise, Amy didn't have to go far to find Roper. He was waiting in her office.

Roper had received enough phone calls and e-mails about the Internet photos to know he'd better reach Amy before she had a chance to build up emotional walls against him.

She burst into the room quickly and stopped short, obviously shocked to see him. She was dressed for work, in a blazer and slacks. Professional and cute at the same time.

As usual, his heart beat faster at the sight of her. He'd accepted his feelings for her.

She hadn't.

He welcomed them.

She was still running.

"Hi." She straightened her shoulders and turned away for a second, obviously wiping tears from her eyes. He guessed she'd heard about the photos.

Anger gripped him, as it had when he'd seen the pictures the first time. This wasn't the usual paparazzi photo. Someone was going to pay.

Clearing her throat, she met his gaze. "You saved me a trip. I was just coming to find you," she said calmly. Too calmly.

Everything inside him chilled. "Well, I'm glad I saved you a trip. What's up?" he asked, trying to gauge her mood.

She walked past him, retreating behind the safety of her desk. "Let's put it out on the table, okay? I'm sure you've seen the pictures." She clasped her hands in front of her, but not before he noticed that they were shaking and her cheeks were flushed pink in embarrassment.

He wanted to wrap her in his arms and protect her from everything that had and could hurt her, but he knew better than to think it was possible. She needed to face this challenge. They needed to face it together if they ever wanted to have a future.

"I've seen them," he said, his jaw clenched tight. "And I'm going to kill the bastard who doctored them and put them up there."

"You'll have to find the person first."

He inclined his head. "I intend to. But I'm more worried about you." This composed, sedate woman sitting in front of him wasn't the Amy he thought he'd find.

He'd figured she'd be angry and fired up. Furious at him just because he was the easiest target.

"I know how you feel about this kind of thing and I'm sorry," he said. "I can't promise you something like this won't happen again, but I swear, I'll do my best to see it doesn't."

She shook her head. "I'm afraid that's not enough. You are who you are. You're John Roper, center fielder for the best team in New York. You're a celebrity, and let's face it, you love being one. I can't ask you not to be you."

Was that a glimmer of deeper understanding he saw? A flicker of hope rose inside him that maybe, just maybe, being in this job, in this city, had taught her to come around. Could that explain the calm aura around her.

"Thank you for that. But *you're you.* We can certainly work around both," he assured her.

He stepped closer, intending to circle around the desk and take her in his arms, but her words stopped him.

"That's not possible, John, and it's naive to think it is." She drew a deep breath. "Being a couple isn't working for me. The photographers are relentless. Being friends won't work, either. Even if I were just your assistant, it wouldn't keep me out of the media spotlight. And that's just not a place I want to be. So I've decided to ask Micki to reassign me. Permanently." Her voice cracked but her composure didn't.

The only sign that she was upset was the fact that her knuckles had turned white.

But Roper didn't have her composure. He snapped, losing his patience. In a heartbeat he strode around the desk and grasped her by the shoulders, spinning her chair around to face him.

She gasped and squirmed, but he didn't release his grip. "What is wrong with you?" she asked, emotion showing at last.

"You're wrong. This is wrong."

"Because I don't want to sleep with you anymore?" she said without meeting his gaze. "Or because I don't like your high-profile life?"

"Because you care about me as much as I care about you. You're using this 'I hate being in the public eye' thing as an excuse not to be with me," he said, his frustration at an all-time high.

She finally met his gaze. "Pardon me if it bothers me to see myself naked on the Internet!" she spat.

"We both know it isn't your body. I'll take a freaking billboard in Manhattan if that's what it takes to convince you I love you!" he yelled at her.

She stilled and stopped pulling away from him. Her eyes filled with tears. "I love you, too," she said softly.

Relief swamped him. "Then get angry at whoever is doing this to us. React, instead of being this monotone robot without feelings. Fight for us, dammit!"

She shook her head. "I can't."

He leaned closer. "Why the hell not?" he asked, seeking an answer to the one question he didn't understand. "We can ignore the press and focus on us. It isn't easy, but we can do it."

"You can. I can't."

"Because . . ." he prompted.

"Because when I'm with you, I'm everything I've spent a lifetime trying to avoid."

He gentled his grip on her shoulders. "In English, please. I'm just not understanding."

She swiped at a tear running down her face. "I don't want to be the crazy lady arrested by airport security for making a scene. I don't want to be caught making love to you in front of a glass window by paparazzi with cameras. No, those photos on the Internet aren't of us, *but they could have been!*"

He finally got it and let out a low groan. "You don't want to end up like your mother, and being with me increases the chances that when you finally let go and act like yourself, you'll be caught by the press."

"I lost my job once thanks to her antics. I've spent years since making sure that won't happen again."

This time he brushed her tears away with his thumb. "You can't keep running from who you are. You can't suppress your true self forever and be happy. You aren't. You won't be."

She stiffened her shoulders. "Who are you to say I'm not happy?"

"I'm the man who made love to you in front of that window. I've seen you making snow angels for the first time. I saw you dancing and singing in the corner with Hannah when you thought no one was looking. I've seen the real you and I'm here to tell you that if you keep running away from yourself, you'll spend the rest of your life out of the spotlight like you think you want — and you'll be perfectly miserable." He lowered his hand from her face.

He looked into her eyes, and although

he'd obviously hit a nerve, he hadn't changed her mind. His heart sank at the thought of walking out of here as alone as he was when he'd walked in.

"I can't do this anymore. I'll talk to Micki and she'll take care of you from now on."

"Did you hear anything I said? Or did you tune me out completely?"

"I heard you. I just don't think you're right about what I need to be happy." She folded her arms across her chest.

He was through. If Amy couldn't see she was running away, there was nothing more he could do to convince her. He had a season to prepare for and he was leaving for Florida to join the team soon. "I guess you're right. You know what you need and what you want. It sure as hell doesn't seem to be me."

She didn't argue.

"It's ironic, though. You helped me get my shit together with my family but you can't do the same for yourself." And until she was willing to try, he had nothing left to say.

Heart heavy, he turned to go.

And she didn't stop him as he walked through the door and out of her life.

Amy left work early. She wasn't in the mood to deal with people today. She couldn't look them in the eye with those photographs circulating, and to add insult to injury, she'd lost the man she loved. In fact, she'd sent him out the door without so much as a goodbye because she wasn't convinced she could handle *anything* anymore. What a mess.

She was mentally spent, and the last thing she expected to find was her mother and her aunt cooking up a storm in her kitchen. The scene was reminiscent of her childhood. Big meals, family dinners. A warm, fuzzy feeling surrounded her as she realized that maybe this was exactly what she needed. Retreating to the comfort of home and family without the outside world intruding. It had worked for her when she lived in the retirement community. It could work for her now, helping her forget about what it had cost to let Roper go.

"Hi," Amy said, announcing her presence.

"Oh, you're home," her mother said. She wiped her hands on a towel and strode across the room to give Amy a hug. "Your aunt and I were just making dinner. We thought you could use a home-cooked meal and some cheering up. Between those awful photos and you being silly enough to break up with Roper, we decided you needed your family around you."

"How do you know about my breakup with Roper?" Considering it had just officially happened earlier today.

"He called and said you might need us and suggested we come here. Of course, we pushed for an answer as to why, and when we found out, we just had to wonder what you were thinking!" her mother explained.

"I'm glad you're here." But she wasn't going to argue with them about the wisdom of the choices she made in her personal life. "A home-cooked meal sounds good. Just let me change into something comfortable and I'll be right back."

"Um . . . How comfortable?" her aunt asked.

Amy narrowed her gaze. "Why?"

"We're having dinner company," her mother said.

"Who?" Amy asked warily. If they'd invited Roper over, she was going to throttle them for interfering.

"While we were cooking for you, your phone rang and we answered. It was a gentleman who said he wanted to know your side of the story regarding those pictures on the Internet," her mother said.

"And so you just had to invite him over?" Amy asked, appalled, but not all that surprised.

"Well, of course!" Her aunt waved a spoon in emphasis. "You know how polite we are. Besides, the gentleman explained that you'd need someone on your side and he was the best person for the job."

Amy rubbed her burning eyes. "Does this gentleman have a name?"

"Frank Buckley from eSports," her mother said. "Amy, be a dear and get the wine that's been chilling in the refrigerator?"

Amy glanced at the ceiling and counted to ten and back again but there was no getting away from the truth. Roper had been right. She'd helped him get his life together, but she hadn't been able to do the same for herself. And as a result, she was here with her mother and her aunt, about to discuss pornographic pictures of herself with the reporter who hated Roper the most.

She had to take control and she had to do it now. Before her new life here in New York shattered beyond recognition.

"Listen, we need to talk."

Her mother nodded. "And we will. But first, you might as well change clothes. Our guest won't be here until seven and it's only three-thirty now. Why don't you get comfortable. You'll be able to change back into a nice, unwrinkled, presentable outfit later."

Amy sighed. "I'll worry about how I'm

going to deal with Buckley later. First we're going to talk. The three of us, so sit. Please." She gestured to the small set of couches.

Her mother and aunt gave each other concerned glances before settling themselves on the cushions.

Amy sat down between them. "You both know how much I love you, right?"

"We love you, too," they said at the same time.

Amy swallowed hard. "What I'm going to say isn't easy, but it has to be said." She rubbed her hands against her pants, nerves setting in. These two women meant the world to her. They'd raised her, they adored her, and she felt the same way about them.

They also caused more trouble than two five-feet-one-inch women should be able to. She adored them for their quirkiness, but she needed them to keep their antics in Florida. Far from Amy — except for planned vacations.

"I'm glad you came to visit because I really missed you both."

"We're glad, too. It's been fun," her aunt Darla said.

"What's wrong? You seem sad." Her mother put her hand on Amy's shoulder.

Rose had always understood her daughter and it was no different now. Unfortunately for Amy, she was about to break her mother's heart. "Mom, in case you don't realize it, my life's a little hectic at the moment."

"Which is why it's good your aunt and I are here, right?" Her mother looked at her with her big, imploring eyes.

Amy drew a deep breath. It was now or never, she thought. She might not have been able to fight for her relationship with Roper — something she'd yet had time to analyze. But suddenly she was ready to fight for herself and her future.

She leaned forward. "It's not so good that you're here right now, Mom."

"What do you mean?" she asked, hurt in her voice.

"I came to New York to grow up," she said, looking toward the bookshelves she'd put her favorite things upon. "I thought I was doing that, but it turns out I was just running away from things," she said, more to herself than to them.

"I don't understand," her mother said. "Darla, do you understand what Amy is saying?"

Her aunt shook her head. "No, but I think she does and that's what matters."

"I left Florida to get a life. Instead, I've still been running away from one," she said, coming to the realization as she spoke.

She'd put miles between herself and her family. But it wasn't them she was running from — it was herself. It was time to stop. To deal with her past and embrace her future, one that, she hoped, included Roper.

"All I ever wanted was for you and dad to be proud of me," Amy said, taking her first step.

"I am. And he would be. Just look at you, my beautiful girl."

Amy smiled. "I love you for saying that, but don't you think that this mess with the photographers, the naked pictures . . ." She shook her head. "He'd be appalled."

"At the people who did it to you, yes. But not at you! He admired people with spunk. Why do you think he married me? I was the same crazy woman at eighteen that I am now. And I refuse to discuss my age, so don't ask."

Aunt Darla opened her mouth but Rose shot her a look that clearly said "Don't you dare."

Her sister shut it without speaking.

Amy laughed.

"Amy, you've got the best of both of us — my crazy side and your father's sensibility. He adored you and thought you could do no wrong, no matter what you did with your life." Then she chuckled. "Although I must say, it's a good thing those pictures aren't really of you. That I don't think he could have handled."

Amy glanced at her mother and her heart was filled with gratitude.

As she looked at the mother she'd always loved and the aunt who'd always been there for her, too, Amy came to yet another epiphany. It wasn't so bad to be like the two women sitting here.

She was glad her mother said her father would have approved of her choices. But in reality she'd already come to the conclusion, as she sat here with her mother and aunt, that it didn't matter as long as she herself approved of her choices.

In moderation, what was wrong with having fun? Unlike her relatives, Amy knew where and when to behave. So she'd made love with Roper in front of a set of windows — in a locked room facing a wintry landscape where it had been very unlikely they'd have been caught.

And if they'd been photographed? Could it be any worse than the doctored pictures on the Internet now? Amy shook her head and laughed, feeling lighter than she had in ages. She wrapped her hands around her knees, rocked back and forth and thought of all the ways she'd tried to run from

Roper. All the excuses she'd made.

And that's what they were.

Excuses.

After being fired from her first job, she'd retreated home to lick her wounds — and she'd stayed there. It had been easy and fun and she never had had to worry about what people would think. Her job at the retirement community, by definition, allowed for the eccentric behavior of those around her.

Her move to New York had been more overwhelming than she'd expected, and she'd been running from her fear — fear of not being able to make it here — without knowing it. Not until Roper had pointed it out today. And even then, she'd refused to admit he was right.

"What's so funny?" her mother asked. "First you weren't happy we're here and now you're laughing."

"I think I'm just realizing what a fool I've been." About so many things.

"So is it good we're here? Or not so good we're here?" Aunt Darla asked.

Amy bit down on the inside of her cheek. "It's good you're here now . . ."

"But?" her mother asked.

"But next time can we schedule a visit so I can take some legitimate time off?" And give her time to plan some activities that would keep them busy and out of trouble.

"We can do that," her mother said, nodding.

"And as far as tonight's guest goes, I need you two to promise you'll stay in the background and let me do the talking. Do you understand?"

They both nodded.

"Good."

Between this afternoon and right this minute, Amy had come to some major conclusions about her behavior and her life. Both needed to change.

And Buckley was giving her a chance to do it publicly.

CHAPTER EIGHTEEN

Roper didn't think his day could get any worse. After leaving Amy for what seemed like the last time, he worked out, checked in with his coaches and headed home. He'd taken one look at the houseguests who'd just returned from their tour of the city and he knew he had to send them to be with Amy. She needed them — either for their moral support or to face her frustration with them and send them home. Regardless, it wasn't his problem. Unfortunately, he still cared enough to want her to have her family around her if she needed them.

An hour later, his doorbell rang and he found himself face-to-face with the last person he expected to see — his brother. As much as he wasn't in the mood for company, he hadn't seen Ben in a while.

"What's up?" Roper asked.

"Can we talk? And before you slam the door in my face, I'm not here to ask you for money, a job or anything else," his brother said, red-faced.

Curious now, Roper swung the door wide and gestured inside. "Come on in. Can I get you a beer?"

"Why not."

A few minutes later, they were settled in his living room with the TV blaring eSports Network behind them. "So what's up?" Roper asked.

Ben shifted in his seat. "A few things. First is, I called some of those contacts you gave me a while back and set up some interviews for assistant coaching jobs."

Roper couldn't believe his ears. "That's great!" He didn't want to ask what changed Ben's mind because he didn't want to ruin this step in the right direction.

"I've done some thinking and I've been an ass," Ben said. "Blaming you because my life didn't work out the way I wanted." He glanced down, not even chugging his beer the way he usually did. "A couple of the guys said if things work out and I prove myself, the head coaching position might become available. I know it's because of you but I'll take the opportunity and try."

"What's going on, Ben?" Roper had never seen his brother so subdued.

"There's something that's going to hit the

news and you need to hear it from me first."

"Can't be any worse than doctored porn shots of me and Amy on the Internet," Roper muttered.

"No, but it relates to it. Turns out my friend Dave, who'd been letting me bunk there until I convinced you to fund the gym, was behind those photographs."

"What the hell? *Why?* I don't even know the guy."

Ben swallowed hard. "Yeah, well, thanks to me, he thought he knew you. My old, skewed perspective of you."

"I don't know what I want to know first. Why your view of me changed or more about Dave and the pictures," Roper muttered. "I do know I'm going over there and kill him for what he put Amy through." He flexed and unflexed his hands, anger coursing through his veins.

Ben rose and began pacing the room. "Hear me out first, then you can decide what to do. You know I was jealous of you. You know I thought fate gave me a raw deal and Dave knew it, too. Not only was he my friend, he's a Renegades season ticket holder, too, and last season's World Series disaster pissed him off big-time."

"He wouldn't be the only one," Roper said, acknowledging the truth.

"But he was more out of control than I realized. You know those packages you've been getting? The letters? The media coverage of you lately, excessive even by New York standards?"

"Yes . . ." Roper knew where this was going and his head felt full enough to explode. "He's been behind it all?"

"Anything I heard about you, things I griped about to him, he used against you, bro." Ben strode to him. "I had no idea. You have to believe me. I was whiny and self-centered, but you're my brother. I'd never do anything to hurt you. As soon as he told me, it was like this huge lightbulb went off in my head and I realized how messed up my own thinking has been." Ben pleaded with Roper to understand.

And he tried. Man, Roper tried. Because this was his baby brother and he wanted to believe he'd changed. "Go on."

"I moved out. Well, he kicked me out, so I moved into Mom's hotel until she goes back to L.A. But as soon as those photos surfaced, I knew it was Dave." Ben picked up his beer and took a long swig, then placed the bottle back on the table. "I hadn't given him back my key, so I let myself into his place while he was at work and checked the laptop. And bingo."

"He wasn't bright enough to delete the evidence?" Roper asked in disbelief.

"He's cocky enough to think he wouldn't get caught. But he's wrong." Ben shoved his hands into his back pockets. "Before I came here, I turned the laptop over to the police. Then I called Buckley and gave him a tip."

Roper shook his head hard. "You did that for me?"

Ben shrugged. "Maybe I also did it for me. A little redemption, you know? So maybe I could look at myself in the mirror and not hate what I see."

Roper tried not to wince. For all Ben's faults, he obviously had a good heart. And Roper knew what it was like to hate yourself at least a little bit. "Ben, it's okay. I don't hold what Dave did against you. I appreciate you stepping up to the plate for me. I do."

"Don't thank me, at least not yet. There's one more thing you need to know," Ben said, looking down as he spoke. He drew a deep breath. "You know how Buckley's known a lot about you lately? Where you've been and who you've been with?"

"Yes," Roper said warily.

"It was me. Mom would mention things in casual conversation and I'd tip off Buckley or gawkerstalker.com," he said, self-loathing in his voice.

"I'll be damned." Amy had been right. It had been someone close to him. He shook his head in disbelief. "Why the hell would you do it? Do you hate me that much?"

His brother shook his head. "No. I thought it was funny at first. And things always seemed to go your way. I thought it would be a lark to see you twist in the wind a little. But I realize now how pathetic that is."

Roper could have bashed his brother for what he'd done, not just to him, but to Amy. Obviously, though, Ben was doing enough bashing to himself. Roper couldn't bring himself to tell his brother all was okay, but he wasn't going to add to his misery.

"What did the police say about the laptop?" he asked, bringing the subject back to Dave and what mattered at the moment.

"They need to go through the computer. Since I had a key, they aren't going to press charges against me for taking it. And I don't understand any of the legalities, you know, like whether or not they can use it as evidence. But they'll see what they find on it and go from there."

Roper drew a calming breath. He glanced at Ben and tried to see the baby brother he'd always loved. "We'll have to do the same." Roper walked over to his brother and

430

threw an arm around his shoulder. "We go on from here," Roper said.

Ben inclined his head, meeting Roper's gaze. "I don't know what to say."

"Nothing. We're family and —"

"Hey, isn't that Amy?" Ben asked, jerking a finger toward the TV.

Roper glanced up, took one look at Amy in the pantsuit she'd worn the day they'd met at Sparks Steak House, and he grabbed the remote control to raise the volume.

He lowered himself onto the couch and watched her, interviewed in the comfort of her own living room by none other than Buckley the Bastard, himself.

"I thought it would be entertaining for my listeners to hear about a day in the life of John Roper from the woman in charge of handling his affairs for the past month," Buckley said.

"You do have a way with words," Amy said, shaking her head and laughing. Her curls fell over her shoulder in sensual disarray as she flirted with Buckley.

Roper couldn't believe his eyes.

"She's playing him," Ben said, easing himself back on the couch beside Roper.

"But I appreciate the chance to tell my story," Amy said.

"She'd better be playing him and not

exposing my life for public consumption." Or his fears and insecurities to a world that already thought he was a washed-up loser. In a few weeks he'd prove them all wrong.

"Relax, man," Ben said. "I know a con when I see one. Buckley's so happy to have her talking, he doesn't realize she's the one using him."

"So the pictures that recently surfaced were doctored?" Buckley asked.

"That's right," Amy said with certainty. She didn't even flinch at the subject.

"Can you prove it?"

She shook her head. "Not yet."

"Rumor has it the police have a lead." Buckley leaned in close.

Amy shrugged delicately. "I haven't heard anything about that."

Roper glanced at his brother. "You stole that laptop. Aren't you worried?"

"No. In all likelihood, the police can't use the evidence against Dave. But at least I'll have planted doubt in the public's mind about those pictures. It's the best I can do."

Roper nodded.

He listened as Buckley questioned Amy about Roper, his habits, his dedication, his talent, trying to trip her up or get her to admit that Roper was more of a player than a dedicated athlete. He failed. Not once did

Amy speak in terms other than respectful and in a way that built him up in the public eye.

She was every inch his publicist.

She was every inch the woman he loved.

"I was hoping for some juicier information when I set up this interview," Buckley said. "So far you haven't given up anything."

"I'm a publicist. My job is to be behind the camera, not in front of it."

"Yet you're here. You agreed to talk with me."

"Technically, you conned two elderly women into letting you come here to dig up dirt on John Roper. Isn't *that* the truth?" Amy asked.

Without warning, the camera panned to Rose and Darla who waved from the kitchen. Roper figured Amy must have bribed them but good to keep their mouths shut during the interview.

Buckley turned red in the face. "They invited me."

"Not to worry," Amy said, patting his hand. "I was happy to get in front of the camera."

"You were?" Roper asked aloud.

"And why is that?" Buckley asked, clearly looking for a scoop.

"Go ahead, tell them you dumped the

infamous John Roper and be done with it," Roper muttered.

Beside him, Ben chuckled. "Come on, she isn't going to diss you in front of your home crowd."

"Thanks to me she's bare-assed on the Internet."

"It isn't really her."

"Like that matters?" Roper asked.

"As you can see, I come from an outgoing family." Once again the camera angle widened to include Rose and Darla, who this time hammed it up for the television audience, blowing kisses and calling out the names of friends back in Florida.

Roper winced. He could only imagine Amy's mortification. And yet she'd put this circus in motion by talking with Buckley. He leaned forward, wanting to hear more.

"But I've always shied away from being in the spotlight," Amy went on to explain.

"Which must make your relationship with Roper an uncomfortable one."

Roper didn't miss the satisfaction in the bastard's voice or the man's obvious pleasure in knowing Roper was probably watching and squirming. Which he was.

"At first, yes." Amy glanced down. "You see, I didn't realize that I was afraid of disappointing someone very special in my life. Someone who's no longer with us. My father."

"But what about today? The photos?" Buckley prodded, obviously not willing to let Amy go off on a tangent, even one Roper sensed was of the utmost importance — to him.

"Oh, he'd hate those photos," Amy said. "But he'd understand how they came into being. Just as I now understand that I idealized the man he was, the things I thought he expected of me. But I realize now my dad was just a man in love with my slightly eccentric mother."

"That's me! Darla, she's talking about me!" Rose squealed.

The camera panned back to Amy's mother, who blushed and blew kisses.

Roper grinned.

Buckley squirmed in his seat. "But those photos. Even if they aren't you, which has yet to be proved, they must have made you pretty uncomfortable," Buckley pushed.

Amy sat up straighter in her seat. "Yes, they did. Especially with my family in town, as you can imagine. But when you love someone, you can't run away from your fears."

"What did she just say?" Ben asked.

Roper wasn't sure. "I need to hear it

again." He raised the volume another notch.

"So how do you like your job at the Hot Zone?" Buckley asked, changing the subject.

"I love my job, although I must admit, I wasn't as prepared for the media hype as much as I thought. But I'm ready to handle it now, both in my professional and my personal life. In other words, if you're watching, John, I was wrong. I'm sorry. And I'm ready to fight for us," she said, grinning as widely as Buckley scowled.

Roper didn't wait to hear any more. "Hold down the fort, brother. I have someplace important I need to go."

Amy paced her apartment as time passed. Surely Roper had seen the interview or someone had called to tell him about it. So why wasn't he banging down her door? She'd be breaking down his if she wasn't afraid of them crossing in the night.

It hadn't taken long for Buckley to leave once he realized his exclusive, live interview wasn't going to bash Roper. He and his crew had wrapped up and taken off, leaving Amy alone with her applauding mother and aunt. Of course, they had gotten their own exclusive, realizing Amy had come to her senses about Roper.

Had he seen it? Did he know?

"Mom, you and Aunt Darla need to make yourselves scarce. Go to a movie or something," Amy said, rifling through her purse for money.

"Don't worry, we're leaving. And we won't be back here tonight," her mother said pointedly.

"So you and Roper can do whatever you want," Aunt Darla said. "We'll end up back at his apartment. Anyway, we have to pack. We have a flight tomorrow early in the afternoon."

"You do?" Amy turned to her family, surprised. "You didn't tell me you were going home." To her surprise, despite the chaos their surprise arrival had brought with them, Amy was sad to see them go.

"We didn't have definite plans. But after our talk tonight, we realize you need more privacy. We'll be sure to give you a heads-up before we come next time. At least we can leave knowing that you and Roper are fine," her mother said.

"You are fine, right?" Aunt Darla asked.

Amy, not wanting to worry them, merely nodded. "It's all good. Now, go out. Keep busy, *behave* and we'll have breakfast before you leave tomorrow. Will that work out timewise?"

"Yes."

They opened the door to the apartment and bumped into Roper on his way in. Another ten minutes of conversation passed, and by the time she shut the door behind her mother and aunt, nerves took over. Her stomach was in knots, her throat raw and dry.

"So." She spread her hands out beside her, then clasped them together. "Alone at last."

He glanced around the empty apartment and grinned. "Very."

"You saw the interview?"

He nodded. "I did. Shocked the hell out of me to see you in front of the camera talking about yourself."

"I bet." She bit down on the inside of her cheek. "I realize I've been driving you a little crazy with all the 'I want you but I can't be with you' stuff."

He raised an eyebrow. "Do tell."

"I tried to explain it to you through Buckley. I was living up to an idealized version of me I thought my father would have had. That's why I became a social worker, to make a difference in the world. For him. But it wasn't really right for me. Working at the retirement home was a blast. I could be myself but I had no social life. When I came to New York and started working for the Hot Zone, I found myself. I love my job. I love organizing and compartmentalizing, strategizing and finding solutions to problems like yours."

"You do it well. Just look at how you fixed me. So go on. Tell me more." He needed to hear everything she had to tell him. He wanted to understand what motivated her, her hopes and dreams, her fears and mistakes. He needed to know so they could go forward.

"Well, you know I don't want to be as out there as my mother. It's a deep-rooted fear of mine. You'd have the same one if you'd rescued Lady Godiva from jail."

He nodded. "I suppose I would."

"But I also don't want to be so repressed anymore."

"You're over it?" The wary tone in his voice told her he didn't want to live the roller coaster anymore.

Neither did she. "I'm over it. I realized that even if we'd been caught at the lodge, what's the worst thing that could have happened?"

"I don't know."

"Some sleazy photographer could have posted naked pictures of us in the papers or on the Internet. The worst has already happened and I survived," Amy said. "My family loves me no matter what."

"I'm sure it helps that it wasn't really you in those photos."

"No, but the public thinks it is. I swear to you, I've come to terms with who you are and who I am. I know it seems like a fast turnaround, but it makes sense to me now. Almost as if I've come full circle today." She cupped his face in her hands and kissed him hard on the lips. "You need to trust me. Want to know why?"

He inclined his head. "Why?" Roper asked, going along with her.

"Because I love you, John Roper, center fielder for the New York Renegades. I can live with being plastered on the pages of the *Post* and the *News* if that's what it takes to be with you."

He shook his head, stunned. And yet, at the same time, not really all that surprised. He always knew she had the strength and spunk he'd seen in her other female family members. "Life with you isn't ever going to be boring."

She pursed her lips. "I can try for boring. I really can. I've done it fairly well at times."

He stepped close and pulled her into his arms. "I prefer you free-spirited," he said, kissing her hard on the lips. "Like at the lodge."

A low purr escaped from the back of her

throat. "You know what? I can live with free-spirited," she said. "As long as I'm only that way with you." She let her hand slip between them until she cupped his hard erection in her hands.

He groaned, his body needing to escape his jeans. "I missed being able to touch you, how I want and when I want," he said, running his hands through her hair.

She moved her hand and let their bodies align. *"I love you,"* she said, meeting his gaze.

"I love you, too. Always." If this was the best life had to offer, Roper didn't need another damn thing.

EPILOGUE

New York Post — *Page Six*

New York Renegades center fielder, John Roper, needs extra innings to keep up with the happenings in his life. His career is back on track, as is his personal life with an impending marriage to Amy Stone, a publicist at the infamous Hot Zone PR Agency. And there's more. Somehow Roper managed to pull off a private wedding for his sister at Brandon Vaughn's mountain lodge in Greenlawn, New York, this past weekend without intrusion by the press. What makes this so surprising is that pop star Hannah Gregory and drummer Mike Morris also married this weekend at the same lodge. Roper and his fiancée joined the rest of Hannah's band as bridesmaids and groomsmen. The guests signed a confidentiality agreement, which left yours truly out in the cold. But to quote two older female guests as they exited Roper's sister's affair, it was small and too sedate for their liking. The ladies were overheard heading to the indoor pool to convince the activities director for the weekend to add naked Marco Polo to the events.

Harrison Smith's television series starring movie star Cassandra Lee as the matriarch of a family in need of guidance as they vie for a trust fund was picked up by NBC for the fall lineup.

In a related story, Dave Martin, a sports trainer, was brought in for questioning by the police in conjunction with the nude photos of Amy Stone and John Roper. Charges to be announced. . . .

In other news, eSports columnist and reporter Frank Buckley checked himself into rehab after his wife left him for the Renegades' newest acquisition, twenty-year-old shortstop, Don Andersen. He was replaced at work by Veronica Butler, a long-time reporter at eSports. The Buck won't be stopping anywhere anytime soon, folks.

And they all lived happily ever after. . . .

ABOUT THE AUTHOR

Carly Phillips started her writing career with the Harlequin Temptation line in 1999 with *Brazen,* and she's never strayed far from home! In 2002 Carly's book *The Bachelor,* was chosen by Kelly Ripa for her Reading with Ripa book club, making it the first romance to be chosen by a nationally televised book club. Carly has published twenty-five books, and, among others, she has appeared on the *New York Times, USA Today* and *Publishers Weekly* bestseller lists. An ABC soap opera addict, Carly lives in Purchase, New York, with her husband, two teenage daughters and two frisky soft-coated wheaten terriers who act like their third and fourth children. You can find Carly online at www.carlyphillips.com; www.plotmonkeys.com and www.myspace.com/carlyphillips.